"I could help you with your daughters."

400

Tristan turned to face Rachel, smiled. "That's what I came to discuss with you."

So, he *had* followed her. She'd suspected as much. But just to be clear…

"You followed me out here to talk about your girls?"

He went very still and studied her face with that intensity she found so disconcerting, as if he were trying to look into the depths of her soul. "In a manner of speaking."

She swallowed. This wasn't supposed to be so hard. What she had to offer made sense for all of them. "So you agree I should take over for Bertha."

"No."

No? She waited for him to expand on that. When he didn't she blinked at him in confusion. *That's it*, she thought. Just… no. Not a single word of explanation?

She blew out a frustrated puff of air. "You realize I'm offering to take care of your daughters. It's the perfect solution. I adore them. I'm pretty confident they like me."

He was already shaking his head before she finished stating her case.

She frowned at him. "I don't understand your refusal. You need help immediately. I'm available."

"I had a more permanent solution in mind."

Oh. *Oh.*

* * *

Journey West: Romance and adventure await three siblings on the Oregon Trail

Wagon Train Reunion—
Linda Ford, April 2015

Wagon Train
Lacy Willia

Wagon Tra
Renee Rya

D0388713

Renee Ryan grew up in a Florida beach town where she learned to surf, sort of. With a degree from FSU, she explored career opportunities at a Florida theme park, a modeling agency and even taught high school economics. She currently lives with her husband in Nebraska, and many have mistaken their overweight cat for a small bear. You may contact Renee at reneeryan.com, on Twitter @ReneeRyanBooks, or on Facebook.

Books by Renee Ryan

Love Inspired Historical

Journey West

Wagon Train Proposal

Charity House

The Marshal Takes a Bride
Hannah's Beau
Loving Bella
The Lawman Claims His Bride
Charity House Courtship
The Outlaw's Redemption
Finally a Bride
His Most Suitable Bride

Love Inspired

Village Green

Claiming the Doctor's Heart

To browse a current listing of all Renee's titles, please visit Harlequin.com.

RENEE RYAN

Wagon Train Proposal

HARLEQUIN® LOVE INSPIRED® HISTORICAL

Special thanks and acknowledgment to Renee Ryan for her contribution to the Journey West miniseries.

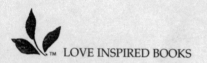 LOVE INSPIRED BOOKS

Recycling programs for this product may not exist in your area.

ISBN-13: 978-0-373-28314-9

Wagon Train Proposal

Copyright © 2015 by Harlequin Books S.A.

www.Harlequin.com

Printed in U.S.A.

There is no fear in love;
but perfect love casteth out fear.
—*1 John* 4:18

To my fabulous critique partner, Cindy Kirk.
Thank you for your wisdom and support through
the years and, most of all, your friendship.
Every book I write is stronger because of
your insights. No matter what trial I face,
I know you always have my back, and I have yours!

Chapter One

⌒

Fort Nez Perce
October 1843

Exhausted, footsore and chilled to the bone from a recent rainstorm, Rachel Hewitt leaned against her family's covered wagon. As she looked out over the organized chaos, one thought emerged. Nearly there.

At long last, the wagon train had reached the final leg of what had turned out to be an arduous, five-month trek across the Oregon Trail.

Despite the hardships along the way, spirits were high among Rachel's fellow emigrants. A brand-new life awaited in Oregon City, with the promise of fertile soil, large land grants. Endless possibilities awaited. And yet…

A sense of quiet despair crept into her usual optimism.

Wrapping her shawl tighter around her shoulders, she traced her fingertip along the edges of a wooden slat. Familiar sounds filled her ears. Hammers striking iron. Saws carving through wood. The creak of wagon wheels and children's laughter and the bleating of worn-out animals.

Soft footsteps approached from behind her. Rachel

moved to the other side of the wagon. She didn't especially want to speak with anyone right now.

Rachel's family, along with many others, had made the decision to build rafts or buy canoes rather than risk the treacherous land route or abandon their belongings. It had seemed the wisest course of action. But as she eyed the rushing waters swollen from the recent storm, she wondered if the worst was yet to come.

The cold wind sweeping off the Cascade Range carried the scent of winter over the land. Time was running short. Little room for mistakes or wrong turns.

Rachel looked around her once again. This time, all she saw was the solitary figure standing on the riverbank.

Tristan McCullough. The handsome, widowed sheriff of Oregon City had joined their wagon train weeks ago. He'd deftly guided their weary group through the treacherous Blue Mountains, past The Dalles and on to Fort Nez Perce.

His strength of character had made an impression on everyone, including Rachel. He was the embodiment of masculine power and something far more troubling. Something her mind shied away from, refusing to acknowledge.

The sun peeked out from a seam in the clouds and wrapped Tristan in a thin, golden beam, turning his sunkissed hair a burnished copper. And his eyes, those intelligent, compelling eyes were probably a full shade lighter now, a cool moss green against his tanned skin.

A shiver passed through her as she watched Tristan eye the rushing waters with a concerned expression.

Was he contemplating another route to Oregon City? Not likely. The only other route was along the sandy, narrow shoreline. But large boulders and steep cliffs, some rising over a hundred feet above the river, would have to be scaled or gone around.

While fraught with its own set of dangers, the Columbia River was still their best option. The one they would take.

Unless Tristan said otherwise. Unless—

"Rachel, what's wrong?" Her sister's soft, lilting voice fell over her. "You're frowning."

Rachel bit back a sigh. Of course the ever-vigilant, fundamentally caring Emma would seek her out.

"I hadn't realized I was frowning." She kept her voice even and her gaze averted. "I was merely lost in thought. Nothing to worry yourself over."

"If you say so."

Something in her sister's voice had her looking up. A mistake. Rachel felt her smile slip the moment her eyes connected with Emma's.

Even with her brows drawn together in worry, her sister exuded happiness. Emma had always been strikingly beautiful, with her golden brown hair and vivid blue eyes. But now that she'd fallen in love with Nathan Reed, she was even more so.

The ex-fur trader and longtime loner brought out the best in Emma. Her confidence grew with each passing day, her innate shyness dissipating with every hour she spent in Nathan's company.

Rachel was pleased for her sister. *She was.* But now that Emma and their brother Ben had both found love on the Oregon Trail, Rachel was feeling a tad lost. For the first time in her life she didn't have a clear sense of belonging.

At least she knew what to expect in her immediate future. Once the wagon train arrived in Oregon City she would take over the care of their oldest brother's home.

Surely Grayson, who'd arrived in Oregon Country nearly two years ahead of them, would welcome her help.

What if he didn't?

"You're frowning again."

Rachel pulled in a deep breath. "I was thinking about Grayson."

"What about him?"

"I…just hope he still needs me to take over his household duties when we finally arrive."

But what if he didn't? she wondered again. She couldn't bear the idea of being useless in her own brother's home, or worse, find herself a burden to him.

"Of course he'll need your help," Emma said. "That's been the plan all along."

Rachel gave a noncommittal nod, then promptly changed the subject. "I'd better get back to work. We have a lot to do before we enter the river."

A vision flashed of their belongings stacked from floor to canvas ceiling inside their wagon. They'd unloaded most of the items already, but there was still more. Several other tasks needed accomplishing, tasks that must be complete before the men finished building their raft. She shouldn't be wasting time feeling sorry for herself.

She started toward the back of the wagon.

Emma reached for her. Not wanting to prolong their conversation any more than necessary, Rachel sidestepped the move as casually as possible. She wanted to be alone with her thoughts, at least until she could manage a shift to a happier mood.

"You're sure that's the only thing on your mind?" Emma's hand fell away. "You're not worried about the river crossing?"

"Of course not." She lifted her chin to punctuate her point. "I trust all will go according to plan."

Before she could say more, a group of young children rushed past them, sized small to smallest. Their unrestrained laughter rang out as they tossed a well-worn ball between them. Rachel marveled at their capacity to find joy in the moment, in their ability to take full advantage of this short respite.

She used to recover from hardships that quickly. She used to take setbacks in stride. But her current situation proved far more difficult. For the first time in her nearly twenty years of life, Rachel was facing a solitary future. With no clear direction. No real purpose.

No one to care for but herself.

Though the youngest in the family, she'd seen to her siblings' needs through the years. After Grayson left Missouri, Ben had worked their small ranch and Emma had nursed their father until he died. Rachel had run the household.

When Grayson sent a letter encouraging them to join him in Oregon Country, Rachel and her siblings had embarked on this journey as a family. Their individual roles had been clearly defined, their stories tightly woven together.

But now, Emma and Ben each had someone else in their lives. Someone they loved and who loved them in return. Rachel's future was no longer linked with that of her siblings.

Not that she begrudged them their happiness. She simply wanted to know where she belonged in the family now that roles were shifting and two more people had joined them.

A sigh worked its way up her throat. This time she let it come, let it leak past her lips.

The worry deepened in Emma's gaze. Or was that pity Rachel saw in her sister's eyes?

Oh, no. She would not be pitied. *Anything but that.* "If we're going to finish unloading the wagon before noon we better get to work."

Not waiting for a response, she pushed around her sister.

"Rachel, wait." Emma stopped her progress with a hand on her arm. "Why do I sense you're hiding something from me?"

"Because you're overprotective of your baby sister?"

"It's not that." Emma gave her a look of exasperation, the kind only one sibling could give another. "You're sad."

Rachel started to deny the shrewd observation, then decided what would be the point? Emma would see through the lie. "Maybe I am. But only a very, very little. I've been thinking about—" she shrugged "—Mama."

And it was all Tristan McCullough's fault.

Though no one spoke of it anymore, he'd joined the wagon train for another, strictly personal reason other than merely to guide them along the last leg of their journey. With Grayson's urgings, he'd also come to determine if Emma would be a suitable mother for his three young daughters. Rachel didn't fault him for that.

She actually admired Tristan's commitment to his children. It was noble of him to want to provide them with a mother. Rachel knew what it was like to grow up without one. Hers had died of consumption when she was barely five years old.

What would Tristan do now that Emma was engaged to Nathan Reed? Would he seek out someone else on the wagon train to marry?

Unable to stop herself, Rachel's gaze sought Tristan once again. As if sensing her eyes on him, he turned his head in her direction.

For a brief moment, their glances merged. The impact was like a sledgehammer ramming into her heart. She nearly gasped.

Her response to the man confounded her.

But, really, he shouldn't be so attractive, so capable and strong, so *disappointed* things hadn't worked out between him and Emma.

Why wouldn't he be disappointed? Emma was beautiful and kind, nurturing and soft-spoken. She would have made Tristan's daughters a good mother.

Nevertheless, Rachel didn't regret pointing out to the good sheriff that Emma wasn't available to become his wife. She was, after all, in love with another man.

Although, perhaps, Rachel could have chosen her words a bit more carefully. *Perhaps*, her delivery could have been slightly less forceful.

"...and who could forget her cinnamon rolls?" Emma's sigh jerked Rachel back to their conversation. "I wish Mama would have shared her recipe with us, or at least written the ingredients down somewhere."

Rachel pressed her lips tightly together. Apparently, her sister had been carrying on the conversation without her, talking about their mother's skill in the kitchen. Rachel liked to think she'd inherited her own gift of cooking from their mother. She tried to pull up Sara Hewitt's image from her memory.

She came away empty, as always, and felt all the more alone for trying.

"I miss her," she whispered, mostly to herself. "So much."

She'd been too young when her mother died to remember her face or many of her physical attributes. But she did remember her soft, sweet voice. Her warm hugs and unending kindness. And how their father had never fully recovered from her death.

"Oh, Rachel." Emma shifted to a spot directly in front of her, a strange of sense of insistence in the bold move. "You know Mama loved you. Never forget that."

Rachel nodded. Of course she wouldn't forget their mother loved her. She distinctly remembered Sara Hewitt whispering in her ear every night at bedtime, *Rachel, my beautiful, precious daughter. You're my very own, special gift from God.*

She hoped one day to say the same words to her own children.

"We all love you. Ben, Grayson, me." Something strange came and went in Emma's eyes. "Never doubt that, not for one moment of a single day."

What a strange thing to say.

"Of course I know you love me." A wave of peace wrapped around her like a comfortable old blanket. Family was everything to the Hewitts. So Rachel's siblings would soon be married. That only meant their close-knit family was growing larger, with more people for her to love.

Yet Rachel still faced an uncertain future. Alone.

You aren't alone, she reminded herself. *You have your brothers and your sister. And their soon-to-be spouses.*

Rachel also had the Lord.

She had to trust His plan for her life would be revealed once she arrived at Oregon City, if not sooner.

"Rachel? Emma?" Their brother's fiancée, Abigail Bingham Black, stuck her head out of the back of the wagon. "Can one of you give me a hand? This trunk is too heavy for me to lift on my own."

"Coming." Welcoming the interruption, Rachel hurried around to the back of the wagon. With a flick of her wrist, she unlatched the tailgate and then lowered it with care.

Smiling her gratitude, Abby moved in behind the trunk and pushed while Rachel pulled. Emma joined in and, after a few grunts and groans, the three of them had the large case sitting on the wet, spongy ground at their feet.

Clapping her hands together in satisfaction, Abby gave the trunk one firm nod, then deftly climbed back into the wagon.

Rachel smiled at the agile move, thinking how far the petite blonde had come since the wagon train left Missouri. Had anyone suggested four months ago that the well-bred, overeducated Abigail Bingham Black would become engaged to her brother, Rachel would have openly scoffed at them. She'd considered the spoiled socialite completely unworthy of Ben, especially since Abigail had broken his heart six years prior.

Rachel had been wrong about the other woman, completely.

Abigail had pulled her weight from the very beginning of their journey. First, by singing to the wagon train children at night. Then, she'd approached Rachel for lessons in daily practicalities in exchange for music lessons. The suggestion had been mutually beneficial. Over time, they'd become friends.

Rachel couldn't think of a better woman to marry her brother. And she liked Emma's fiancé just as much.

A movement out of the corner of her eye pulled her attention back to the riverbank. Back to Tristan.

Their gazes locked and held once again.

A dozen unspoken words passed between them. For a moment, the world seemed to stop and pause. Rachel couldn't catch a decent breath. Then…

Her pulse skittered back to life.

Her breathing picked up speed.

Remorse filled her.

Perhaps she'd overstepped when she'd first met the widowed sheriff.

Rachel had been so caught up in protecting Emma, insisting her sister "follow her heart" and be allowed to make her own choice, that she hadn't considered how doing so would affect Tristan. Or his three young, *motherless* daughters.

She'd never met his little girls, yet Rachel still felt a connection to them and their plight.

More to the point, she owed their father an apology. Not for warning him away from Emma but for the way she'd addressed the situation.

If not now, when?

Tristan felt the corner of his mouth twitch. It was the only outward sign of his irritation as Rachel Hewitt approached him with strong, purposeful strides. She might be small, but she was certainly determined.

He couldn't deny the young woman was pretty, in an untraditional sort of way. Her wild, curly brown hair that seemed to defy any attempts at taming and those dark brown eyes were an attractive combination. Her sweet, youthful face held no guile, and she'd proved herself to be full of life, especially when she was around, or caring for, little children.

Tristan admitted, if only in the privacy of his own mind, that he'd been a bit taken by Rachel Hewitt when they'd originally met.

Then she'd opened her mouth.

Out rolled one unwelcome opinion after another. Although she was almost always right, he wasn't used to a woman speaking her mind with such…enthusiasm.

How like her to seek him out and share one of her *opinions* when he had far too many other concerns on his mind. There were countless tasks that needed addressing before the wagon train set out down the river. He wished there were a better route, but the Columbia was hemmed in by steep slopes and cliffs of hard rock on either side.

Worse still, the soggy bottomlands were flooded, leaving the west end of the gorge unsuitable for foot traffic. While several hearty men had volunteered to lead the animals over the Lolo Pass, the bulk of the wagon train had little choice but to cross the river on rafts, canoes or bateaus. If conditions held, and they put in the water today, the emigrants could make it to Oregon City in less than a week.

Tristan would soon be home. *Not soon enough.*

After weeks on the trail, he missed his daughters. He hated leaving them behind with his neighbor, Bertha Quincy, but he'd been eager to find a woman to marry. And now that things hadn't worked out with Emma Hewitt, they were facing a longer future without a mother.

He had to figure out another solution quickly.

In the meantime, he had a wagon train to assist down the tumultuous Columbia.

He turned his back on Rachel and walked off in the opposite direction. There was movement everywhere. The unloading of wagons, the unhitching of oxen teams, trees being felled and dragged to the makeshift rafts in midconstruction, all created a cacophony of sights and sounds.

A profusion of odors thickened the cool October air. Oxen and horses, canvas and dry rot, quashed campfires, burned tar—and those were the more palatable smells.

Tristan longed for the journey to be complete. He longed to see his daughters again, to hold them close and tell them he loved them. He'd made a mistake, thinking he would find a suitable woman to marry on the wagon train.

There was another concern plaguing him, as well. The emigrants had a thief among them. Before leaving Missouri, nearly fifteen thousand dollars had been stolen from a fireproof safe. As the caravan continued on the Oregon Trail, various valuables had also gone missing.

The thief had yet to be discovered. Tristan wasn't giving up hope, though.

He and the nine-man committee of overseers and regulators, along with the insurance agent from the safe company, could still catch the thief before the wagon train crossed into Oregon Country. *Please, Lord, let it be so.*

A familiar female voice called out his name.

He increased his pace.

"Sheriff McCullough." The call came again, more formal this time but with an equal amount of conviction. "A quick word, if you please."

He could keep walking. He could continue to pretend he didn't hear the perfectly reasonable request. Or he could turn around and deal with the confounding woman.

Tristan did the only thing a man of integrity would do in such a situation. He turned around.

And faced Rachel Hewitt head-on.

Chapter Two

With Tristan's impatient gaze locked on her, Rachel's footsteps faltered and she slowed to a near crawl. Now that she'd secured his attention, she wasn't quite sure what to say to the man. *I'm sorry* seemed too simple, too easy and thoroughly inadequate, given the circumstances.

He was, after all, heading back to Oregon City without a bride *or* a mother for his daughters. Rachel had played a role in that. Although...

The situation wasn't entirely her fault. In truth, it wasn't even a little bit her fault. She'd merely pointed out what should have been obvious. By discouraging him from pursuing her sister, Rachel had saved everyone—including Tristan himself—a whole lot of trouble, possibly even heartache.

But that wasn't the point.

Rachel drew in a tight breath, forced her feet to move quickly over the sodden grass.

Why, *why* had Grayson told Tristan about Emma and then suggested a match between them? Now, Tristan had a glimpse of what might have been. No other woman could hope to rival Emma's serene beauty and soft, caring nature, especially not Rachel.

Not that she was interested in becoming Tristan's wife. No matter how connected she felt to his three motherless little girls, Rachel would not serve as Emma's stand-in. Not nearly as beautiful as her sister, Rachel had spent most of her life falling short in most people's eyes. She'd always been considered second-best, the *other* sister.

No more.

When Rachel eventually married, she would be first in her future husband's heart, or not at all. And…and…

She was stalling.

With a clipped stride, she closed the distance between them. If only Tristan weren't so tall. If only she didn't have to crane her neck to look into his eyes, eyes full of intensity.

Get on with it, Rachel.

She took another step toward him, just one, and immediately regretted the move. The smell of spicy bergamot mixed with leather and something indescribably male washed over her.

"I…I've come to…" Her words trailed off. She immediately firmed her chin and blurted out the rest in a rush. "I've come to apologize."

A winged eyebrow rose.

Better, she supposed, than a verbal response. Tristan's gravelly Irish brogue was entirely too attractive. Once he started talking, Rachel could very possibly lose the remaining scraps of her nerve.

She'd made a mistake, approaching him like this without a plan in mind.

Every instinct told her to forget this conversation, to leave at once and never broach the subject again.

But Rachel Hewitt was made of sterner stuff.

"I…that is, I quite possibly, maybe…" She swallowed.

"That is—" she swallowed again "—I spoke in haste when we first met."

Silence met her words, followed by a slow, thoughtful scowl. Then came a long, tense moment when Tristan's gaze roamed Rachel's face.

His inspection was altogether too thorough, too disconcerting.

She forgot to be uncomfortable, forgot her nervousness and jammed her fists on her hips. "You could make this easier for me."

"I could," he drawled, that Irish brogue as appealing as she'd feared. "But I find I'm quite charmed at the moment. It's so rare to see you tongue-tied."

Her mouth fell open. "You're *enjoying* my discomfort?"

"On the contrary, I'm attempting to lighten the mood." A slow, attractive grin slid across his lips. "I suspect, Miss Hewitt, apologies do not come easy for you."

"You have no idea," she muttered, her shoulders stiffening.

"It's a trait that I must regretfully admit—" he leaned in close, so close their noses nearly touched "—we share."

She couldn't help it. She laughed. The man wasn't supposed to make her laugh, while also—mildly—insulting her. "I'm trying to do the right thing here, be the bigger person and all that."

"I'm well aware."

"I…" She trailed off, blew out a puff of air and tried again. "I can't seem to find the proper words."

"*I'm sorry* is always a good place to start."

Wasn't he oh-so-helpful? Rachel would be annoyed with the man if he wasn't also oh-so-right.

She puffed out another breath. "I'm sorry, Sheriff McCullough, I may have—"

"Tristan."

"Excuse me?"

"Considering our history, you should probably call me Tristan."

Oh. *Oh.* "I'm sorry...*Tristan.*"

He smiled.

Unfair. The man was far too handsome when he looked at her like that. Her heart took an extra beat. "When I warned you to stay away from my sister, I may have spoken a bit more harshly than the situation warranted."

There went that eyebrow again, traveling the same path as before. *"May have?"*

Rachel sighed. Of course he would latch on to that part of her awkward little speech.

"I spoke too harshly," she amended, eliminating the qualifier this time around. "I could have used more grace with my delivery and less disapproval in my tone."

"You were attempting to protect your sister. Your loyalty does you credit."

The unexpected compliment sent a bolt of pleasure straight through her, catching her completely off guard.

This was the point in the conversation where she was supposed to say farewell and walk away. But no. She had to keep talking, had to make a point of being painfully, brutally honest. "I am not sorry for warning you away from Emma, you understand, only for my delivery of the message."

As soon as she said the words, she regretted them. *Let your conversation be always full of grace.* Why did she seem to forget her manners around this man?

He chuckled softly, shaking his head in wry amusement. "You really are bad at apologies."

She didn't disagree. "What I meant to say—"

"I know what you meant."

"I'm not sure you do."

He chuckled again.

She considered walking away. But, again, she held her ground. "My sister has spent most of her life caring for everyone else. For once, I wanted to ensure she made a choice with only herself in mind. She deserves a chance at love. *Everyone* deserves a chance at love."

"Yes, they do." For a brief moment, his gaze turned unreadable, distant, as if he was somewhere else. Lost in the past perhaps? A split second later his smile returned, lightning quick and even more devastating than before. "Let me save us both some time and accept your apology."

She sighed. "I didn't mean to overstep, Tristan. It was unconsciously done."

"I know that, Rachel."

She liked the way her name sounded wrapped inside his Irish brogue, liked it perhaps a bit too much. She sighed again. When had she become the sighing sort? "I'm also sorry you won't be bringing home a mother for your daughters. My intention wasn't to make matters worse for you, or them."

"I know that, as well." Looking up at the sky, he lifted the brim of his hat off his head then shoved it back in place.

The gesture was so thoroughly…him.

"What will you do now?" she asked.

It wasn't really her concern. And yet, Rachel felt as though his daughters' care *was* her concern. She couldn't explain why, precisely, except that she'd insinuated herself into the matter and now she was invested in the outcome.

"I'll come up with another solution." He rolled a shoulder. "Eventually."

Let it go, she told herself. *Walk away.*

She pressed on. "Who watches your daughters now?"

"My neighbor, Bertha Quincy. She's exceptional. But she's due to give birth to her own child in a few months and won't have the time or, I predict, the inclination to care for my girls."

Rachel's heart filled with distress. This widowed father was about to find himself in a very difficult situation, with no easy answer in sight, save one.

"You could always find someone else on the wagon train to marry." She made a vague gesture toward the bulk of the activity behind her. "There are several available women besides my sister."

Including me.

He was already shaking his head before she finished speaking. "As much as I'd like to find a mother for my daughters, I have to think of their welfare and safety first. I need to know the woman I bring into my home. Moreover, I need to trust her completely."

Did he not hear the contradiction in his own words? "You were willing to consider Emma, sight unseen."

"Your brother is my closest neighbor and friend. I trust Grayson's judgment unequivocally."

Rachel wondered why Grayson hadn't considered her as a possible candidate for Tristan's wife. Had her brother thought her too young? Or was it because Emma was the more beautiful of the two Hewitt sisters?

A spurt of bitterness tried to take root. Rachel shoved it aside. Her days of living in Emma's beautiful shadow were over. She was unique and special in her own way, a treasured child of God, worthy of her own happy ending. One day.

Some day.

Tristan looked as though he had something else to say, when the trail boss, Sam Weston, trotted over.

"Sheriff McCullough." Ignoring Rachel completely, the tall, lanky man reached up and tugged on his thick, bushy brown mustache. The gesture implied distress. "Mr. Stillwell and I have a matter of grave importance we need to discuss with you."

Tristan looked to Rachel before answering.

"There's just one more thing I wish to say," she informed him. "It'll only take a moment."

He turned to Mr. Weston. "I'll be with you shortly."

The trail boss started to argue, but something in Tristan's piercing gaze must have made him reconsider. He shrugged and went back the way he came.

Once they were alone again, Rachel spoke quickly, before she lost her nerve. "When we arrive in Oregon City, if you ever find yourself in need of someone to watch your daughters, I'd be happy to do so."

He looked at her oddly and started to speak but was cut off by another person calling out his name.

The sheriff was a popular man this morning.

"I'll let you know." A short nod in her general direction and he was gone.

Rachel stared after him a full ten seconds, wondering why she suddenly felt more alone than ever before.

Thankfully, Johnny Littleton waddled into view. The one-year-old was just learning to walk. A triumph, considering he'd faced death twice already on the crossing. He was nearly killed the day before the wagon train left Missouri when a bunch of young rabble-rousers had taken it in their minds to shoot off their guns in a crowd of people. It was a blessing the baby wasn't killed, only nicked. But then he'd taken ill during the measles epidemic and the concern for his life had been far worse.

Rachel scooped the child off the ground and cuddled him close. She'd discovered recently that if her hands were idle for too long, an odd sense of loneliness crept over her. Perhaps that explained the emptiness she struggled to contain now.

No, no. She would not give in to self-pity. Squaring her shoulders, she reminded herself she was a Hewitt, born and bred. Strength of character was in her blood, as well as the fortitude to face any challenge with unwavering courage. Even an uncertain future, in an unknown land.

Attitude adjusted, she shifted the baby in her arms. "Come on, Johnny, let's find your mother."

Tristan headed over to the spot near the river where the trail boss stood in conversation with James Stillwell and Ben Hewitt. By their pinched expressions, he had a good idea what they wanted to discuss with him.

Another robbery had occurred.

He wondered what had been stolen this time. With his mind sorting through possible scenarios, he joined the other men. Just as he pulled to a stop, he caught sight of Rachel out of the corner of his eye. She was holding the Littleton boy, whispering something in the child's ear. She lifted her head slightly, then pressed a kiss on the light brown hair.

The little boy giggled.

Laughing with him, she set the child on the ground and took his hand. Johnny wobbled through several unsteady steps, then plopped down on his bottom. Incredibly patient, Rachel helped him stand and encouraged him to try again.

Watching the two together, something warm moved through Tristan. Rachel looked good leading the infant back toward his family's wagon. She was the picture of a young, unflappable mother.

Had he set his sights on the wrong Hewitt sister? Was the answer to the problem of his daughters' care right in front of him? His own needs hardly mattered. He'd had his chance at love, had been blessed with a wife he'd adored with all his heart and considered his best friend. When it came to finding a woman to marry this second time around, the girls were his primary focus, his *only* focus, his—

"We've had another robbery, Sheriff."

The words dragged his attention back to the problem at hand. Tristan wasn't with the wagon train in an official capacity, only as a representative of Oregon City. The nine-man committee was technically the law, while the money missing from the safe fell in Stillwell's jurisdiction.

Nevertheless, the thief was heading to Oregon City, and that made him Tristan's problem. "What'd he take this time?"

Ben rubbed the back of his neck, frowned at something in the distance. The blue-gray eyes beneath messy, light brown hair revealed a mix of frustration and outrage. "Sally Littleton's wedding ring."

Her wedding ring? "How'd the thief get it off her finger?"

"He didn't," James Stillwell said, inserting himself in the conversation. An agent of Thayer & Edwards safe company, he'd joined the wagon train soon after the safe robbery in Independence.

He'd insisted on remaining undercover. With jet-black hair, equally dark eyes and a tough, muscular build and unassuming clothing, he fit in well enough. Only the men standing in their tiny circle knew his real identity.

"It appears Mrs. Littleton was so busy answering Amos Tucker's questions about the best way to pack dishware, she burned the oatmeal," Stillwell explained. "She then took off her ring to scrub out the bottom of the pot. The thief lifted the piece of jewelry when she wasn't looking."

Slick, Tristan thought. Dastardly. The question remained. Were they dealing with a cunning thief, or someone who took advantage of opportunities when they presented themselves?

Either scenario came with its own set of trouble.

"Was anyone else near Mrs. Littleton at the time of the robbery?"

Tristan aimed the question at Stillwell, but Ben Hewitt answered. "Mostly women from our section of the wagon train, and…Clarence Pressman."

Tristan's shoulders stiffened. There was something not quite right about Mr. Pressman. He walked oddly, hunched over like a man three times his age. He rarely spoke beyond a grunt or a rough, one-syllable response. Emma Hewitt had befriended the man. She was one of the few people on the wagon train Clarence seemed to trust. Her fiancé was another.

"Have you questioned the women and anyone else who might have seen something?"

"Everyone but Clarence," Stillwell said.

Tristan absorbed this piece of information. "One of us needs to question him before we put the rafts in the river."

"Won't be me." Sam Weston lifted his hands, palms facing out. "My only job is to get the wagon train to Oregon Country."

"I could do it," Stillwell said. "But I'm not sure it's worth risking my cover."

Before Ben Hewitt could chime in, Tristan caught

sight of Clarence. Head down, face completely covered by an ugly, floppy hat, he approached Nathan Reed near the river's edge. Nathan set down his ax and began a hushed conversation with the man.

"He's over there," Tristan said. "With your future brother-in-law."

Ben followed the direction of Tristan's gaze. "I'll speak with him. I was on my way over to assist Nathan, anyway."

"I'll join you."

As they drew close, Nathan rose to his full height and shifted to his left. The move put his large, rangy body directly in front of Clarence.

It was a peculiar gesture, almost protective.

Tristan frowned.

Clarence peered around Nathan, squeaked out something unintelligible and then scurried away.

Staring after his retreating back, Tristan couldn't get it out his mind that he'd seen that wide-legged walk before, a cross between a waddle and a shuffle. In fact, he'd seen that exact stride three distinct times—when his wife had carried their daughters in her belly.

Puzzle pieces began fitting into place. Tristan's mind was just about to shove the last one in place, when Nathan stepped in his line of vision, his face scrunched in a ruthless scowl.

"Leave Clarence alone, Sheriff." His voice held no emotion, his eyes equally flat.

In a gesture similar to the one the trail boss had given, Tristan lifted his hands, palms facing toward the other man. "I just want to question—" he held the pause for emphasis "—*him* about the robbery this morning."

"Clarence didn't take Mrs. Littleton's ring."

"If you say he didn't do it, Nathan," Ben interjected

before Tristan could respond, "we believe you. Isn't that right, Sheriff?"

Tristan gave a single nod of his head, deciding to let the matter drop. For now. He figured Nathan's hostility had more to do with Tristan himself than his suspicion of Clarence.

Tristan couldn't say he blamed the man. When he'd first arrived at the Blue Mountains Pass, he'd been eager for a quick match with Emma Hewitt.

The moment he'd realized that Nathan and Emma were falling in love, he'd immediately backed off. Having experienced a happy, loving marriage himself, Tristan wished them well.

Unfortunately, his daughters were still without a mother. And Tristan was no closer to finding them one than when he'd left Oregon City.

A familiar laugh pulled his attention to a handful of children gathering near the Hewitt wagon. Rachel was organizing them in a circle, a ball in her hand, probably with the idea of keeping the boys and girls out of their parents' way as they prepared for the trip down the Columbia.

Abigail Black joined the group a moment later.

Just as the women formed a makeshift circle, one of the smaller boys broke away from the others. Looking back over his shoulder, laughing at his friends, he ran flat out.

The child wasn't paying attention to where his feet were taking him—straight for the river.

Tristan's breath lodged in his throat. He moved without thinking. But not fast enough. The terrible sound of a splash rent the air. He dropped to his knees at the water's edge and reached out, catching hold of a tiny arm.

Heart pounding, he plucked the child from the water and set him on dry land.

Soaking wet, water dripping off his dark hair, the little boy grinned up at him. "That was fun, Sheriff. Can I do it again? Can I, huh? Can I?"

He had opened his mouth to explain the dangers of running off from the group when Rachel skidded to a stop beside him. By the set of her jaw, and the uneven cadence of her breathing, Tristan knew he had an ally. No matter who did the talking, the little boy would not be playing by the river anymore today.

Chapter Three

Lungs burning, her pulse pounding in her ears, Rachel divided her attention between Tristan and the wet child staring expectantly up at him. The sheriff appeared outwardly calm, in complete control of the situation.

Rachel wasn't nearly as composed.

A slower uptake on Tristan's part, a clumsier snatch, and the six-year-old would have been swallowed up by the river.

She didn't know whether to sigh in relief or scold the child for his recklessness.

Tristan made the decision for her, choosing something in between the two responses. "The river is a dangerous place, Donny." He met the boy's gaze. "You must stay near the wagons. You will give me your promise."

Huffing out a sigh, Donny scuffed his foot on the grass. "I promise, Sheriff."

Tristan's shoulders relaxed and he patted the boy on the back. "Good man."

Donny's chest puffed out with pride, either from the praise itself or being called a man, Rachel couldn't say. One thing she did know. From the glint of adoration in the child's expression, Tristan was the boy's new favorite adult.

Unfortunately, he was becoming Rachel's favorite adult, as well, which was rather inconvenient. She had enough to worry about without a growing admiration for a man she hardly knew, a man who was more interested in finding a woman to mother his children than a wife for himself.

Depressing thought.

Still, his quick reflexes had saved a young child's life. She gave him a grateful smile.

His lips lifted in response.

A silent message spread between them, solidarity in their shared concern for a little boy. In that moment, Rachel felt more connected to Tristan than anyone else on the wagon train.

She wrenched her gaze free and focused on Donny. A beat later Delores Jensen rushed across the soggy grass, calling out her son's name. Her voice held a frantic, high-pitched note.

"Oh, Donny." She dropped to her knees and tugged her son against her. Complaining she was holding him too tight, the boy squirmed free.

Attention still on her son, Mrs. Jensen regained her feet. She pressed a kiss to the boy's head and then gave Tristan a shaky smile. "Thank you, Sheriff." Her wide gaze was filled with equal parts terror and relief. "Donny can't swim. You saved his life."

"I was merely in the right place at the right time. Rachel was only one step behind me." His voice came out low and gruff, but his eyes were gentle as they fell on her. "I'm confident she would have caught Donny if I hadn't gotten to him first."

Not true.

Rachel had been too far behind the boy. She started to say as much, but the other woman spoke over her. "Nevertheless, your quick reflexes prevented certain disaster."

Donny, already losing interest in the adult conversation, asked his mother if he could go back and play with the other children again.

All heads swung in the direction of the Hewitt wagon. Abby had taken over where Rachel had left off. Mandolin in hand, she set about organizing the boys and girls in a semicircle, their backs facing the riverbank. Clearly, she was about to sing a song for them.

It was a perfect ploy to keep the children away from the unfolding drama at the water's edge. Rachel smiled as one of the smaller girls climbed onto her future sister-in-law's lap. Her brother's fiancée would make a superb mother one day.

Her smile slipped as a startling wave of longing took hold. She desperately wanted what her siblings had found on the trail. Family. A secure future. *Love.* She had to believe her time would come.

She just needed a little faith.

"Thank you, again, Sheriff." Mrs. Jensen pulled her son close to her side. "Come on, baby, let's get you into some clean, dry clothes, *then* you can play with the other children."

Mother and son ambled away, Donny grumbling over the delay.

The moment they were alone again, Rachel became enormously attuned to the man standing beside her. She could feel his focus on her, intent and unflinching and, while he hadn't moved, it was as though he'd grown larger, more solid.

Aware of his presence, of his strength and big, broad shoulders, she stifled a sigh. Every one of her senses seemed unnaturally heightened, her every heartbeat full of raw emotion.

Had to be a result of her scare with Donny, and not because the handsome sheriff was standing a little too close, a little too large and imposing.

An uncomfortable sensation swept through her, something she'd never experienced before meeting Tristan. "We both know I wouldn't have caught Donny in time."

"You would have." There was more than just kindness in the remark. But also a certainty in her ability to save the child that had her glancing his way and taking in his handsome profile.

He stared out over the rushing water, his expression thoughtful.

"How can you be so sure?" she asked aloud.

He turned his head, held her gaze. "I've watched you with the wagon train children. I've seen the lengths you go to in order to ensure their safety. If necessary, you would have jumped in the river to save that boy."

"Which is practically what you did, yourself."

He reached to the ground, picked up the hat that had fallen off in the commotion and shoved it back on his head. "I did what needed to be done."

He was such a good man, humble and brave, and if Rachel wasn't very, very careful, she could find herself caring for him beyond what was wise. "It was more than that. Had you not acted with lightning speed, Donny would have drowned."

There. She'd said the words aloud. No more dodging the reality of the situation, no more pretending he hadn't saved a child's life this morning.

"I'm glad I saw the boy heading toward the river when I did." His gaze turned inward, his thoughts hidden from her in the shadows created by his hat. "There's been enough loss on this journey already."

He was right, of course. The outbreak of measles had taken a toll on the emigrants, hitting many families hard. Not to mention the snakebite that had killed Abby's mother, and the other mishaps along the way.

The journey across the Oregon Trail had been truly harrowing. Yet many blessings had occurred, as well. Several potential disasters similar to the one today had been averted, and love had been found.

Rachel promised herself she would focus on the positive aspects of the journey from this point forward. She would thank God daily. Offer up her praise for the things that had gone right rather than lament over the things that had gone wrong.

She sneaked a glance at Tristan's face. Beneath the brim of his hat, his eyes had turned sad. Had his thoughts turned to his own loss? A loss he shared with his three precious daughters. Daughters he hadn't seen in weeks.

"You must miss your girls terribly."

The silence that followed her words seemed to last an eternity. "I do." He rubbed a hand across his mouth. "Violet, Lily and Daisy are the heart of me."

Even the girls' names captured Rachel's awe, inspiring thoughts of delicate petals. Soft pastel colors. Sweet, guileless faces. "They must be adorable little girls."

"They're beautiful, three tiny copies of their mother." The smile he gave Rachel was full of poignant emotion and that same look of tempered sadness. "They have Siobhan's petite build, her red hair and pale blue eyes. They also have her personality. Most of the time, they're like any other children their age. But at others they seem unsure of themselves. They need a mother's love and encouragement."

No wonder Tristan was disappointed things hadn't worked out with Emma. Rachel's sister was soft-spoken, caring and would have been a perfect choice to mother three little girls.

Wishing to offer him comfort, knowing the potential danger to her heart, she reached out to touch his arm. She immediately thought better of the move and quickly dropped her hand back to her side. "Grayson's letter mentioned you've been a widower for two years. Is that correct?"

And there she went, overstepping again, speaking out of turn, bringing up a subject that wasn't any of her concern.

Instead of pointing out the inappropriateness of her question, Tristan nodded. "It is."

The sorrow she felt for this man and his daughters made her want to weep. Thus, she continued asking questions. Either that, or give in to her tears. "How old are your girls now?"

"Daisy is six and takes her role as big sister seriously." He let out a breath of air. "She's far too mature for her years. Lily is four, sweet and full of imagination, a little wild at times, which I must say, I kind of love about her. Violet is but two years old."

Rachel did a quick mental calculation. If his youngest was only two years old that meant his wife had died in childbirth. *Just like Grayson's wife, Susannah.* Both men had suffered a similar tragedy, though Tristan's loss was newer.

Only two years had passed since his wife died. During that time, he'd raised his daughters on his own while also serving as the town sheriff. Friends and neighbors had provided some help, but that wasn't the same as a wife. "I'm truly sorry it didn't work out with Emma."

She meant every word.

"A match between us wasn't meant to be." He swung his gaze down to meet hers. "I'm confident the Lord will provide another solution, in His time."

Such faith. Rachel found herself admiring him even more. She had so many questions, questions about his daughters, about his life in Oregon City. Now wasn't the time.

She turned to go, then spun back around. "Tristan?"

"Yes?"

"I hope you find someone who will make a wonderful mother for your daughters." She would add the request to her daily prayers.

"Thank you, Rachel."

With nothing more to say, she left him to the various tasks he still had in front him.

Though it took incredible strength of will, she did not look back to check if he was still on the riverbank. Not even once.

Tristan watched Rachel walk away, her head high, her shoulders perfectly square with the ground. She had him good and rattled, which was nothing new. The woman put him on edge. What was different this time around was the reason for his unease.

Something about Rachel Hewitt made him want to spill his secrets. Secrets he hardly knew he carried, so deep had he buried them in his mind.

The piercing cry of an eagle slashed through the air, jerking his attention to the sky. The clouds had disappeared, leaving a hard, brittle blue that looked ready to crack with the slightest provocation.

Lowering his gaze to the fast-flowing water swollen

from the morning's rainstorm, a belated sense of relief nearly buckled his knees.

Not only had he saved a little boy's life but he feared he'd saved Rachel's, as well. Tristan knew enough about the youngest Hewitt's personality to know she would have jumped in the river to save the child. Though she'd proved herself anything but fragile, she was a small woman, with fine bones and delicate features. Regardless of her intent, the rapids were strong at this juncture in the river. She would have been carried her away with Donny.

Tristan's gut twisted at the thought. He instinctively rolled his shoulders, as if the gesture alone could shrug off his agitation.

Frowning, he surveyed the immediate area, left to right, right to left, widening the arc with each additional pass. Fort Nez Perce was busy with motion. Fatigued yet hopeful emigrants readied themselves for the final leg of their long journey.

The noise was constant, sounds of people coming and going, bartering for one last load of supplies, striking deals, negotiating bargains.

A thief was among them and headed straight for Oregon City.

Tristan snatched a quick breath of air.

Though still small by American standards, Oregon City was growing rapidly. Set on the east side of the Willamette River, just below the falls, the town boasted several businesses, including a blacksmith, a cooper, a general store and the new mercantile Grayson Hewitt had opened several months ago. They also had a small sawmill and a recently built flour mill.

Most of the residents were farmers working their own homesteads. But more and more people were choosing to live in town. Tristan had worked hard making Oregon City safe for its residents. Even without the threat of a thief, this current influx of emigrants would change the face of his town.

He prayed it would be for the better.

Mind on the future, he wove his way around the perimeter of the fort. The intense bartering dragged him back to the past, to his early days in Oregon Country. He and Siobhan had arrived with their two young daughters, with nearly no money and unspeakable hope in their hearts. So optimistic, both of them. So naive.

He missed Siobhan desperately. They'd weathered many storms together. The loss of her was like a gaping hole in his soul.

There'd been a dangerous moment when he'd nearly told Rachel how Siobhan's death had nearly destroyed him. If it hadn't been for his daughters, he didn't know if he would have survived the grief. For the girls' sake, he'd put aside his sorrow and had done what needed to be done. One step at a time.

One day at a time.

It hadn't been easy at first. It still wasn't. Most days were just plain difficult. With Siobhan it had been the two of them against the world. They'd grown up on neighboring farms in Ireland. Had fallen in love at nearly the same moment. Had left for America with the promise of a better life compelling them.

Tristan had acquired a piece of property east of the falls with the idea of farming the fertile land. But Siobhan's third pregnancy, fraught with problems, had necessitated abandoning the property and moving to town. Things had started to look up. And then she'd gone into labor.

Darkness filled Tristan's soul at the memory. He

shut his eyes momentarily and shoved aside his bleak thoughts.

"Sheriff, can you give us a hand?"

Welcoming the distraction from the depressing memories, he strode over to the raft where Ben Hewitt and Nathan Reed were laying out logs. He counted ten of equal length resting side by side. Matching triangular dovetail notches had already been cut on either end of each log.

Tristan took a quick count, grimaced. They would need at least six more logs if the Hewitts hoped to put all of their belongings on the finished raft.

"What can I do to help?"

"After we set this support beam in place, we need you to go behind us and secure each log with this." Ben tossed him a thick, sturdy length of rope. "Once we're through here, we'll start on the next raft."

Tristan looked at the pile of raw timber, realizing the men had cut down enough trees for two complete rafts, one for their family and one for Ben's fiancée and her father, or so he assumed.

Taking the rope, Tristan started securing the crossbeam to the first log, cinching each knot tighter than the one before. The Littleton and Jensen men worked on their own rafts a little farther down the river.

Amos and Grant Tucker were another hundred yards beyond that point, already loading their belongings onto their raft. A favorite among the other emigrants, the fraternal twins presented the picture of honor and Christian integrity.

Although their loyalty to each other was without question, something about the two didn't sit right with Tristan.

His instincts hummed a warning. Perhaps he was on edge because of Donny's near-drowning, or perhaps it was more.

Tristan narrowed his eyes.

Amos and Grant had already finished building their raft and were almost done loading up their considerable belongings—a lot of material possessions for two young, single men.

Once he was through here, Tristan would make it a priority to have a word with the Tucker brothers. He predicted a very interesting conversation.

Chapter Four

Midday approached with alarming speed. To Rachel's utter dismay, the Hewitt wagon was still nearly half-full. While Abby continued entertaining the children with her singing, Rachel and Emma unloaded the rest of their belongings.

On their immediate left, Abby's father quietly organized the contents of his own wagon. Over the past few months, Rachel had grown fond of Vernon Bingham. A short, thin man with a slight paunch, he sported a horseshoe patch of gray hair beneath a bald pate. Though not especially handsome, he had a pleasant disposition. And a ready smile.

Even with a hint of the sadness lingering in his blue eyes, he looked younger and healthier than when they'd left Missouri.

Prior to the fatal snakebite, his wife had been the heartier of Abby's parents. Martha Bingham's untimely death was a startling reminder that disaster could, and often did, show up at the most unexpected moments on the trail.

Rachel attributed the sting she felt in her eyes to thoughts of Mrs. Bingham's shocking demise and the void the woman's death had created in her family. Though no longer a child, Abby was now motherless. And Mr. Bingham was a widower.

That last thought brought to mind another widower.

Pressing a hand to her heart, Rachel glanced in the direction of the river to where Tristan worked side by side with her brother and Nathan. All three men had rolled up their sleeves, but Tristan's forearms were especially strong and muscular.

She knew he was a carpenter by trade. That certainly explained his dexterity with hammer, chisel and rope.

Watching him now, Rachel's stomach dipped before she had a chance to prepare for the sensation. She blinked and looked away quickly. Unfortunately, she couldn't stifle the sigh that leaked past her lips.

"Rachel?" Emma's concerned voice rang out from the interior of the wagon. "Is something the matter?"

"Oh, Emma, no. I'm sorry." To her embarrassment, she realized she'd been wasting precious time staring at Tristan. "I was…just—" she swallowed "—lost in thought."

Hoping to avoid additional questions, she took the stack of folded blankets from her sister's arms and set the pile on top of a nearby trunk.

Emma stared at her a long moment but thankfully ducked back into the wagon without voicing her thoughts aloud.

For the next half hour they worked in silence, Emma handing Rachel items from the wagon, Rachel finding a place for them with their other possessions.

The sky up above was clearer now, mostly blue and speckled with small patches of fluffy white clouds. A sure sign they'd seen the end of the rain. At least for today.

Not that another shower would slow down the wagon

train. Rachel's fellow travelers were a tenacious, hard-working bunch. With single-minded focus, they completed their tasks quickly and efficiently.

Rachel had witnessed countless displays of teamwork throughout the arduous journey. Though, originally, neighbor helping neighbor had been necessary for survival, the emigrants had become a makeshift family in recent months, sharing highs and lows, joys and tragedies, celebrations and sorrow.

Sighing, Rachel reached for the next load from Emma, a box of dry goods and kitchen utensils. Out of the corner of her eye, she saw Tristan tie off a rope and then step back to study his handiwork.

Even from this distance, she could make out the furrow of concentration on his brow. Or was that concern Rachel saw in his eyes? She couldn't quite decide.

He turned his head and focused on a spot farther down the river. He said something to Ben and, a second later, strode off in the direction he'd been looking.

He seemed to have a specific destination in mind with his ground-eating stride—very determined, very sheriff-like.

Rachel glanced ahead of him, past several clumps of men and women working, to where Grant and Amos Tucker were already loading up their raft.

She cocked her head, confused. Surely Tristan wasn't heading toward the brothers with that hard look on his face. Everyone liked the young men, Rachel included.

Grant, tall and wiry, with dark hair, gray eyes and a thin mustache, was a charmer and very likable. Amos, equally tall but more muscular, with eyes that tended toward greenish-brown, was always the first to offer compassion when someone was hurt or possessions went missing.

"We're nearly finished," Emma called out from the interior of the wagon. "Only a few things left to unload."

Realizing she was staring at Tristan *again*, Rachel reached out and accepted the next item from her sister.

The moment her fingers closed around the small wooden box, a sense of peace washed over her. Of all the possessions her family had packed in their wagon, the contents of this tiny keepsake held the most value for Rachel.

Perhaps packing the box had been self-indulgent on her part. Nothing inside was necessary for survival; nor did the meager contents carry any monetary value. Yet these had been her mother's most treasured possessions and represented a connection to the woman Rachel had lost far too soon, long before she was ready to say goodbye.

Watery images of her mother swirled through her mind, moments she couldn't quite bring into focus.

Her siblings had real memories of their mother. Rachel had only this box.

"That's all of it. We're officially unloaded." Looking pleased, Emma climbed out of the wagon and brushed her hands together once, twice, three times. "I'll let the men know we're finished."

Not waiting for Rachel's response, Emma headed toward the riverbank, her gaze riveted on her fiancé.

Happy for a brief moment alone, Rachel rounded the other side of the wagon. The children were still circled around Abby, settling in as she began weaving a cautionary tale about a greedy dog and his bone.

Her mother used to tell a similar story. If Rachel closed her eyes, she could almost hear Sara Hewitt tell the tale. Her voice had been as sweet and as musical as Abby's.

Feeling nostalgic, and maybe a bit sad, Rachel sat on the wagon's tailgate and spread her fingertips over the lid of the keepsake box she'd insisted on packing. The wildflowers painted on the lid were all but faded. The wood was smooth to the touch.

Overwhelmed with an urge to connect with her mother, Rachel removed the lid and studied the contents inside. There wasn't much. Several dried flowers, a miniature painting of a famous Philadelphia street, a tin rattle and matching cup, a handful of buttons that must have had significance at one time. And, lastly, the most precious possession of all—Sara Hewitt's journal.

Rachel pressed her palm to the worn leather binding. For years, she'd wondered what her mother had written on these pages. She'd attempted to read the first entry on several occasions, but something always kept her from continuing beyond the initial opening sentences.

These were Sara Hewitt's innermost private thoughts. Reading them seemed somehow wrong, intrusive even.

But now that her siblings were engaged to be married and Rachel was facing a future alone, she sensed her mother would understand her need to bond.

Refusing to think too hard about what she was doing, Rachel flipped open the book and read the first few lines.

At Pastor Wellborne's continued urging, I have decided to write down the thoughts I cannot speak aloud. I find myself both compelled and revolted by the idea of revealing the contents of my heart to anyone, even the Lord Himself.

Rachel flexed her fingers beneath the journal. She'd never read beyond this point before. She didn't know if she should continue now. In truth, she didn't know if she could.

And yet, she wanted this connection with her mother.

Bottom lip clamped between her teeth, she lowered her head and picked up where she'd left off.

> *We buried my precious daughter a fortnight ago, yet the pain of her loss is still fresh. I try to be brave. I try to hold back my sorrow, at least until I am alone. I do not succeed. How am I supposed to pretend all is well?*
> *My baby is dead.*

Rachel gasped at the pain she felt leaping out of those four words. *My baby is dead.*

"Oh, Mama." Rachel checked the date scrawled at the top of the page. *November 19, 1822.* Her mother had lost the child exactly a year before her own birth.

Had Rachel known that?

She couldn't remember ever being told about the strange coincidence. Why hadn't anyone told her?

Why did she sense it mattered? Shrugging, she carefully shut the book, hugged it tightly to her. Her mother's anguish was so real that Rachel's own sorrow swelled. And her breathing came far too quickly, in hard, painful snatches.

She lowered her head, thinking to pray, *needing* to pray. But for whom?

For her mother? The dead sister she'd never met?

A set of raised, angry voices captured her attention. She automatically turned her head toward the river.

Grant Tucker, his arms flailing wildly in the air, was talking—arguing—with Tristan. He appeared highly agitated.

Tristan, on the other hand, held himself perfectly still. There was something in the angle of his shoulders that didn't fit with the picture of his apparent tranquility. He was too composed, too unmoving. A storm brewed inside all that calm.

What had Grant and Amos done to garner such a reaction?

Rachel hated not knowing.

Tristan is a lawman, she reminded herself. He's trained to handle all sorts of unpleasantness. She should let him deal with the situation as he saw fit. She should sit back, watch and wait.

The very idea went against her nature.

What harm could there be in moving a few steps closer? Just a smidge closer…

Standing toe to toe with Grant Tucker, Tristan kept his temper buried behind a bland stare and a deceptively mild tone. Against his advice, the brothers were determined to travel down the river ahead of the other emigrants.

Not only was Grant unmoved by Tristan's repeated warnings about the dangerous rapids along the route, he didn't have a problem vocalizing his displeasure.

Even now, as Tristan attempted to reason with the man yet again, Grant's voice hit a decibel that could be heard at least a hundred yards away. Maybe two hundred, if the interested stares from the other emigrants was anything to go by.

"Stay out of our business, Sheriff."

As Grant made a point to hold Tristan's stare, Amos casually slipped the edge of their overloaded raft into the water.

Tristan caught the move anyway and frowned.

"Do not head out alone," he warned. "It's a mistake."

Grant snorted. "We'll just see about that, now won't we?"

Tristan instincts hummed. Grant's continued belligerence didn't fit with his charming reputation. The man wasn't what he seemed; nor was his brother.

Had Tristan found the wagon train thief? Or rather, *thieves*?

Before he made any accusation, he needed to get a better look at their possessions, primarily the large trunk situated on the port side of the raft.

Buying himself a bit of time, he studied the raft with a carpenter's eye. "You didn't cut those notches deep enough and you failed to secure the logs properly on the port side."

"The raft will float."

Possibly. However…

"It won't withstand the rapids, or the—"

Grant cut him off midsentence. "We've forded a river before."

"Even if that's true, the Columbia can be tricky this time of year."

"We'll be fine." Grant gave his brother a quick nod.

Amos shoved the rest of the raft into the water. He climbed on top, then tested the sturdiness and buoyancy with a few foot stomps.

The raft tipped dangerously to port. For a moment, Tristan thought the trunk might slip into the water, but eventually the raft settled into an unsteady bob.

Grant shot Tristan a smug grin. "Guess this is farewell."

Not quite. Tristan eyed the large piece of luggage the brothers had foolishly placed on the far edge of the raft. "That your trunk?"

"Yeah, it's ours."

"Looks like it belongs to a woman." The ivy and floral design were a dead giveaway.

"Yeah, well…" Grant maneuvered his rangy body in

an attempt to block Tristan's view. "It was our…ma's, and now it belongs to us."

Tristan heard the lie buried inside the hostile tone, could see the deception in the man's shifting eyes and curled upper lip.

Amos picked up a long pole and placed it in the water, digging around until he found purchase on the rocky bottom. "Time to get a move on."

Tristan peered around Grant. "What's the rush?"

Amos avoided eye contact. "No rush, just don't like to waste daylight."

Another lie.

"Your raft is unevenly weighted," Tristan pointed out. "I suggest moving that trunk to the middle and—"

"It stays where it is." Amos shot out his hand and set his palm flat on top of the trunk's lid.

The swift gesture hiked up his sleeve, revealing a long scar from wrist to elbow. From the angry red puffs at either end, the wound wasn't fully healed yet.

Tristan's eyes narrowed. "What happened to your arm?"

"Childhood accident."

And the lies just kept piling up.

Again, Tristan leaned forward for a better glimpse of the trunk beneath Amos's hand. "What you got stowed in there, anyway?"

"That's none of your concern." Grant waded thigh deep into the water, shoved the raft slightly forward and then hopped on board.

The additional weight threw his brother off balance. A string of muttered oaths ensued, followed by a round of weaving and bobbing. With the help of his pole, Amos regained control of the raft. Barely.

Once he found his sea legs, Grant rose to his full height and touched the brim of his hat. "See ya, Sheriff."

"You're making a mistake," Tristan called out over the sound of rushing water.

The words had barely left his mouth when the current caught the back end of the raft and spun it in a quick, sharp circle. Grant dove on top of the trunk and hung on with a white-knuckled grip.

Amos frantically dug his pole into the river bottom. His efforts only added to the chaos, spinning the raft in harder, faster circles. With each turn, more of the twins' possessions splashed into the water.

From behind him, Tristan heard the sound of footsteps pounding toward the riverbank, followed by shouts of warnings and suggestions.

Tristan cupped his palms around his mouth. "Amos, stop fighting the current. You're better off riding it out."

Ignoring him, Amos continued battling the rapids.

Rachel Hewitt joined the other emigrants on the shoreline. "Hold on, Grant, Amos." She rose onto her toes. "We'll get someone out to help you."

The raft listed heavily to port, dumping more of the men's possessions in the water. The pole slipped out of Amos's hand.

The river had complete control of the raft now, carrying it straight toward a cluster of mean-looking, jagged rocks that stuck out of the water barely fifty feet up ahead.

Running on the shoreline, Tristan shouted out a warning. Ben Hewitt and James Stillwell came up beside him. The three of them kept even pace with the out-of-control raft.

Rachel was only a few steps behind them. "Look out for the rocks," she shouted. "Grant, Amos, look out."

Her warning came too late.

The raft smashed headlong into the rocks.

Amos immediately lost his footing and fell into the water. His shout for help was nearly lost in the sound of crashing waves. He went under fast but then popped up a few seconds later near the opposite shoreline.

Battered by rock and waves, Grant still managed to hold his position atop the raft as he clung to the trunk. Man and luggage swirled in a hard, tight circle. The second crash was as ugly as the first. This time, Grant lost his hold. He went into the water screaming for help.

Amos was close enough to reach out and grab his brother's foot. He pulled Grant free of the raging water and dragged him to shore. Both men then fell to their hands and knees, gasping for air.

Grant recovered first. He jumped to his feet and glanced frantically around. His eyes landed on the trunk, now stuck atop a group of rocks near where Tristan stood.

He waded back into the water.

Tristan did the same on his side of the river.

"We have to get to that trunk before Grant does." He directed his words at Ben and James Stillwell.

Neither man questioned him. They simply followed his lead.

When Rachel attempted to step into the water, as well, Tristan placed a palm in the air to stop her progress. "Stay back."

"But Grant and Amos need our help." Her chin tilted at a determined angle. "They need—"

"*I* need you to keep the crowd at bay."

"What crowd?" She glanced over her shoulder. "Oh, my."

Tristan's sentiments exactly.

Dozens of gawking men, women and children were

lining up along the riverbank. At least a dozen more were in the process of abandoning their tasks and heading over.

Frowning, Rachel stretched out her arms. "Everyone step away from the river and give the sheriff room to work."

As she herded her fellow travelers away from the river's edge, the trail boss shouldered in next to her. The two quickly restored order.

With Ben and Stillwell's help, Tristan wrestled the Tuckers' trunk out of the water and onto dry land.

The latch sprung open.

"Well, well." Tristan tossed back the heavy lid and peered inside. "What have we here?"

Chapter Five

The trail boss proved far more skillful at crowd control than Rachel. Not that this surprised her. Sam Weston had considerable experience managing disasters along the trail. Throughout the hazardous five-month journey he'd employed whatever technique was necessary to keep the emigrants calm, focused and, as was the case today, out of the way.

"Let's get back to work, people." He stalked back and forth among the concerned onlookers. "We leave in one hour."

Amid grumbles and rapid-fire questions concerning the Tuckers' accident and the potential for more calamities on the water, he remained firm.

"One hour," he repeated. "We wait for no one."

Sam Weston never issued empty threats. Therefore, despite obvious concern over the next leg of their journey, the crowd dispersed.

At last, Rachel was free to return to the water's edge. By the time she had picked her way across the rocky beach, Ben and James had rescued most of the twins' possessions from the river.

Tristan rifled through a large trunk that Rachel recognized as belonging to the Tucker brothers. The expression in his sharp green eyes was solemn, even a little austere. With that tight jawline and rigid set of his shoulders, he looked pure male, all lawman.

Every ounce the dedicated sheriff.

Curiosity drove Rachel closer, close enough to peer at the contents inside the trunk.

Her throat tightened in outrage.

For several long seconds she couldn't speak. There were so many familiar items, items that had randomly disappeared in recent months.

Mind reeling, she took a quick mental inventory. There, atop a pale gray blanket, sat the lace shawl that had once belonged to Abby's mother. And there, smashed up against the far right corner, was Mrs. Jenson's silver hairbrush.

Torn between shock and utter dismay, Rachel counted at least twenty pieces of jewelry. Necklaces, bracelets, a lovely cameo and—she gasped—Sally Littleton's wedding ring that had gone missing just this morning. There was also money inside the trunk, so much of it her mind boggled.

As if all that wasn't bad enough, her gaze landed on her sister's missing hair combs. The very ones Nathan Reed had been accused of stealing before he and Emma had fallen in love. He'd even been brought to trial by the wagon train committee and had only been cleared when new thefts occurred while he was incapacitated.

Anger surged, blurring Rachel's vision. She opened her mouth, closed it, felt her cheeks grow hot. Lips pressed in a grim line, Rachel reached out, ran her fingertip across the combs.

All this time, all these months, Grant and Amos Tucker had been the thieves. They'd remained silent throughout

Nathan's trial. They'd been willing to allow an innocent man to take the blame for their treachery.

The vile reprobates.

A fresh spurt of fury rushed through Rachel. Her cheeks grew hotter still. She practically trembled with the dark emotion.

"Where are they?" She spit out the question even as she searched the river. "Where are Grant and Amos?"

"Over there." Tristan angled his head toward the opposite side of river.

Rachel looked in the direction Tristan indicated. The moment her gaze swept over the Tuckers, she opened her mouth, but again nothing came out. Not a whisper, not a squeak.

All she could do was watch in stunned silence as the twins faced off with each other. They seemed to be engaged in a verbal battle, which quickly escalated to pushing and shoving.

Amos slammed his hands against Grant's shoulders. Grant returned the favor, sending his brother back several steps.

"Hey, boys, looks like you left a few things behind."

Pausing midshove, Grant pulled away from his brother and stomped to the river's edge. The thunderous expression on his face distorted his features, giving him a twisted, almost sinister look. "You got no right searching through our stuff."

"*Your* stuff? Now see, that's where you're wrong. This does not belong to you." Tristan waved the hairbrush, then reached inside the trunk and retrieved the cameo. "Nor does this."

He picked up Mrs. Bingham's shawl, studied the design with casual slowness. "Or *this*."

Grant shouted out something foul concerning Tristan's

heritage. Rachel gasped at the venom in the other man's words, could only marvel at Tristan's calm demeanor as he carefully returned the stolen items to the trunk, then prowled like a large menacing cat to the water's edge.

Feet planted in a wide-legged stance, his expression turned so hard, so threatening, that Rachel shivered.

"Come over here and say that to my face," Tristan said through gritted teeth.

"Maybe I will." Grant splashed into the water up to his knees. He looked prepared to dive into the river, but Amos grabbed his arm and yanked him backward.

Struggling against his brother's grip, Grant fought for release.

Amos refused to let him go. He muttered frantically to him about something Rachel couldn't quite make out.

Finally, Grant broke free of Amos. But instead of jumping into the water, he stayed put. "This ain't over, Sheriff. You'll pay for interfering in our business." Grant shook his clenched fist in the air. "I'll see to it personally."

Tristan smiled at the threat. "You're welcome to try."

One last foul oath, then Grant spun around and headed in the direction of the Cascade Mountains.

Amos trailed closely behind him.

At some point during the heated exchange, Rachel's brother and James Stillwell had commandeered a canoe.

The two approached the river, discussing various strategies for apprehending the brothers. Tristan joined them, adding his own opinions and a sense of urgency to the discussion.

As a section leader and one of the elected committee members for the wagon train, Ben's involvement made sense. What Rachel couldn't understand was why Mr. Stillwell had insinuated himself into the matter.

She voiced her confusion aloud.

"I'm an agent with Thayer & Edwards safe company," he said simply.

Rachel wasn't quite sure what that had to do with his desire to apprehend the Tucker twins. Then she remembered right before the wagon train left Missouri someone had broken into a special heavy-duty safe containing a considerable amount of money belonging to several local merchants.

"You're here because of the robbery back in Independence," she said. "The safe that was broken into was made by your company?"

"That's right," he confirmed. "I joined the wagon train when I discovered evidence that suggested the thief, or rather *thieves*," he corrected, glaring across the river, "were using the journey to hide their escape."

"Oh, does that mean…you—" Rachel paused, considered the man through narrowed eyes "—aren't meeting up with family in Oregon City?"

"Correct." He reached inside the trunk and picked up a handful of loose bills. "My job was to recover the stolen money, no matter how long it took."

Rachel dropped her gaze to the interior of the trunk. "There must be hundreds of dollars in there."

"Thousands," he said, his eyes troubled. "The Tucker brothers have gone to a lot of trouble transporting this trunk across miles of difficult, rugged land."

Rachel sighed. Grant and Amos had seemed so charming, so likable. In reality, they were nothing but liars and thieves. Now her brother and Tristan were leading the charge to capture them.

Rachel's heart tightened with fear. Ben had been keeping order and breaking up fights since their first day on the trail. Tristan was a town sheriff. She had to trust they could handle themselves in this situation.

Still, she lifted up a prayer for their safety, then added, *Lord, bring Grant and Amos to swift justice.*

The moment she finished the prayer, she caught sight of Tristan climbing into the canoe with Ben.

Tristan's a lawman, she reminded herself. Of course he would set out to apprehend the Tucker brothers. Nevertheless, she lifted up yet another prayer for Tristan's safety.

James attempted to join the two men in the canoe, but Tristan waved him off. "We'll pursue the brothers," he said. "You stay with the money."

The agent looked prepared to argue, then seemed to think better of it. "Good plan."

Ben and Tristan navigated the rapids quickly, but the twins had covered a lot of ground already.

Another rush of fear rose to the back of Rachel's throat and stuck. No amount of swallowing dislodged the sensation.

James Stillwell's voice dropped over her. "I should probably determine which of these items were stolen and which actually belong to the Tuckers."

The suggestion was exactly what Rachel needed to distract her from worrying about Tristan and her brother. "I can help with that."

"I was hoping you would say that." They shared an awkward smile, then simultaneously dropped their gazes to the trunk.

Rachel sighed again. "I find it hard to believe Grant and Amos could be so, so…" She shook her head. "Deceitful."

"They fooled everyone, Miss Hewitt, including me."

Bottom lip caught between her teeth, Rachel watched Ben and Tristan pull the canoe onto the opposite shore and set down their oars.

A short nod passed between them, and then off they went, Tristan leading the way over the first ridge.

Refusing to allow her fears to overwhelm her, Rachel reached inside the trunk and picked up the first item. The silver hairbrush. "This belongs to Delores Jensen."

Better, she thought, now that she had something to do with her hands.

What seemed like hours passed. In actuality, Ben and Tristan returned barely twenty minutes later.

They were alone.

Eyes locked with hers, Tristan climbed out of the canoe.

Pleased to see him, and mildly surprised by the depth of her reaction, Rachel went to meet him. She desperately wanted to touch his face, to assure herself that he was unscathed, but that wouldn't be proper. Or appropriate.

She settled for searching his features with only her gaze.

"What happened?" she asked, somewhat alarmed at how breathless she sounded.

Lifting his hat a moment, Tristan ran a frustrated hand through his hair. "We lost them in the cliffs."

"We could see them, but couldn't get to them." Ben wiped sweat off his brow. "They had too much of a head start on us."

James slapped his hand on the trunk's lid. "I doubt they'll leave all this without a fight. We'd be smart to come up with a plan to keep the money safe and—"

"Ben! Oh, Ben, I heard the Tucker brothers are the thieves and that you went after them." Eyes slightly wild, Abby lifted her hand to touch Ben's face. "Are you all right? Are you hurt anywhere?"

"I'm fine, Abby." He cradled her small hand inside his. "Frustrated. No, make that *angry,* but fine."

The two leaned in close and spoke in hushed whispers. Pulling back slightly, Abby took Ben's hand, pressed a kiss to the inside of his palm.

The gesture was brief, even casual, yet somehow intimate, as well. Rachel felt like an intruder, watching Abby fuss over Ben while he attempted to soothe away her concerns with soft words and gentle touches.

Turning her back on the two, Rachel tried to stifle a sigh.

Tristan looked up at the sound. For a moment, his eyes softened and the stiffness in his shoulders eased. She tried to smile at him, but her mouth wobbled instead. A rush of…*something* spread through her, a brief, unexpected need to belong to someone, to anyone.

To Tristan?

Too soon, her mind told her. It was entirely too soon to fall for the man, to think about belonging to him, to wish for something that might never be possible.

She must be logical.

She must remember to guard her heart.

Too late, her traitorous heart whispered. *Too, too late*.

Giving in to that sigh, after all, she pressed her hands tightly together. Either that or go to Tristan and…and…

She cut off the rest of her thoughts. "I have to go."

"Go?" He tilted his head to one side. "Go where?"

"I have to…" *Think, Rachel, think*. "I have to return these stolen items to their rightful owners."

Not waiting for his response, she gathered up an armload of objects that belonged to fellow travelers and hurried away.

Later that afternoon, just before sunset, Tristan decided that Sam Weston was the most competent, efficient trail boss he'd ever met. Despite the trouble with Grant and Amos Tucker and the shock among the emigrants over the twins' deception, the wagon train left Fort Nez Perce at high noon. Right on schedule.

Now, with the sun bumping up against the horizon and leaving a spectacular array of color in its wake, Weston waved his hand above his head.

The day's travel had come to an end.

More than ready for a break, Tristan guided the raft he shared with James Stillwell and another emigrant through the rough current toward the shoreline.

Hopping onto the rocky beach, he looked around, fought off a surge of dark foreboding. His encounter with the Tuckers had put him on edge, making him feel scraped raw on the inside. He hated that they'd escaped, hated knowing they would show up again yet not knowing when.

When they returned, and they *would* return for the items they wrongfully believed belonged to them, they would probably be desperate. Desperate equaled reckless. Reckless equaled innocents being harmed. That was the most troublesome part of all.

With Abby and her father's assistance, Ben Hewitt guided the Bingham raft to shore next to where Tristan stood.

Nathan Reed guided the Hewitts' raft in beside the Binghams'. Rachel, Emma and Clarence Pressman rode with him, but only Rachel appeared to be of any help.

Emma, usually the more graceful of the two Hewitt sisters, couldn't find her balance without assistance. Her face had taken on a greenish tint. Clearly, the woman wasn't meant to travel by water. By the looks of her, Tristan doubted she would find her sea legs before the wagon train arrived in Oregon City.

Rachel, on the other hand, was poetry in motion.

Tristan couldn't take his eyes off her. Her strength and ease of movement belied her small stature. The moment the raft was secure on dry land, she immediately focused on her sister.

"Emma." She took the other woman's arm and carefully guided her to a large flat rock beyond the shoreline. "Sit down and rest."

"But we have to unload our supplies for the night, and then start supper, and—"

"I'll take care of everything from here. All you need to do is focus on catching your breath."

She looked over her shoulder, barely glanced at Clarence and said, "You there, I need your help."

"M-m-me?"

"Yes, you. Come here."

Tristan bit back a smile at Rachel's curt order. She might be a little bossy, but no one could accuse her of failing to get the job done.

Case in point, Clarence obeyed Rachel's command without question.

"Don't let Emma move from this rock until Nathan and I are finished unloading the raft."

"O-okay." Not meeting Rachel's gaze, Clarence tugged a floppy hat over his—*her*—eyes, then sat on the ground beside Emma.

Seemingly satisfied the two would stay put, Rachel went to work unloading the Hewitts' raft.

Tristan offered to assist.

"Oh, I…" She paused, as if just realizing he'd been standing there watching her. "Yes, thank you, Tristan. I could use your help."

For the next half hour they worked side by side, unloading only what the family would need for the night.

They functioned in perfect harmony, silently anticipating each other's move without the need for words.

Tristan couldn't help sneaking a glance at Rachel out of the corner of his eye. Her hair had come loose from her braid, spilling past her shoulders in coffee-colored spirals.

Something clutched at his heart, something soft and tender, making him pause to take in the view of her working. Rachel Hewitt really was quite pretty, even after a full afternoon of uncomfortable travel. She was also competent and unafraid to exert herself, loyal to a fault and clearly loved her family with a ferocity he admired.

For weeks, Tristan had convinced himself he'd joined the wagon train to find a mother for his daughters. Now he wondered—did he want a wife for himself, as well?

The thought brought a pang of something sharp and sad in his gut. Not quite guilt, not quite loneliness, and he realized two years had come and gone since Siobhan's death. Two long, lonely years. He missed having someone in his life, missed sharing the ups and downs, the hardships and the triumphs.

No, that wasn't completely true. He had someone in his life. Three very special, very precious little girls who needed his full attention, his protection, his daily love and support. Something vaguely like homesickness spread within him.

A soft female voice slid over him. "Tristan?"

He found Rachel staring up at him, her dark eyes searching his face. He immediately smoothed out his expression, evened out his tone. "Yes?"

"You're welcome to join me, I mean…my family tonight for supper. I often make too much food, no need to let it go to waste."

The invitation itself didn't catch him by surprise, but

rather the way Rachel issued it, with a shyness he didn't often attribute to her. He cleared his throat, hooked his hands behind his back, looked out over the mountains in the near distance. The idea of sharing a meal with her felt…somehow…right.

And yet completely and utterly wrong.

Allowing himself to become too close to her, even over a simple meal, could prove a mistake.

Or the wisest decision you've made in years.

He shook his head.

"I appreciate the offer," he began carefully, fighting off a fresh wave of loneliness and an unwanted surge of longing. "But I must decline."

She didn't understand his response. He could tell by the way her eyebrows pulled together.

"I have too many duties pressing in on me," he found himself explaining, "and…"

He faltered, made another attempt to explain himself, but words failed him and so he just stood there, hands still clasped behind his back, feeling stubborn and awkward and far too out of control for his liking.

"I tell you what." Rachel's fingers closed over his arm, squeezed gently, then dropped away. "I'll make you a plate and keep it warm until you have time to eat."

The offer was given casually yet again carried a hint of shyness in the tone that he didn't usually associate with this woman.

Instantly charmed, he relented. "Thank you, Rachel. I'd appreciate that."

"Well, then, consider it done." She locked gazes with him, smiled. Warmth wrapped around his heart and gently caressed the ache there, an ache he'd lived with for so long he'd nearly grown used to the sensation.

This small, outspoken, opinionated woman had somehow slipped beneath his guard, made him wish for things he'd forgotten existed. He didn't like it. Not one bit.

Breaking eye contact, he said a few quick words of farewell. It wasn't until twilight turned the big open sky a deep lavender hue that he made his way back to Rachel, er, the Hewitt family. All around him crickets chirped, fires snapped, conversations buzzed. The sound of a mandolin accompanied pretty female voices singing a favorite hymn of his from childhood. Tristan could pick out Rachel's above the others.

He realized he actually liked Rachel Hewitt.

Would his daughters like her, as well?

Although they needed a mother, Tristan wasn't sure Rachel was the woman he wanted to fill that role. Something about her put him on guard. He couldn't—*wouldn't*—allow just anyone into his home. Especially a woman who made him think as much about himself as his daughters.

No good would come from mistaking what he needed in a wife, or what he was able to provide a woman in return. He'd already had his chance at love. He didn't want another. Somehow, he doubted a marriage in name only would satisfy a young woman like Rachel Hewitt.

He approached the Hewitt campfire. As if she'd been watching for his arrival, Rachel rose to meet him.

Eyes glittering in the firelight, she handed him a tin plate. He bit back a grin at the large helping of salt-cured ham, beans and three—*three!*—biscuits. "Looks good."

"Sit." She motioned to an empty spot next to her future brother-in-law. "Eat."

Dangerously charmed by her no-nonsense manner, Tristan settled on the ground and, avoiding eye contact with the disturbing woman, dug into his food.

"Where's Ben?" he asked when his plate was nearly empty.

Abby's father answered. "He and my daughter are out walking. It's become a tradition of theirs."

Tradition. The word stuck in Tristan's mind, swirled there a moment, tugging at him, nagging at his composure. Siobhan had been one for traditions. His thoughts turned to his daughters and the Spartan existence the four of them lived. He had his hands full caring for them. He didn't think much beyond getting from one day to the next.

What new traditions had he given his daughters? None, he realized, and decided a few changes were in order.

His gaze found Rachel. Perhaps, he thought with a slice of panic, the changes had already begun.

Chapter Six

Over the next three days Rachel and her fellow travelers endured an unending cycle of miserable sameness. Each morning, just before the sun peaked out from the horizon, they pushed their rafts into the river. They traveled until noon, paused only long enough to eat a quick meal, before casting off again.

The unpredictable current, coupled with the brutally fierce winds, battered Rachel's attempts to maintain her usual optimism.

Endless bobbing and weaving. Endless hours stretching into endless days. Endless. Endless. Endless.

From atop the Hewitt raft, Rachel pressed her lips firmly together and faced out over the water. Acres upon acres of trees lined the shores. Under normal circumstances, she might have enjoyed the colors in the autumn leaves.

Under normal circumstances, she might have found the wild, untamed underbrush somewhat pretty.

These were not normal circumstances.

At least the Columbia River was behind them and they were now floating down the Willamette. One more day to go, according to Tristan.

Tristan.

Rachel felt a familiar flutter in her stomach. There'd been a moment the other night when their eyes had met over the campfire and held. She'd felt the impact of his stare all the way to her spine. Even now, days later, her heart began to thump with a curious mix of hope and despair.

Was he starting to see her as a woman in her own right, not merely as his friend's youngest sister? Did she *want* him to see her that way?

Lifting onto her toes, she defied her own good sense and searched for his tall, muscular form. She caught sight of him several rafts up ahead. He traveled with James Stillwell and another emigrant. The stolen money was enclosed in the large trunk placed between the three of them.

Just then, Tristan looked over his shoulder and caught her staring at him. He smiled at her just a little, more a crooked slant of his lips, yet everything inside her trembled.

She tried to break the connection, but she could hardly move, could barely breathe. Mr. Stillwell seemed to be talking and, thankfully, Tristan looked back in the other man's direction.

Good timing.

Another series of rapids approached.

Before Rachel could fully prepare, the raft beneath her dipped and swayed. She lost her footing, reached out and gripped a nearby box to steady herself. Once she had her balance restored, she let go. Water splashed across her face.

Sighing, she raised her hand to swipe at her cheeks but dropped it when a throaty boom of thunder rolled across the sky.

"No point," she whispered. *No point.* Not with water everywhere and yet another rainstorm poised for attack.

She gave the darkening sky a cold, hard glare. No lightning yet. By now, Rachel should be used to the random downpours.

She was not.

Water beneath her, water falling from the sky above, would she ever feel warm and dry again?

At least she wasn't seasick. Her sister wasn't so fortunate. Poor Emma. She looked so pale, and nearly as miserable as her friend Clarence, who clung to the edge of the raft with a white-knuckle grip.

The two had been inseparable over the past three days. Oddly enough, Nathan didn't seem concerned by the unusually close relationship Emma had with another man.

Was it because Clarence was so timid, so reluctant to connect with others? Rachel couldn't think of a time when she'd actually seen Clarence's face. She'd never once made direct eye contact with the man. Even now, head hung low, Clarence stared at his lap. In that slumped posture, he looked wilted and downtrodden and Rachel suspected he was as seasick as Emma.

On cue, the pitiful man leaned over the edge of the raft.

Emma, likely battling her own wave of nausea, rubbed Clarence's back and cooed soothing words. Words that seemed out of place for a man. Maybe a young boy, or even a...

Rachel narrowed her eyes. She moved closer, dropped low enough to get a better glimpse of the man's face but couldn't find the proper angle.

"Just think," Emma murmured to her friend. "When this is over, you'll have your very own tiny blessing."

What an odd thing to say, Rachel thought, scooting closer. Was he married?

Clarence croaked out a mumbled response in a high-pitched voice, a voice that was nearly female in nature. Female?

"Now, now, none of that," Emma scolded. "You aren't alone. You have Nathan and me, and you will soon have your…"

The rest of her words were swallowed up by another crash of thunder.

One more step closer and Rachel could finally see Clarence's face. The skin was smooth, nearly poreless, like a young boy's, or…

Rachel gasped. "You're a woman."

"Shh, not so loud." Emma's panicked gaze swung up to meet hers. "No one must know she's not a man."

"But why?" Rachel searched her mind for a reason, could think of none, at least none that would matter at this late date. "We're nearly to Oregon City. Surely whatever made it necessary to disguise her gender can't be an issue anymore."

"Please." The plea came from Clarence as he, or rather, *she* collapsed against Emma. "You can't reveal my secret. An unattached woman isn't allowed on the wagon train."

"That's not precisely true," Rachel countered, thinking of two other unattached women who'd each hired themselves out to a family on the wagon train. "Mary Connor is unattached, as is Lucy O'Brian."

Emma came immediately to her friend's defense. "It's not that simple."

Frowning at her sister, Rachel lowered to her knees and considered Clarence more closely. No, not Clarence. "What's your real name?"

"Clara."

Rachel took in the rounded cheeks, bow-shaped lips and pretty brown—albeit poorly cut—hair. "You look like a Clara." She touched the other woman's hand in the same manner she might a frightened child. "I still don't understand the need for all the secrecy."

Clara glanced at Emma. Emma patted her friend's hand.

Seeming to draw courage from the obvious support, Clara pulled in a shaky breath of air. "My husband and I sold everything we owned to join the wagon train. But Adam fell ill not long after we left Pennsylvania. He died before we reached Missouri. He…"

She stopped speaking, choked back a sob. The sound was so full of grief Rachel felt the woman's pain as if were her own. Though she'd never been married, she knew what it was like to lose a loved one. "I'm sorry for your loss."

"Adam was my whole world. He took care of everything and made all our decisions. When he died, I had no idea what to do or where to turn, especially those first few days. Afraid someone would try to take advantage of a woman traveling alone, I dressed as a man, in his clothes, and continued on as planned."

"That still doesn't explain why you didn't attempt to hire yourself out to a family."

"By the time I made it to Missouri all the available positions had been filled."

Ah. "So you continued on as Clarence."

Clara nodded. "It seemed the only option. My sister and her husband are all the family I have left. They live in Oregon City and are awaiting my arrival."

What a tragic tale. Though she couldn't imagine making the same choices as Clara, Rachel couldn't be sure. She'd never been alone and desperate and without family close by. Knowing Clara's sister awaited her arrival in Oregon City, Rachel couldn't deny there was an odd sort of logic to her decisions.

Rachel glanced over at Nathan, only now realizing he was watching the three of them in silence. His protective behavior of Clarence—Clara—made better sense, as did his encouragement of a friendship between Emma and the other woman.

"Who else, besides the people on this raft, knows your secret?" Rachel asked.

"No one," Emma said. "We must keep it that way, at least until we arrive in Oregon City."

At this, Nathan broke his silence. "I fear we aren't the only people who know about Clara."

The woman's eyes filled with terror. "Someone else knows I'm a woman?"

"Sheriff McCullough has it figured out." Nathan looked out over the water, connected his gaze with the man in question. "Nothing gets past him."

The hard tone in Nathan's voice disturbed Rachel. She understood Nathan's original distrust of Tristan. After all, they'd been pursuing the same woman, at least at first. But when Tristan had discovered the truth about Nathan and Emma's feelings for each other, he had done the right thing and backed off. He'd behaved with honor and integrity.

He would do so in this situation, as well.

"You can trust Tristan with your secret." Rachel defended him without question, willed Clara to accept the truth of her words. "He's a good man, moral and upright. He won't hurt you. In fact, he'll help you, I'm sure of it. He'll—"

Clara cut her off. "There's more."

Rachel didn't like the sound of that. Because it seemed

the right thing to do, she closed her hand over Clara's and waited for the other woman to continue.

Clara pulled away from her and placed her fingertips to her rounded belly. "I'm not traveling alone."

Not quite grasping what the words meant, Rachel blinked at the other woman, felt her eyebrows slam together. "But you said your husband died and there was no one left except your sister and her husband in Oregon City."

"I'm with child."

Stunned, Rachel dropped her gaze to the woman's belly, the overly large, rounded belly. For five months on the trail Clara had kept her condition a secret? It hardly seemed possible that others hadn't noticed the changes in her body, even hidden beneath the men's clothing.

Lies and deception, though well-meaning, had brought them to this uncomfortable place. And now, Rachel was a part of the pretense, whether she liked it or not. "How far along are you?"

"Eight months." Clara screwed her face into a scowl. "Maybe a bit longer."

Rachel's stomach knotted with apprehension. "Are you saying you could have the baby at any moment?"

"Yes."

Oh, my. There'd already been too many tragedies on the trail so far. If Clara had the baby before they reached Oregon City, there could very well be another one to add to the list. Perhaps even two.

Please, Lord, Rachel prayed. *Please keep Clara's babe from coming until we make it to Oregon City.*

The rain chose that moment to let loose, coming down in hard, unforgiving blasts of cold, needlelike pellets.

Sighing, Rachel looked up at the sky and wondered if

the rain was a good sign or the precursor of a very challenging day ahead.

Only time would tell.

Later that night, after leaving the stolen money in James Stillwell's care, Tristan found himself with too much free time on his hands. Nothing needed his immediate attention. The rain had stopped, but now a cold chill hung in the air and a dark feeling of gloom permeated the campground.

After days of river travel, the emigrants were exhausted, water-logged and ready for the journey to end. Tristan sympathized. But if they thought the hardships were nearly over, they were in for a disappointment. Oregon country was mostly wild frontier. The land was fertile, yes, but uncultivated and refused to be tamed easily.

Some of the people that survived the hardships of the trail wouldn't live through winter.

Tristan closed his eyes against the thought, forced himself to listen to the sounds of the night. He could almost hear the Willamette Falls in the distance. The sound of home.

Close, so close. A few more miles and he would be with his daughters once again. He brought their sweet faces to mind. So pretty, all three of his girls, so in need of a woman's influence in their lives. They needed more than a woman's influence. They needed a mother.

Opening his eyes, he looked around, wondered why he'd come on this journey at all. No, he wouldn't allow himself to feel regret over failing to find a mother for his daughters on the wagon train. He must have faith the Lord would provide.

Faith, such a simple word with such a lofty, often slippery meaning. Faith had never come easy for Tristan, harder still since losing Siobhan. The pain of her passing would always be with him, but it had become more manageable lately.

Tristan no longer argued with the Lord about the unfairness of his wife's death. He no longer questioned why her and not him. In truth, he no longer prayed much at all, other than to ask the Lord to give him the endurance to get through each day as it came.

Tristan would provide his daughters with a suitable mother. However, now that he'd had time to think on the matter during several sleepless nights, he was more convinced than ever that he needed to secure a marriage in name only. He refused to put another woman through the dangers of childbirth. Surely, there was someone out there who would agree to his terms. He simply had to find her.

In the meantime, he had other concerns, such as luring the Tuckers out of hiding. He and James Stillwell had discussed possible scenarios, traps really, but nothing firm had been decided. Frustrated they hadn't come up with a workable plan, he took off his hat, slapped it against his thigh and scowled into the night.

"Tristan?" A soft hand touched his arm. "Is something the matter?"

As he jammed his hat back on his head, he knew he would find Rachel's concerned gaze when he turned his head. Despite their awkward beginning, they'd somehow managed to forge a tenuous friendship during this final leg of the journey.

He felt a closeness to this woman that defied logic. The realization left him feeling oddly hollow, maybe even a little angry. Guilty, as well.

Siobhan had been the heart and soul of him, the only woman he ever loved. The hole left in his life after her death was filled by his daughters now. There wasn't room for anyone else.

His scowl dug deeper at the thought.

"I'm bothering you." She drew in a small breath and her hand fell away from his arm. "I'll leave you alone."

He didn't want to be alone. He wanted…

Truthfully, he didn't know what he wanted.

"You aren't bothering me," he found himself saying. "I was just thinking about tomorrow."

"Ah." She smiled at him, a pretty, soul-soothing smile.

Instead of calming him, the gesture sent his pulse roaring through his veins.

His earlier anger dug deeper, taking root, morphing into something equally disturbing.

Something that felt like…coming alive again.

Tristan had given up feeling alive. Though he told himself that he waited on the Lord, he didn't really know how to wait. He certainly didn't know how to surrender his will to an invisible, silent God. Best to make things happen on his own, through his own power and on his own timetable.

He frowned, realizing the implications of his current approach to life. How was he supposed to teach the girls to believe in God when he struggled with his own faith?

"You miss your daughters." It wasn't a question and so he didn't treat it as one.

"Always."

Rachel nodded and that light of understanding in her eyes made him feel a surge of hope again, followed by another burst of anger. He preferred the anger, relished it even. "I need to walk."

"Do you mind if I walk with you?"

Actually, he did mind. But there was something in her

tone, something he recognized as loneliness. How well he understood that emotion.

Apparently, like him, Rachel had too much free time tonight, with no task needing her immediate attention.

Not your concern. And yet, he said, "Join me."

They strolled under the inky fabric of the night sky in silence. Considering his earlier mood, he didn't expect to feel comfortable in her presence, but he did.

He allowed some of his anger to dissipate as they wove their way toward the river, away from the others. The sounds of low chatter, soft laughter and frogs croaking melded with the oddly musical pounding of water against rock.

At the river's edge, Rachel shifted her gaze to the sky. Tristan did the same.

"There's something you should know," she began. "Something I only just discovered this afternoon."

Still looking up at the stars, wondering at her tone, he clasped his hands behind his back. "I'm listening."

"Clarence is a woman."

"Yes." He lowered his gaze to meet hers. "I know."

She jammed her hands on her hips. "How long have you known?"

"I figured it out back at Fort Nez Perce."

"Yet you haven't confronted her about it?"

"I have not." He held her gaze. "Until she arrives in Oregon City her situation is a matter for the wagon train committee."

She gaped at him for several long seconds. "Aren't you curious as to why she's pretending to be a man?"

He lifted a shoulder. "I have a theory or two."

"Oh, really." She released a feminine sniff. "And what have you concluded?"

Her irritated tone brought a smile to his lips. Rachel

Hewitt might not be soft-spoken like her sister. She might not be one to hold back her opinions, but she was never boring. And she continually surprised him.

"Evidently," he began, "she assumed it would be safer to travel on the Oregon Trail in the guise of a man."

"Well, aren't you clever?"

"I'm a lawman, Rachel. I'm required to be observant."

She lifted onto her toes, probably in an attempt to bring them to eye level. Her gaze fell just below his chin.

"Well, then, *Sheriff*." His title had never sounded sassier. "I assume you've also figured out that Clara is with child."

Clara, not Clarence. He filed that piece of information away for later. "I'd say she's at least seven months along."

Muttering something he couldn't quite make out, Rachel leaned toward him. "Try eight, maybe more."

His gut clenched. Memories of the darkest night of his life threatened to overwhelm him. He shoved them down with a hard swallow and focused on the woman staring up at him. "Why are you telling me this, Rachel?"

She gave him a pitying glare, the kind women reserved for naughty children caught in the act of being, well, naughty. "Because you're the sheriff of Oregon City."

"You do realize," he said, clearing his throat, beating back the terrible, unwanted memories, "assisting a woman in the birthing process is not part of my job."

His voice came out even, but a shudder passed through him. His thoughts brought him back in time. He'd been with Siobhan for the birth of every one of his daughters, including the last one that had taken her life. He knew the dangers of childbirth firsthand. He would not be the cause of another woman's death.

Memories tried to take root, dragging him back to that terrible night when his beloved wife had died in his arms.

Darkness filled his soul. Black ringed his vision.

A sharp voice cut through his growing despair.

"Well, of course, I know it's not your *job*." Rachel shook her head as though she thought him daft.

Desperate to stay in the moment with her, he clung to the sound of her voice, appreciated more than she could ever know the frustration he heard in her tone.

"I told you about Clara so you'll be prepared when we arrive at Oregon City. There must be a doctor or a midwife or *someone* who knows about these things. And…" She paused, studied his face a moment past polite. "I can see by your expression that I've overstepped my authority again."

There was something in her voice, a desolation that brought him firmly into the moment. *At last.* "You're simply being helpful, taking it upon yourself to assist a friend in need."

"Yes, exactly. Oh, Tristan, I really was just trying to help."

"I know that, Rachel."

They shared a smile. For that one instant, with the stars glistening overhead and the sound of rushing water filling his ears, Tristan felt less…chaotic. Not quite at peace, but closer.

"Tristan, I… That is…" She dug her toe in the gravelly sand. "I better head back before someone notices I'm gone."

She didn't sound overly excited about the prospect of returning to her campsite. What must it be like for her, now that both her brother and her sister were engaged to be married?

Lonely, he suspected.

Familiar with the sensation, he took her hand. "When

we get to Oregon City, if you need anything, anything at all, you just have to ask and I'll see to it at once."

Eyes studying his, she gave him a slow, sweet smile. "Thank you, Tristan. I'll keep your offer in mind."

"Good." He paused. "Rachel, I…" He paused again, offered his arm. "It's getting late. Let me escort you back."

"Yes, of course." Her smile turned sweeter still. "What a lovely way to end a long, trying day."

He couldn't agree more.

Chapter Seven

At last. After five grueling months and more than their fair share of misfortunes, the wagon train arrived at Oregon City.

Desperate for a glimpse of her new home, Rachel leaned so far over the raft's edge she nearly toppled into the water. She quickly righted herself just as a stiff breeze whipped a clump of tangled curls across her face. She shoved the unruly mess aside and breathed in deeply. The threat of winter hung in the frigid air.

Nevertheless, sunlight danced off the water in glittering flashes. The hiss of Willamette Falls grew louder as Nathan guided their raft around a small bend. Another bend and, yes, *yes*, Oregon City came into view.

Rachel's heart soared. *I'm home.* Three terraces of land rose above the east side of the river. However, only the lowest section showed signs of development. The streets stretched northward from the falls for several blocks, but there was no order to building placement. She liked the town all the more because of eclectic way the simple single-story clapboard structures were tucked in haphazardly beside sturdier two- and three-story buildings.

Emma came up beside Rachel and linked an arm through hers. Rachel's heart soared once again. Emma looked less pale today, as though the prospect of reaching Oregon City had cured her seasickness.

"Well?" Emma asked. "What do you think of our new home?"

Rachel studied the town. "Smaller than I'd anticipated, but it's—" she searched for the right word, discarded several before settling on "—charming."

"Oh, Rachel, it *is* charming." Arms still linked, they braced through a series of dips and bumps.

Once the ride smoothed out, Emma released her hold and went to stand by Nathan. He paused in the middle of steering their raft to drop a kiss on her forehead. It was a lovely display of affection and familiarity. Nathan and Emma were living proof that when two people were meant to be together nothing could keep them apart.

Seeing the expression of their love refreshed Rachel's faith in the possibility of finding someone for herself. Was he among the emigrants or already a resident of Oregon City?

Her gaze tracked over the surrounding area, landed on Tristan standing beside James Stillwell farther down the river.

Even from this distance, Rachel could see that Tristan's gaze was locked on a spot up ahead. The look in his eyes spoke of longing. Her breath caught painfully in her lungs.

Was he thinking of his daughters? Did he regret not finding them a mother on the wagon train?

Oddly stricken for three little girls she'd never met, Rachel forced her attention back to her own raft. Nathan's dark head was bent over Emma's lighter one. He whispered something in her ear and they both laughed. The sound reached all the way to Rachel's heart and squeezed.

Did they know how blissful they looked?

A jaw-cracking yawn drew her attention away from the happy couple. Clara was awake.

Rachel crouched down beside her new friend. "Clara, our journey is over at last."

Clara rubbed at her eyes. "Truly?"

"Truly."

"Oh." Clara clasped a hand to her belly. "Oh, thank God."

Rachel couldn't agree more.

Smiling, she assisted Clara to her feet. By the time they worked their way onto the rocky shore, many of the Oregon City residents were already showing up on the riverbank.

Emma took over with Clara, urging her to sit on a nearby rock.

Clara protested, but Emma remained firm. "Nathan and I will help you locate your sister once the crowd thins out."

Finally giving in, Clara nodded.

Almost immediately, Ben, Abby and Mr. Bingham joined them on the shoreline. "Anybody see Grayson yet?" Ben asked.

Rachel scanned the loud, boisterous crowd. "Not yet."

She continued looking, lifting onto her toes. She caught sight of Tristan again. He and Mr. Stillwell, working as a team, hoisted the trunk of stolen money up a steep riverbank.

Rachel tried not to stare.

But how could she not? Tristan had competence layered all the way through him. He'd been such a godsend on the trail. She wanted to thank him for his assistance, not only for herself, but for her fellow emigrants, as well.

She started out. Unfortunately, he disappeared over the rise before she could take more than a few steps.

Her heart did a long, slow roll. She'd missed her opportunity. Later, she told herself. She would seek out Tristan and thank him later.

For now, she went back to searching for her brother's familiar face. She spotted him less than thirty feet from where Tristan had just disappeared. Grayson hadn't seen her yet, or any of their family. Rachel took the opportunity to study him. He looked the same, and yet…not.

His hair was still a rich, dark brown, and his eyes were still an unusual gray. Yet he stood taller than Rachel remembered, held his body with strength and power, as if he were fully confident in his place in the world. Grief no longer edged his gaze or showed in the stoop of his shoulders.

Rachel took a step toward him, then paused when she realized he wasn't alone. A young, rather pretty woman stood beside him. Somewhere close to Emma's age, she was willowy thin and wore a lavender dress that highlighted her curly blond hair and small, distinct features.

Grayson bent his head to say something to the woman. She smiled, and when he straightened, Grayson wore a smile, as well. Her brother and the woman looked friendly.

No, Rachel corrected, they looked together.

Had Grayson found love since his last letter? Was he, like their siblings, no longer facing the world on his own?

Every muscle in her body tensed. If Grayson had a woman in his life, and if that woman was soon to become his wife, he wouldn't need Rachel to take care of his household.

What if Grayson doesn't need me?

It was a selfish, ungrateful thought, but one she couldn't seem to shake. A sharp breath escaped her lungs. She forced herself to calm down. She was getting ahead of herself.

Firming her chin, she lifted her voice over the loud din of travelers reuniting with their loved ones. "Grayson," she called out. "We're over here."

Eyes alight with pleasure, he took hold of the woman's hand and the two ventured forward together.

Rachel rushed ahead of the rest of her family and, forgetting everyone but Grayson, flung herself into her brother's arms. Tears she couldn't fully attribute to joy sprang into her eyes. "Oh, Grayson, it's so good to see you."

Laughing, he spun her in a fast circle, then set her on the ground and stepped back. "Look at you. You're all grown up."

Emma moved in and took her turn hugging their brother, then introduced the man hovering by her side. "I'd like you to meet my fiancé, Nathan Reed."

Grayson clasped Nathan's hand, then paused. "Wait, what? Did you say your fiancé?" His confused gaze flitted from one to the other. "But what about Tristan? He and I had an understanding. He went out to meet the wagon train for you, Emma. The plan was for him to begin a proper courtship while on the trail. What happened?"

Prepared to give her brother the same speech she'd once given to Tristan, Rachel opened her mouth. But before she could begin, Ben stepped in front of her and explained the situation.

When he finished, Grayson's eyebrows drew together in a frown. "Well, this is certainly unexpected. Tristan must be disappointed."

Ben lifted a shoulder. "You'll have to ask him about that yourself." Smiling now, he reached behind him and pulled Abby forward. "You remember Abigail Bingham Black."

Grayson said nothing as his eyes narrowed over Abby. "I didn't realize you'd be on the wagon train, Mrs. Black."

"Abby won't be Mrs. Black much longer." Ben smiled into his fiancée's eyes. "We're engaged to be married."

Grayson's gaze stayed locked with Abby's. "Aren't you already married?"

Once more, Ben presented an explanation. He told Grayson a story even Rachel hadn't heard in its entirety. She hadn't known that Abby had been as heartbroken as Ben when she'd agreed to marry the man her mother had chosen for her.

Nor had Rachel realized that Abby's marriage to Frank Black had been a complete disaster. "Her husband was a wastrel and a gambler," Ben went on to explain. "He left her penniless when he died. She was forced to move back in with her parents. By then they'd been struggling financially, as well."

At this point, Abby's father stepped in and explained how he'd fallen on hard times and thus had joined the wagon train. He finished with, "halfway through the crossing my wife died from complications after she was bitten by a snake."

"I'm sorry for your loss," Grayson said, his tone solemn and full of sincerity. Never let it be said that Grayson Hewitt held a grudge.

"Thank you, Mr. Hewitt."

"Call me Grayson."

Mr. Bingham nodded, drew in a hard breath. "Grayson, your brother and my daughter have forgiven one another for the past and are ready to start their life together. I've given them my blessing. I hope you will do the same."

Grayson held the older man's stare for several tense heartbeats, then turned his attention to Ben. "Are you happy?"

"Very."

"Then I offer you my sincere congratulations." His gaze merged with Abby's. "Welcome to the family, Abigail."

Abby gave him a shy smile. "Thank you, Grayson."

Brows still pulled together, Grayson dropped a dark scowl onto Rachel. "Are you engaged, too?"

She sighed. "No, I am not."

"Good. You're far too young to marry."

Too young? Now she was insulted. "I'm nearly twenty."

Grayson opened his mouth to respond, but the young woman beside him laid a hand on his arm. "Grayson, aren't you going to introduce me to your family?"

"Of course." He closed his hand over the woman's. "This is Maggie Hewitt, my wife."

A beat of stunned silence met the declaration. Then, after a loud whoop from Ben, congratulations flowed between the happy couples.

Rachel stood frozen in place, unable to move. Her breathing quickened, coming in hard, painful snatches as the joyful scene unfolded before her.

Grayson was married. He didn't need her to take care of his household.

No one in her family needed her.

What was she going to do now?

His eyes searching the general area, a habit as much as a precaution, Tristan directed James Stillwell into the heart of town. They carried the trunk of stolen money between them.

"Where we headed, Sheriff?"

"The jailhouse is the second building on your left." With a quick nod, he indicated the plain clapboard structure. "I have a small safe in the back room where we can lock up the money until we decide our next step."

"I fear locking up the money in the jailhouse won't deter the Tuckers from coming back to take what they think belongs to them."

"Probably not, but the money will be safer in there than anywhere else in town."

Stillwell nodded his agreement. "Can't argue with that."

Setting down his end of the trunk, Tristan waited for the other man to do the same before unlocking the door and twisting the knob. "Safe's located in the room behind the jail cells."

Tristan led the way inside. Walking backward, he moved past the jail cells, past the lone desk and chair, and stopped inside the room he'd mentioned earlier. Stillwell set down his end of the trunk and looked around. Tristan did the same.

"You're welcome to bunk in here through the winter," he offered, knowing the insurance agent wouldn't be able to make his way back to Missouri before spring. "Stay as long as you like, or not at all, up to you. We don't have a hotel in town, but there's a decent boardinghouse one block over."

Stillwell walked past the cot, over to the potbellied stove. He swung open the door and peered inside. He then rose, spun in a tight circle and nodded. "Here is fine, at least for now. Only after we catch the Tuckers will I consider other lodging."

"Good enough," Tristan said.

A commotion outside drew both men's attention. Perhaps it was talk of the Tucker brothers or just basic instinct, but both men dashed out of the jailhouse. Tristan's feet ground to a halt when he realized the source of the shouting.

Reverend Mosby, the local preacher, stood atop a large crate. He waved his hands in the air, demanding everyone's attention. The pastor from the wagon train, Reverend Pettygrove, moved through the dense crowd to join the other preacher. With equally tall, rail-thin builds, scraggly beards and piercing brown eyes, the two men could be brothers.

Only after a modicum of silence descended over the gathering did Reverend Mosby lower his hands. "I'd like to be the first to welcome the wagon train to Oregon City. We're happy you made the journey and have chosen our humble town as your destination."

As the preacher continued his welcome speech, Stillwell muttered something about needing to go back inside and watch over the money. Tristan made an attempt to join him, but the other man told him he had it under control for now.

With a promise to return shortly, Tristan turned back to the crowd. A part of him wanted nothing more than to reunite with his girls, to hold them, kiss them and tell them how much he loved them. But another part of him hoped Bertha Quincy had kept his daughters home, safe and away from the large crowds.

Eyes meeting his, Rachel Hewitt tossed him a jaunty little wave. He found himself smiling and returning the gesture with a quick nod of his head.

The preacher droned on.

"Now, if you will bow your heads we'll lift up a prayer of thanksgiving. Brother Pettygrove, would you do the honors?"

"I'd be delighted."

A quick look over the crowd, and the wagon train preacher began his prayer. "Father God, we thank You for Your daily presence throughout our journey. Just as You guided the Israelites through the desert so, too, You remained with us every step of the way. We pray for Your continued mercies and protection. We ask this in Your Son's name, Amen."

The crowd lifted their heads.

Reverend Mosby smiled benignly over the people. "We hope to see many of you at church later today. We have a special surprise planned. The general service will begin in two hours."

The crowd slowly dispersed, giving Tristan a direct view of the Hewitt clan. His gaze on Rachel, he watched her take a step to one side. The move wasn't enough for anyone to notice, unless they were looking closely.

She turned her head and caught him watching her. She gave him a shy smile. In that moment, he couldn't help thinking Rachel needed a friend. Before he could lecture himself over the wisdom of his actions, he set out.

When he was but a few steps away, she shifted to face him directly. "Hello, Tristan."

"Rachel." He greeted the rest of the Hewitt clan and smiled kindly at Clara Pressman, who clung to Emma and refused to meet his gaze.

"Ah, Tristan, we were just discussing living arrangements," Grayson told him. "Rachel and Emma will stay with Maggie and me. Abby and her father can live in the space above our mercantile, and—"

"That's going to be a problem." Ben cut off his brother midsentence. "Now that the journey is complete, I see no need to wait any longer to make you my wife. What do you say, Abby?" He took Abigail's hand and lowered to one knee. "Will you marry me this afternoon at the welcome service?"

She gasped at the question. "Can...can we? Is such a thing possible?"

"I spoke with Reverend Pettygrove this morning and he's agreed not only to officiate, but to arrange all the particulars."

"Oh, Ben." Her hand went to her heart. "Yes, of course I'll marry you this afternoon."

Smiling broadly, he stood and kissed her. "Once the ceremony is over," he said, turning to Grayson, "Abby, her father and me will stay in the cabin you built on the land you acquired when you first arrived. I want to get back to ranching and I want to do so immediately, before winter sets in."

"If that's what you want to do, then by all means," Grayson said. "Nathan can bunk above the mercantile by himself."

"Not necessary." Nathan shook his head. "I'll set up a tent by the river until I can acquire my own parcel of land."

"You're family now," Grayson reminded him. "The Hewitts take care of their own."

Emma urged her fiancée to accept her brother's offer. Still, he didn't appear convinced.

"I'll feel better knowing you're living in town," she said.

"Moreover," Grayson added, as if sensing he was stepping on the other man's toes. "I'd feel better knowing someone was there to watch over the shop at night. We haven't had any trouble, but that doesn't mean we won't."

Nathan seemed to consider this, then slowly nodded before turning to speak to directly to Emma. "I'll only agree to live above the mercantile if you agree to join me there as my wife." He took her hand and, following Ben Hewitt's lead, lowered to one knee. "Emma Hewitt, will you marry me this afternoon?"

"Oh, Nathan." Her pretty blue eyes filled with tears. "Are you sure you're ready?"

"Of course I'm sure. I love you, Emma. I want to marry you right away."

"What a splendid idea," Abigail said, interrupting before Emma could give her answer. "Say yes, Emma. Then we can have a double wedding."

Emma's gaze locked with her future sister-in-law's. "You wouldn't mind sharing your special day with me and Nathan?"

"I'd consider it an honor."

"Well, my darling?" Nathan asked from his position in front of her. "Is that a yes?"

"Yes." Emma laughed through her tears. "Yes, I'll marry you."

A flurry of hugs ensued. Rachel joined in the celebration, but Tristan recognized the detached look in her eyes. He opened his mouth to say something to her, not sure what, when a high-pitched squeal cut him off. "Da!"

The joy of hearing the familiar voice eclipsed all other thought. Out of the corner of his eye he saw Lily launch herself in the air, straight at him, no concern for her safety.

My fearless middle daughter, he thought with his heart in his throat. She was so full of childlike faith, never once doubting that he would catch her.

He reached out and trapped her against his chest.

"My dear, sweet girl," he said in a low, choked voice. "How I've missed you."

Overcome with emotion, he buried his face in her baby-fine hair that smelled of lilacs and fresh soap. Out of the corner of his eye, he noted how his other two daughters remained dutifully beside Bertha Quincy. His youngest finally broke away, a determined look in her eyes.

Tristan set Lily on the ground and opened his arms. But instead of approaching him, Violet marched straight to Rachel and tugged on her skirt.

Rachel smiled down at the child. "Well, hello there."

"Hello," Violet said, then stuck her thumb in her mouth.

Tristan heaved a weighty sigh. The child had reverted to sucking her thumb in his absence. They'd have to work on that now that he was home.

Bending over so she could meet Violet at eye level, Rachel ran a hand gently over the child's head. "My name is Rachel. What's yours?"

Out came the thumb. "Violet."

"Violet," Rachel repeated, sweeping her hand over the child's head again. The gesture was full of unconscious tenderness. "A very pretty name for a very pretty girl."

Violet poked her thumb back in her mouth.

"You know—" Rachel lowered to her knees and placed her hands on her lap "—I've never met anyone named Violet before."

Violet grinned around her thumb.

Watching the two interact, Tristan felt a sting in the back of his throat. Bertha was good with his daughters, but not like this. Not like Rachel. She spoke to Violet as though the little girl was as important as any adult.

Not one to be left out for long, Lily rushed to join her sister. "I'm Lily."

Still kneeling, Rachel turned her attention to the other child. "Another pretty name for another pretty girl."

Lily seemed to think over her response, then made a grand show of pronouncing, "I like you."

"I like you, too." Tristan could tell Rachel meant every word.

Another crack opened in his heart.

Evidently deciding she'd been obedient long enough, Daisy released Bertha's hand, marched over to the group and shoved in between her sisters.

Tristan knew that determined look in his daughter's eyes. He knew, and dreaded, what was about to come out of her mouth.

In an attempt to forestall the inevitable, he closed a hand over his daughter's shoulder. "Daisy, baby, come over here and say hello to your father."

As was often the case in situations such as these, Daisy wanted nothing to do with conversation. She wanted answers.

The little girl set her fists on her hips and stared hard at Rachel.

"Are you my new mommy?"

Chapter Eight

Rachel blinked in stunned silence at the child staring back at her. Despite the outrageous nature of her question, or perhaps because of it, she immediately felt a connection to little Daisy McCullough.

Truth be told, she saw a lot of herself in the precocious six-year-old. Not in physical appearance, but in the determined angle of her tiny shoulders. In the bold tilt of her head. In the desperate hope simmering in her big, sorrowful blue eyes.

Tristan had once remarked that his daughters were three tiny copies of his wife. Siobhan McCullough must have been a real beauty, if this child with the ruby-red hair and ivory skin favored her mother.

For a dangerous moment, Rachel had a powerful urge to tug the little girl into her arms and give her the answer she so clearly wanted.

Careful, she warned herself. *Think before you speak.*

"Well?" Hands still perched on her hips, Daisy's small mouth turned down at the corners. "Are you my new mommy or not?"

Rachel shot a glance at Tristan. His chest rose and fell

in a noiseless sigh, but she forestalled any response he might give his daughter with a quick shake of her head.

"I'm sorry, Daisy, no." A wave of disappointment swept through her, the sensation so profound she would have stumbled had she not already been kneeling on the ground. "I'm not your new mommy. However, I am your new neighbor and I'll certainly see you often, perhaps even daily."

Tristan cut in then, touching his daughter's shoulder to gain her attention. "Daisy, my darling girl, we've talked about this before. You cannot go around asking every woman you meet if she's your mommy."

"But Da." The little girl's lower lip jutted out. "You said you were bringing us back a new mommy when you got home."

Daisy's words surprised Rachel. Tristan didn't seem the type of man to make promises he couldn't keep.

"No, Daisy." He pulled his hand away from her shoulder, then shoved it in his pocket. "I said I *might* bring you home a new mommy. I made no promises."

Unmistakable regret threaded through his words.

Her brows knit in concentration, the child seemed to consider this new bit of information. However, Rachel suspected Daisy didn't quite capture the difference between what she thought she'd heard her father say and what he'd actually said.

When tears formed in the little girl's eyes, Rachel found herself interceding. "I may not be your new mommy," she began, taming a stray wisp of the child's hair behind her ear. "But I can be your very good friend."

The little girl's eyes lit up. At the same moment, Tristan's youngest plopped into Rachel's lap. No longer able to resist, Rachel wrapped her arms around the child and hugged her close. Violet snuggled against her and sighed contentedly.

In that moment, Rachel understood what had driven Tristan to travel all the way to the Blue Mountains Pass to meet Emma. His precious children not only needed a new mother, they wanted one.

Lily attempted to join her sister on Rachel's lap. When Violet refused to budge, the little girl settled for pulling on Rachel's sleeve. "You don't want to be our new mommy?"

The poor child sounded so despondent Rachel's heart twisted. "Oh, Lily, it's not a matter of want. You see, I'm already committed to—"

She cut off her own words, realizing she had no other commitments now that Grayson was married. He didn't need her to run his household. *No one* needed her. Except, maybe, this tiny family.

Before the thought could take root, Tristan cleared his throat. All gazes swung to him. "Girls, tell Miss Rachel goodbye." There was gravel in his voice. "It's time to go home now."

The inevitable grumbling began. "Already?" Daisy asked. "We just got here."

"Nevertheless." His tone brooked no argument.

Reluctantly, Daisy held her tongue. The child's bent head and stooped shoulders were the very picture of quashed hope. In a gesture far older than her four years, Lily reached out and patted her older sister on the back. Violet, thumb in her mouth, joined the other two and attempted to copy Lily's movements.

Trying not to sigh over the scene the three little girls made, Rachel stood. She understood their disappointment on a deep, personal level. She had wished for a new mommy after her own had died. Because she sympathized so completely, she should be able to find the right words to comfort the children.

Unfortunately, nothing concrete came to mind.

While she contemplated how best to broach the subject, a young woman approached Tristan. Her rounded belly, along with their easy familiarity with one another, suggested this was his neighbor Bertha Quincy, the woman who regularly took care of his daughters.

Tristan confirmed her suspicions when he motioned Rachel to join them. "Let me introduce you to my neighbor, Bertha Quincy." He turned to the other woman. "Bertha, this is Grayson Hewitt's sister newly arrived on the wagon train."

They greeted each other with a smile.

Rachel couldn't help but think that Bertha Quincy looked familiar. Her hair was a common chestnut brown, but her eyes were a unique shade of green she'd seen before. The connection was there, just on the edge of her mind, when Violet broke away from her sisters and gazed up at Rachel with big, round eyes, her thumb still in her mouth.

She took the little girl's hand and squeezed gently.

Bertha Quincy's smile widened. "I don't mind saying, Miss Hewitt, your arrival has been a long time coming."

Mildly confused, Rachel angled her head. "Oh?"

"Indeed, yes. Your brother has told us quite a lot about you." She looked meaningfully at the child clinging to her hand. "You are a true answer to prayer for our good sheriff and his family."

Rachel's confusion vanished, only to be replaced by distress. Evidently, this woman had mistaken her for Emma.

Not knowing quite what to say, Rachel looked to Tristan for help. His eyes were gentle as they met hers, even affectionate. Odder still, he didn't correct his neighbor's mistake.

A fiber of hope eased through Rachel, followed by a heavy dose of reality. If Tristan wanted her to mother his daughters he would have already said something to her.

Besides, he'd made his position clear when they'd discussed his situation in Fort Nez Perce. *I need to know the woman I bring into my home. Moreover, I need to trust her completely.*

Rachel sighed. "I believe you have me confused with my sister, Emma." Needing something to do with her hands, she ran her fingertips over Violet's head. "I'm Rachel, the youngest of the family."

"But, you're not… That is, I assumed…" Bertha looked from Rachel to Tristan then back again. "You're so pretty, and clearly have a way with the girls. I would have immediately assumed you were the woman Sheriff McCullough went out to meet on the trial and…"

The rest of her words dissolved in a puff of air as if she only just realized she had a tiny audience of three listening intently to her every word.

Still, Rachel's heart swelled. No one had ever mistaken her for Emma, and they'd never, *never ever*, called her pretty.

She slipped a glance at Tristan from beneath her lowered lashes. An achy sort of warmth filled her heart at what she saw in his eyes—thoughtful speculation, as if he were looking at her for the very first time and liking what he saw. A delicious sort of terror filled her heart. Was he considering…

Did he think maybe she could…

Flustered by the direction of her own thoughts, Rachel focused once more on Bertha Quincy. She started to thank the other woman for her unexpected compliment but was cut off by an uncertain little yelp coming from behind her. Rachel looked over her shoulder in time to see Clara Pressman hurrying over, arms waving wildly in the air.

"Bertha," she shouted with unmitigated joy. "Bertha, it's me, Clara."

Bertha's eyelashes fluttered, her breath caught. Then, she too squealed in delight. "Oh, sister, I've been so worried. Praise God you made the journey, after all."

The two women all but leaped into each other's arms. Unfortunately, their rounded bellies got in the way and their reunion turned into a shuffling, clumsy mess. Laughing in perfect harmony, the sisters stepped back, shifted their individual stances and tried again.

The second attempt was far more graceful.

Rachel rubbed at her eyes over the beautiful reunion, so similar to many others she'd witnessed since climbing off her family's raft.

Caught up in the excitement, Tristan's daughters joined the celebration between Bertha and Clara, their childish giggles mixing with the women's happy laughter.

Emma came up beside Rachel and linked arms, her eyes riveted on Clara and her sister.

"Another happy ending," she whispered, a gleam of satisfaction glowing in her eyes.

Rachel nodded as she and Emma stood silently watching the scene unfold before them. Wiping at her eyes, Emma muttered something about needing to find Nathan so she could tell him that Clara had found her sister.

She turned to go, only to pause when she realized Rachel remained firmly rooted to the spot. "Aren't you coming?"

"Yes." Rachel started out after her sister, but then stopped abruptly. "I'll be along in a moment."

Emma's eyebrows pulled together. She looked about

to say something but must have thought better of it because she simply shrugged and walked away.

Tristan gathered up his daughters and herded them over to Rachel. She said farewell to each child individually, then turned her gaze onto their father. "Thank you for your help on the trail. Goodbye, Tristan."

"Goodbye, Rachel."

His smile, slow and devastating, made her heart ache again.

Why did the man have to be so handsome, so kind, so patient with his daughters? Maybe, if he was overly strict with them, or not so obviously in love with all three, Rachel could resist his charm.

With nothing more to say, she turned to go.

Tristan caught her arm with a light hold. "Will I see you at the church later this afternoon?"

She swallowed, offered a wobbly smile, then finally found her voice. "Yes."

"Good. You and I need to talk." He said this quietly, in a tone that held determination while his eyes held unspoken promises.

Her stomach tumbled to her toes. "Oh…I, of course."

After one final glance over her shoulder, she hurried away from Tristan's family and approached her own. The men were in some sort of discussion. Rachel thought she heard something about obtaining land grants before winter set in but couldn't be sure.

"Rachel, there you are." Emma waved her over to where the women were huddled together in their own conversation. "Maggie has offered to help us dress for the wedding and we were thinking you could help us with our hair."

"I'd consider it a privilege."

"We have so much to do and so very little time to prepare and, and…" Emma let out a delighted laugh. "And I'm babbling. I'm just so excited, I guess, and flustered, and—"

"Really, really happy," Rachel supplied, letting her sister's joy help wash away her melancholy.

"Oh, Rachel, I am happy. Blissfully so." Emma glanced over at the men. "Just think, in a few hours I'll be Mrs. Nathan Reed. I've never wanted anything more."

Rachel was reminded of a favorite verse from Ecclesiastes. "To every thing there is a season, a season and a time to every purpose under the heaven."

The season for hardships and suffering was over. Now it was time to look to the future with gladness. It was the end of one journey, Rachel thought, and the beginning of another. Even she was embarking on a new adventure. Would she find joy and happiness as her siblings had?

She glanced over her shoulder, caught sight of Tristan picking up Violet and swinging her onto his shoulders. The other two girls skipped along beside him.

Rachel swallowed, felt her heart melt at the sight of the devoted father with his daughters.

They need me.

The thought skittered through her mind, instantly followed by another, more disturbing revelation. *And maybe, just maybe, I need them.*

Two hours after arriving in Oregon City, Tristan guided his daughters in the direction of the church one block from their house. The girls hadn't stopped talking since his arrival and he couldn't be more delighted. The sweetest sound in the world was their tinkling baby voices that held the barest hint of Ireland, picked up no doubt from him.

Their favorite topic since meeting Rachel Hewitt had

been…Rachel Hewitt. She'd made quite an impression on them. Now Tristan couldn't stop thinking about her, either. He couldn't stop thinking that maybe, perhaps, she was the answer to his problems.

He would know more after they spoke.

Only a light breeze stirred the unseasonably warm afternoon. The trees were in full autumn splendor, a kaleidoscope of red, yellow, orange and green. A perfect day for a wedding.

The first strains of piano music wafted from the plain white building on their left. He directed his daughters toward the steps leading inside the church.

"Can we sit in the front?" Daisy asked.

He visibly shuddered at the suggestion. Tristan preferred the back pew, where he could corral his wriggling daughters and keep some semblance of order. "We'll sit in our usual seats."

"But Da." Lily picked up the argument where her sister had left off. "Miss Bertha always lets us sit up front with her."

"You're sitting with me, in the back, and that's the end of it," he said, his tone gentle but firm. "Besides, the front pew is reserved for family members of the brides and grooms."

Daisy scuffed her foot. Violet sucked harder on her thumb. Lily opened her mouth to continue arguing, but one stern look from him and all three girls quieted down.

Now that he'd dealt with his daughters' short-lived rebellion, Tristan scanned the people gathering outside the church. He let out a quick burst of air. No sign of Grant and Amos Tucker. Perhaps they'd given up on the idea of reclaiming the stolen money.

His gut said otherwise.

He continued searching the assembled crowd. His gaze

landed on Bertha Quincy and her husband, Algernon. A pretty young woman with a very large belly stood beside them.

It didn't take a trained lawman to notice that Clara Pressman had dispensed with her disguise. Her choppy brown hair wasn't much of an improvement over the men's cap she'd worn to conceal her identity. But at least her blue gingham dress with the lace collar was better than the ridiculously baggy pants and oversize jacket.

Her fellow emigrants didn't seem to notice, or care if they did, that Clarence was actually a woman named Clara. Not that surprising, Tristan thought, with all they had on their minds. Most of the new arrivals were facing a difficult winter with nothing more than a flimsy tent for shelter.

Tristan would protect the new residents of his town to the best of his ability, but there was little he could do about the weather. Many families would have to fight for their lives on the harsh frontier.

He prayed they found success.

With half his mind on the long, cold months ahead, he led his daughters up the steps and into the crowded gathering area beyond the large double doors. Rachel Hewitt was already in the foyer with her sister and Abigail Black. The two brides spoke excitedly to each other, looking eager and slightly apprehensive at the same time. Head down, Rachel hustled around them, smoothing and straightening their dresses.

"Miss Rachel!" Daisy pulled away from Tristan and rushed over to her. "You're here already."

Rachel stepped away from the brides. "And now so are you."

Daisy smiled.

Lily, following hard on her sister's heels, tapped on

Rachel's arm, then lifted her own hands in the air. Clearly understanding the silent plea, Rachel picked up the child and swung her around to rest on her right hip.

The move was so natural, so easy and ordinary, that Tristan's gut took a hard roll. The sensation was not altogether unpleasant.

Rachel spoke softly to Lily. The child bobbed her head up and down, then pointed to where Tristan stood holding Violet's hand.

Turning slightly, Rachel smiled at him. "Hello, Tristan."

He felt another roll, then a hard tug, this time in his heart. "Hello."

For some reason, he and Rachel were uncomfortable. Where was the easy camaraderie they'd shared on the trail?

Disconcerted by the change between them, he focused on Emma Hewitt. Realizing she'd yet to meet his daughters, he made the introductions. Then he repeated the process with Abigail Black.

Daisy eyed both women closely. A crease of concentration dug across her forehead. Tristan braced for the inevitable *mommy* question but his daughter surprised him. Bouncing her gaze from one bride to the other, she said, "You're very pretty."

"Thank you," Abigail said, while Emma added, "You're very pretty, too."

The child responded with a tilted grin.

"Are you the ones getting married today?" Lily asked.

Daisy let out a big-sister huff. "Of course they're getting married. They're holding flowers."

Both women smiled at the children. Their individual joy seemed to come from the depths of their souls. "We are indeed the brides," Emma said in confirmation. "And we're so very, very happy."

Tristan laughed. "It shows."

Emma's smile momentarily slipped. Something like an apology, with a hint of guilt around the edges, moved in her eyes. In that, at least, he could ease her mind. "I wish you and Nathan nothing but the best, Emma."

She visibly relaxed. "Thank you, Tristan."

Grateful *that* was finally over, he offered similar words to Abigail Black.

"Thank you, Sheriff McCullough."

As people shuffled past them, offering up their own congratulations, Lily tapped Rachel on the shoulder. "Are you getting married today, too?"

"No, sweet girl, I'm not." She punctuated the statement with a soft, self-conscious laugh. The sound was a little sad.

Tristan felt his hand reaching out to her of its own accord. He wanted to offer her more than momentary comfort. He wanted to offer her a place in the world to call her own.

Perhaps there was a way, if she agreed to his terms. Terms he wasn't sure he had the right to impose on such a lively, spirited young woman.

"When the ceremony is over," he found himself saying despite his reservations, "I'd like a word with you in private."

"All right."

He held her gaze a moment longer, praying he was making the right decision, not only for him, but for her, as well. He wouldn't know until he explained the entirety of the situation. What he could give her.

And what he could not.

The preacher stuck his head in the foyer. "We're ready to begin. Those not getting married this afternoon—" he looked pointedly at Tristan "—need to find their seats."

Tristan had started to hustle his daughters toward the back pew when Rachel asked them to join her up front. He opened his mouth to protest, but she spoke over him.

"Please, Tristan, with the short notice of this wedding, and the small size of the church, I have no part in the actual ceremony. Like you, I'm merely a spectator today." Something came and went in her eyes. "I'd really like you and the girls to sit with me up front."

Her plea sounded casual, but Tristan recognized the desperation in the tight angle of her shoulders and the loneliness beneath her outward control.

Perhaps that explained why he found himself agreeing to her request, much to his daughters' glee. "Yes, we'll sit with you."

She gave him a grateful smile. Drawing in a sharp breath, she took a moment to hug Abigail Black, then repeated the process with her sister, whispering something that made the other woman tear up.

Sniffling herself, Rachel turned toward the church and, after a quick swipe at her eyes, took Daisy's hand. She reached out and took Lily's hand next. Tristan picked up Violet and the five of them marched down the center aisle.

Chapter Nine

After a short-lived argument over who would sit where, Rachel settled in the middle of the pew with Lily on her lap. Violet sat on her left, Tristan and Daisy on her right.

They'd barely claimed their seats when Reverend Pettygrove, in his role as wedding officiator, took his place between Nathan and Ben. An expectant hush filled the air. The preacher nodded to the woman sitting at the piano. Music flooded the small building.

As one, the congregation stood and turned their collective gazes toward the back of the church.

Emma and Abby made their entrance.

Rachel's eyes immediately filled with tears. Both women were beautiful in their new dresses from Grayson's mercantile. The designs were nearly identical, all the way down to the sloping sleeves, pointed waistlines and bell-shaped skirts. But while Emma's gown was a pretty silvery blue, Abby's was soft pink.

Abby's father stepped between the beaming brides and offered an arm to each of them. The three made the short trek down the aisle with little fanfare.

A perfectly coordinated shuffle of positions allowed Mr. Bingham a spot on the front pew with the rest of the family. After one more bar of music everyone took their seats.

A brief welcome and thank-you to the local preacher followed before Reverend Pettygrove delivered the opening words of the wedding ceremony.

"Dearly beloved, Benjamin and Abigail, as well as Nathan and Emma—" he paused to smile at each couple "—have invited us to share in the celebration of their marriage. We come together not to mark the start of your relationship, but to recognize the bond that already exists…"

As the preacher continued, Rachel dabbed surreptitiously at her eyes. Conflicting emotions rolled through her—joy and excitement, restlessness and anxiety. The combination made her strangely pensive. She didn't feel deserted, precisely, but…all right, yes, she felt a little deserted. As if she was losing the last fragments of her family with each spoken vow.

She was glad Tristan had agreed to sit with her. She didn't feel comfortable around Grayson's new wife yet, primarily because there hadn't been much time to speak with her during the whirlwind of wedding plans. Sitting with Tristan and his precious daughters was easier, less complicated and somehow helped Rachel feel less alone.

Unable to stop herself, she swung her gaze to meet his. Something quite wonderful passed between them, something that nearly stole her breath. Biting back a sigh, she quickly swiveled her gaze back to the front of the church.

It would be unwise to allow her mind to wander toward something that could only end in heartache. Although Tristan had professed to wanting a wife, he was primarily interested in finding a woman to care for his daughters. There'd been no mention of anything more than a marriage in name only.

Any woman—Rachel, for instance—could take over the children's daily care without actually marrying Tristan. According to Grayson, Tristan wasn't just his neighbor, he was his *next door* neighbor. Since she would be living in such close proximity, Rachel was in a convenient position to offer her assistance, at least temporarily.

The idea had merit.

Ben's strong, steady voice broke through Rachel's ponderings.

"I, Benjamin Hewitt, take thee, Abigail Bingham Black, to be my wife, to have and to hold from this day forward, for better, for worse, for richer, for poorer, in sickness and in health, to love and to cherish till death do us part."

Abby repeated the same vows, the sound of pure love in her voice. The preacher, looking especially touched, turned slightly to his left and then guided Nathan and Emma through the same litany of promises.

From her position on the front pew, Rachel noted how Nathan's eyes shone with the love he felt for Emma. The same look was on Ben's face as he stared at Abby. Rachel tore her own gaze away from all that...adoration, only to confront the *same* look in Grayson's eyes as he smiled down at his pretty new wife.

Rachel's heart lifted and sighed. Four siblings. Three happy endings. How she yearned for someone to love her with unbridled affection. How she wanted her own happy ending.

Lowering her head, she placed a soft kiss to Lily's head. The child cuddled closer. Tristan reached out and closed his hand over hers. Cheek resting on the little girl's head, Rachel smiled over at him.

He smiled back.

Her world instantly felt a little less...gloomy.

But then Tristan pulled his hand away and she became aware of the preacher's voice once again.

"…before this gathering, Benjamin and Abigail, Nathan and Emma, have promised their love and have given each other rings to wear as sign of their deep commitment."

Rachel gasped softly. She'd missed the part of the ceremony that had always been her favorite. The giving of rings. She firmed her chin and resolved to listen more carefully to the rest of the ceremony.

"Marriage is a gift from God," the preacher continued, straying slightly from the traditional service. "The union of a man and a woman is the Lord's beautiful plan for His children. Your goal isn't to become one. You are already one by the sacredness of your vows. I urge you to honor your commitment to one another the way the Lord intended from the beginning. Leave your family, cleave to your spouse. Be fruitful and multiply."

Rachel cast a quick glance in Tristan's direction. His eyes were different now. They'd taken on a faraway, distant appearance. Was he thinking of his own wedding?

What must he be suffering?

The thought had barely materialized when a choked sob had Rachel glancing behind her. Clara Pressman wore an expression of loss.

"Let love rule your household," Reverend Pettygrove said. "Hold fast to what is good and right and true. Outdo one another in showing mercy. And…" He paused with a self-deprecating laugh. "And that's enough preaching for one day."

The congregation joined in his laughter.

"It is with great honor that I declare you husband and wife. Gentleman, you may kiss your brides."

Applause filled the church as they did. Someone whispered, "Lovely, simply lovely."

Rachel couldn't agree more.

The preacher nodded again to the woman at the piano.

Fingers poised over the keys she waited for the applause to die down before pounding out a popular hymn celebrating God's glory. The happy couples walked down the aisle. Ben and Abigail led the way, with Nathan and Emma only a few steps behind.

Once they completed their march, Grayson stood. The rest of the congregation followed his cue. Rachel, however, remained seated. She didn't want to let Lily go just yet. She liked having her close, and felt somehow useful. The child had other ideas and scrambled off her lap without a backward glance.

Head bent, Tristan helped Violet to the floor. Daisy jumped off the pew on her own. Amid their excited chatter about the wedding, Rachel smiled and laughed and debated if this was the right time to broach the subject of their care.

Unfortunately, Tristan seemed determined to avoid making eye contact with her. He also seemed to be in a hurry.

"Come, girls." He took Violet's hand, looked meaningfully at his other two daughters. "We'll wish the couples well and then head home."

Thinking she understood his shift in mood, and hurting all the more for him, Rachel followed silently after the McCullough family. She should just let them leave, she told herself. She should wait for a more appropriate time to present her idea about taking over the girls' daily care.

Unfortunately, Rachel had never been one to keep her mouth shut when she had a solution to a pressing problem. "Tristan, I thought you wanted to speak with me after the ceremony. In…private?"

Still not looking at her directly, he gave a single shake of his head. "Another time."

He directed his daughters outside and continued guiding them to where the newly married couples stood surrounded by other well-wishers.

Unable to let the matter drop, Rachel fell into step beside Tristan. "I don't understand. You seemed eager to speak with me earlier. What's changed?"

He stopped walking and, finally, looked her in the eye. He let his gaze linger on her face a moment. And then, something astonishing happened. Everything seemed to go back to normal between them. It wasn't anything she could pinpoint, just a sensation that she didn't need to be on her guard around him.

Rachel actually felt the tension drain out of her shoulders. But a loud shout from inside the church had them tensing up again.

"Sheriff McCullough." Reverend Pettygrove called out to him from atop the church steps. "Come quick."

Tristan's gaze snapped in the preacher's direction. "What is it?"

"We have a…situation inside the church."

With one hand on Daisy, the other on Violet, Tristan and the girls retraced their steps.

"You better come alone," the other man suggested. "It's a matter of some delicacy."

There was no mistaking the insistence in his tone or the urgency.

"Go on," Rachel said, reaching out to take the girls' hands. "I'll watch your daughters while you take care of whatever problem has occurred."

Without waiting for him to argue the point, she spun

around and issued a question sure to garner the children's attention. "Who wants to hear how your da saved a little boy's life?"

Three tiny arms shot in the air. "Me," they shouted simultaneously.

Tristan's lips pressed into a thin, tight line. "Rachel, you don't have to—"

"Go on, Tristan." She made a shooing motion with her hands. "I have everything under control here. I promise we'll stay close." She looked around her. "We'll sit right over there."

She pointed to a wooden bench across the street.

"Thank you." He gave her a half smile, told his daughters to "mind Miss Rachel" then took off toward the church at a fast jog.

Rachel followed his progress with her gaze. Right after he disappeared inside the building, a loud female wail rent the air. Wincing, she thought she saw Clara Pressman swaying in the middle of a group of women. But then the poor woman dropped out of sight and the church doors slammed shut.

Oh, my.

Tristan scanned the crowded area inside the church, assessing the situation as quickly as possible. No blood, no broken bones, no shots fired. So far so good.

He stepped deeper into the building. The rising panic among the small gathering of mostly women hit him like an iron fist. Some internal instinct urged him to turn around and leave the premises at once. *Run, don't walk.*

He remained where he was and forced himself to continue quickly gathering information. Only after he knew what he was dealing with would he decide on a course of action.

Another sweeping glance over the general area and his gaze landed on his neighbor Bertha Quincy. At the terror he saw in her eyes, ice slid through his veins.

"Sheriff, help us. Please."

All eyes turned to him. "What's happened? Is someone injured?

"It's my sister, the poor, dear girl is in the throes of—" The rest of her words were lost in the sound of a panicked, high-pitched female shriek of pain.

Tristan knew that sound, felt his own spurt of terror deep in his bones. Another scream followed yet another and another. Clara Pressman's obvious pain took him back in time, back to the worst day of his life, a day full of fear and helplessness and paralyzing grief.

For a dangerous second, Tristan stood frozen in immobility. Memories of his wife's final hours threatened to overwhelm him. Stay, go. Stay, go. He couldn't make up his mind which action to take. There was only one choice, of course.

Stay.

He wouldn't—couldn't—allow another woman to die in childbirth, not if he was able do something to prevent such a tragedy. He shouldered through the crowd.

By the time he managed to weave past the tangle of humanity, Bertha was already sitting on the floor, cradling her sister's head in her lap. Every ounce of her concern showed in her shaking hands, in the quivering of her lips, in the tears swimming in her eyes.

"Tell me what I can do," he said, careful to keep his voice calm for all their sakes.

"Emma," Clara gasped between sporadic gulps of air.

"Please, Sheriff. Get Emma Hewitt. She'll know what to do."

Although Emma wasn't a midwife, Tristan had seen the way she cared for the sick on the trail. She probably would know how to ease Clara's suffering.

He rushed out of the church, found Emma, explained what was happening in short, clipped sentences and all but dragged her back inside the building with him.

Emma immediately collapsed onto her knees and began whispering softly to her friend. The fear in the young woman's eyes cut Tristan to the core. His first instinct was to move her to a safer locale, where there would be fewer people creating unnecessary stress.

Unfortunately, Clara was already deep in the birthing process, too deep. No moving her now. The best they could do was make her as comfortable as possible. First order of business, clear the premises as quickly as possible.

Driven by resolve, Tristan located the preacher. "We need to clear the building."

Between the two of them, they managed to herd the majority of the crowd outside. Once that was done, Reverend Pettygrove offered up his own suggestion. "I'll organize a prayer group."

Tristan held back his thoughts on the futility of such an endeavor. He simply nodded at the other man.

Calling out Tristan's name, Grayson joined him in the doorway. "Maggie and Abigail are collecting blankets, rags and other supplies."

Tristan set a hand on his friend's shoulder. There were dark memories in the other man's gaze, the same ones Tristan struggled with in his own mind.

"Childbirth doesn't always end in tragedy," he said, as much for himself as for Grayson.

The other man nodded, but his eyes were still haunted. They'd both lost their wives in childbirth, but Grayson had also lost his son. Tristan had no words to alleviate the other man's pain. He would not offer the empty platitudes they'd both heard too many times to count.

A wail of pain cut through the air.

Grayson and Tristan both flinched.

Thankfully, Maggie and Abigail arrived, arms overflowing with blankets and rags and, as Grayson had mentioned, other supplies. Abigail also carried a bucket of water.

Catching a glimpse of her husband's face, Maggie shoved her load at Tristan. She barely waited for him to secure the bundle in his arms before she took Grayson's hands and pulled him away from the church.

Maggie must already know what her husband had gone through before he'd arrived in Oregon City and was attempting to ease him through the terrible memories.

At the moment, Tristan had no one to offer him such comfort.

He felt momentarily lost. Empty.

But he wasn't truly alone. He had friends and neighbors and three precious daughters he'd left outside the church, where he hoped they couldn't hear Clara's screeches of pain.

Lily had been two years old when Siobhan died giving birth to Violet, Daisy barely four. Did they remember that night?

Panic filled his every fiber. He had to get to his daughters. Had to make sure they weren't scared or afraid.

He headed in their direction, then paused a few steps later when he remembered the blankets in his arms. He quickly reentered the church but paused again at the sound of Clara's desperate moans.

"You're doing wonderfully," Emma cooed. "The worst is nearly over."

Bertha added her own words of encouragement. "You'll be able to push soon."

Unable to bear another moment, Tristan thrust his armload of blankets at Abigail. "I'll be just outside if you need anything else."

"Thank you, Sheriff."

He beat a fast retreat and only felt a moment of relief once he shut the church doors behind him.

Taking the steps two at a time, he strode over to Rachel and his daughters. Halfway there, his feet ground to a halt. The four of them looked…they looked like a…

Family.

His breath hitched in his throat. The contrast between Rachel's cloud of dark, thick curls next to his daughters' straight red hair actually looked…somehow…right.

The four of them hadn't noticed him yet. He took the opportunity to watch them a bit longer. Lily leaned heavily against Rachel, her gaze riveted on the young woman's face. Violet sat in Rachel's lap and had popped her thumb in her mouth.

Daisy stood facing Rachel, her back to Tristan and the church behind him.

It was then that he realized Rachel had positioned his daughters so that their attention stayed focused on her and away from the drama unfolding inside the church.

He would have to thank her for that small blessing later.

Noticing his approach, Violet grinned around her thumb. "Da!"

Lily immediately hopped to her feet and rushed over to him. "Miss Rachel just told us about how you saved a little boy's life. She said you're a hero."

He lifted an eyebrow in her direction. "Did she now?"

"I only told them the details of what happened." The sassy, unrepentant tone was pure Rachel.

Smiling, he lowered onto the bench beside her. He experienced a moment of profound peace when Lily crawled into his lap and pressed her tiny head against his shoulder.

This. This was what he'd needed. A reminder of what he had, not what he'd lost.

Violet tapped him on the arm. "Can we go home now?"

"Not yet." As the town sheriff, Tristan needed to stick around a little longer in case something bad happened. He shuddered at the many possibilities.

"How's Clara faring?" Rachel's worried expression indicated she knew what was happening inside the church. She was right to be concerned. Childbirth was a dangerous prospect, ending far too often in death.

Holding her gaze, forcing himself to stay in the present, Tristan lifted a shoulder. "As well as can be expected."

"What about you?" She gripped his hand and squeezed gently. "How are you doing?

"As well as can be expected," he said, then promptly changed the subject. "If memory serves, you're a masterful storyteller. Now would be a good time to entertain us with an intriguing tale or two."

Clearly recognizing his tactic, she gave him a tender smile. "Any specific requests?"

"I have one." Daisy, as was typical, spoke up first. "Will you tell us the story about the woman you're named after, the one from the Bible?"

Rachel shot Tristan a questioning gaze.

He considered, then nodded. "That'll be fine."

"I'll keep it simple," she promised.

"Even better."

One more squeeze to his hand and she launched into the story.

Chapter Ten

The Biblical story of Jacob and Rachel was full of intrigue and suspense, favoritism and deception, misplaced loyalties and greed. But it was also a love story that showed how far a devoted man would go to win his beloved's hand in marriage.

With so much material to choose from, Rachel decided to focus on her favorite part of the tale—the love story. "There was a man named Jacob," she began, "who needed to find himself a wife."

"Oh-oh." Daisy fluttered her hands back and forth in a show of little-girl excitement. "That sounds just like Da!"

Rachel hadn't made the connection until now. "Well, yes, Jacob's situation was somewhat similar to your father's, but not entirely the same."

Daisy frowned. "How come?"

"Because Jacob didn't have any daughters who needed a mother. He was only looking for a wife for himself."

"Oh, you mean like the men who got married today."

"That's right." Wondering what Tristan thought of the story so far, Rachel glanced in his direction.

He didn't seem to be listening. His gaze was locked on some unknown spot in the distance. There was something in his eyes. A vacancy she'd seen before. For a second, Rachel wondered if he was even aware she and the girls were sitting here with him. She wondered if he was aware of his surroundings at all.

Lily tapped her on the shoulder. "Did Jacob find a wife?"

Oh, right, she was supposed to be telling the girls a story. "Yes, he did, but we're getting ahead of ourselves. We need to back up a bit."

Three pairs of big round eyes flooded with expectation.

Rachel looked over at Tristan again. She could practically feel the turbulent emotions rolling off him, but he still didn't seem to be listening to the story.

"Jacob had a twin brother. The two didn't get along." She paused and, remembering her promise to keep the tale simple, chose her next words carefully. "One day Jacob and his brother fought so fiercely that Jacob had to leave home for a while."

Lily shifted closer to Rachel. "Where did he go?"

Keep it simple, Rachel reminded herself. "He went to live with his uncle. On his first day there, he met a woman named Rachel."

"That's your name," Violet said around her thumb.

"Yes, it is." Rachel swept her hand over the child's head. "Jacob's Rachel was very beautiful and he fell in love with her on the spot."

All three little girls sighed, as did the storyteller.

"Unfortunately, Rachel's father was a greedy man and he didn't want to let Jacob marry her without—"

The church door swung opened with a bang.

Distracted, they all looked toward the loud noise. A woman Rachel recognized as the pianist from the wedding stepped outside. "It's a girl," she declared. "A beautiful baby girl sporting a head full of brown hair just like her mother's."

With the faintest trace of nerves, Rachel glanced at Tristan again. He was still staring straight ahead, but now his eyes were on the church, or rather on Emma, who'd just exited the building and started across the street.

"Well, girls, looks like I'll have to finish the story later," Rachel said when it became evident Emma was heading their way. Her sister looked drained. Her dress was rumpled and would require a lot of effort to get rid of all the wrinkles. Her hair was a tangle of loose curls, but she was smiling.

Tristan climbed to his feet. "How are mother and child?"

Emma's smile turned exultant. "The baby is healthy, Clara is exhausted, but both are doing well. I'm here because Bertha Quincy asked me to find you," she told Tristan. "She wishes to speak with you as soon as possible."

He nodded. "I'll go talk to her now." He turned to Rachel, drew in a tight breath. "This shouldn't take long. I already have an idea what she wants to discuss."

So, too, did Rachel.

In the span of a single afternoon, Bertha Quincy's life had changed dramatically. She now had her sister and brand-new niece living with her. They would need her full attention. She would no longer be able to watch Tristan's daughters.

Rachel had prayed for a place to belong. Though not quite what she had in mind, she realized she wanted to watch Tristan's daughters. Not only in an effort to help him out, but also because she actually enjoyed Daisy, Lily and Violet. Caring for them wouldn't be a chore. It would be a blessing.

Emma lowered onto the bench beside Rachel, closed

her eyes and released a long, exhausted breath of air. "It's been quite an eventful day."

"Yes." Nothing would ever really be the same again, Rachel thought, realizing it was time she accepted that things weren't going back to the way they used to be

Eyes still shut, Emma smiled serenely. "Lots of changes ahead."

"Yes," Rachel said again. She needed to focus on the future. *Her* future. One that wouldn't involve her family in the same ways as before.

Daisy walked over to Emma and tugged on her arm. "I know you. You got married today."

Emma opened her eyes. "I did."

"Where's your husband?"

"He's right here," Nathan said, striding over to them. "I've come to steal away my bride."

He took Emma's hands and drew her to her feet. For what seemed an eternity he stared into her eyes. "Hello, Mrs. Reed."

"Hello, Mr. Reed."

All that love and happiness flowing between them made Rachel's throat close up tight. She cleared away the lump with a delicate cough. Nathan finally stepped back and attempted an apologetic grimace in her direction, but he failed miserably. Clearly, the man was too happy to frown.

Rachel watched as the newlyweds said their farewells and walked away holding hands.

Tristan reappeared atop the church steps. His face tight, he hiked back across the street with a stiff, impatient gait. Whatever he'd discussed with Bertha Quincy wasn't sitting well with him. He seemed in an especially edgy mood.

As he came closer, Rachel watched an array of emotions chase across his face and wondered what he was feeling. Relief, to be sure, relief for Clara and her baby, but sorrow still lingered.

Out of a desire to offer him comfort, Rachel reached out to him. He took her hand without hesitation.

"Rachel." He held her gaze and appeared about to say something profound, but then he let her go and stepped away from her. "Your family is gathering at Grayson's house. He requested I escort you home. Evidently, Maggie has plans to feed us all before we go our separate ways."

Though a kind gesture on her sister-in-law's part, it was yet another reminder that Rachel wasn't needed anymore, at least not by her family. She would be living under a roof where she had no duties, no purpose. What would she do with her day? How would she fill the endless, empty hours?

Ah, but another family needed her.

Taking that to heart, Rachel gathered Tristan's girls. They elbowed one another and fought for position until Rachel stepped in and organized them from shortest to tallest.

"Violet, you stand here." She pointed to a spot just to the child's left. "Lily, you line up directly behind her and, Daisy, you come in right behind Lily."

The little girls hurried to their places.

Pleased they accepted direction so well, Rachel took up her position directly behind Daisy. "All right, then. Let's go."

With Violet in the lead, they set out at a relatively slow pace. They'd barely taken three steps when Rachel called their tiny group to a halt. Tristan was staring at her, mouth slightly agape. Even in a state of mild shock he was still imposing, almost as if he were silently demanding something of her.

She felt a little light-headed under all that intensity focused on her. But when he continued staring at her, with his eyebrows cocked in silent inquiry, she angled her own questioning stare at him. "What?"

"Do you know where you're going?"

Of course she did.

She thought she did. She was pretty sure she did. Or, maybe, she didn't. She looked quickly around, suddenly unable to get her bearings. It would seem she hadn't paid close enough attention to the route she'd taken from Grayson's house earlier in the day.

"Uh…we need to head…" She adopted a confident air and pointed toward the mountains in the distance. "That way."

"Actually, it's *that* way." Tristan pointed in the opposite direction.

"Oh." Mortified, Rachel felt her cheeks grow hot. Not only had she overstepped her authority with Tristan's children, she'd been taking them, quite literally, down the wrong road.

"I apologize." She forced herself to hold his gaze without flinching. "I didn't mean to take charge."

"Yes, you did." Amusement twinkled in his eyes, softening the impact of his words. Almost.

He continued watching her with smiling eyes. But now his lips were twitching, too. Any minute he'd break out laughing.

She sighed. "You could have stopped me before I headed out with the girls."

"True."

"And yet, you didn't."

He lifted a nonchalant shoulder. "I wanted to see how long it would take you to realize your mistake."

The girls giggled. But they refrained from joining in the conversation. They seemed happy to remain silent spectators.

Still unable to determine their exact location in the town, Rachel looked around her again.

"Are you sure we aren't supposed to go that way?" She jerked her chin toward the mountains.

Tristan chuckled. "I think I know where my own house is, which happens to be right next door to your brother's."

She sighed again. "Point taken."

Chuckling louder, he turned each of his daughters in the proper direction and led them away. Two steps out, he glanced over his shoulder. "You coming with us?"

Rachel refused to sigh another time. Twice in one conversation was more than enough. "Of course I am."

She took up her position behind Daisy and paid very close attention to her surroundings. Next time she found herself on this side of town, she would know the way home.

An hour later, Tristan watched Rachel interact with her family from a position near the back of the main living area. He shifted his stance, leaned a shoulder against the wall and continued to observe the Hewitt family dynamics. Did Rachel know how much her siblings loved her? Did she understand how worried they were about her?

Tristan had his doubts, primarily because she seemed determined to hold herself separate. Even when one of her family members engaged her in conversation, she kept a slight physical distance.

He'd witnessed this same behavior from her earlier

today. It was as if she was deliberately setting herself apart.

The invisible barrier she'd raised between her and her family was disconcerting. Rachel had been so vibrant and full of life on the trail. He'd watched her laugh with her siblings during the day and sing songs with them around the campfire at night. She'd stood up for them against any real or perceived threats, including him.

Tristan felt an urge to go to her, to draw out the animated woman he knew was underneath all that artificial reserve. Now that his daughters sat at the feet of Abigail's father, listening to him regale them with life on the wagon train, Tristan had no reason not to approach Rachel.

He pushed away from the wall.

A soft, lilting voice stopped him mid-step. "You look tired, Tristan."

Forcing a lightness in his tone he didn't especially feel, he looked into Maggie Hewitt's sympathetic, understanding eyes. "I'm a bit tired, but no more than usual."

"You push yourself too hard."

He lifted a shoulder in response.

"When I was speaking with Bertha this afternoon about an order she'd placed at the mercantile, she told me she can't watch the girls anymore now that her sister and baby are living with her." Maggie's gaze turned worried. "Do you have another plan?"

He shrugged again. Although Bertha had left him in a bind, the situation wasn't entirely unexpected. "I'll figure something out."

There were several options available to him, but only one he really wanted to pursue.

"Seems nothing's turning out the way you planned." Maggie shot a meaningful glance in Emma's direction.

"Things are as they should be," he countered. "Emma

and Nathan belong together. I'm happy they found one another when they did."

"Still…" Maggie patted his arm. "Grayson and I had hoped it would work out for you. Your girls need a mother."

He said nothing because, well, she was right. His daughters did need a mother. He'd been willing to offer Emma a marriage of convenience for their sakes. But now, seeing her so happy with Nathan, understanding the love they shared, Tristan was doubly glad he hadn't pursued a match with her.

"What will you do now?"

He had a plan, one he wouldn't share with anyone until he'd spoken to Rachel first. She could still turn him down. And maybe she'd be right to do so. He wanted a wife he couldn't hurt, a woman he couldn't fail. And fail he would, if Rachel wanted things from him he couldn't give.

He wanted no part in breaking her heart.

"Leave the poor man alone, Maggie. Tristan's going to be fine." Grayson entered the conversation at the perfect moment, thereby rescuing Tristan from having to give Maggie a suitable response to her question.

Maggie wrinkled her nose. "I didn't say otherwise."

Grayson simply looked at her.

She attempted to stomp away, but Grayson caught her by the arm. "Aw, now, Mags, don't walk away in a huff."

She lifted her nose in the air and sniffed delicately.

Laughing, Grayson kissed her square on the mouth, then whispered something in her ear.

Eyes twinkling now, she halfheartedly slapped at his arm. "Fool."

"You got that right. I'm nothing but a big, sloppy fool in love with my wife."

"Oh, honestly." She walked away, laughing and shaking her head.

When she was out of earshot, Grayson turned to face Tristan. "I haven't thanked you for not telling my family about my marriage when you joined up with them on the wagon train. That's not the kind of news you want to find out about from a second party."

"Wasn't my tale to tell." Tristan watched Maggie laugh over something one of his daughters said. She was a different woman than the one he'd known two months ago. She was happier, everything about her seemed lighter. And Tristan knew why.

"You're good for her," he told his friend, remembering how Maggie had suffered her own tragedy. Her parents had been killed in a flash flood a month before her wedding to Grayson. He'd helped her through her shock and grief.

"She's good for me, too." Grayson's expression sobered. "I daresay she saved my life."

Tristan didn't argue the point. Before meeting Maggie, Grayson had been a hard man, full of anger, especially at God. Tristan had experienced a similar disillusionment after Siobhan's death.

But unlike Grayson, Tristan didn't plan to fall in love again. Siobhan had been his life, his whole world, and had left him three tiny blessings to remember her by. He didn't need or want anything more, except a mother for his daughters.

His gaze went to Rachel, locking with hers. A moment of peace filled him.

Grayson followed the direction of his gaze. Understanding dawned in his eyes, followed by unmistakable horror. "Rachel is too young to get married."

"She's not a child, Grayson. She's a grown woman more than capable of making her own decisions."

His friend continued staring at his sister. "I know that."

"Do you?" Surprised at the anger in his tone, Tristan lowered his voice. "You shouldn't dismiss her, or make her decisions for her, simply because she's the youngest in your family."

"She's not just the youngest, she's also…" He broke off, clamped his mouth shut. "I'm not discussing this with you."

There was a protectiveness in the man's behavior that went beyond the usual big brother/little sister bond.

Something didn't add up. "What aren't you telling me about Rachel?"

"She's…unique, special."

"I completely agree. She's kind. Funny. And has a wonderful way with children. The girls already adore her." He decided to give his friend the truth. "And I'm thinking about asking her to marry me if she'll—"

"No." Grayson's scowl turned fierce. "She's too young to get married."

"So you already said. But correct me if I'm wrong—" Tristan compelled his friend's gaze "—isn't she around the same age you were when you got married the first time?"

"It's not the same."

"You're right, it's not." Tristan faced the other man head-on, determined to be as clear as possible. "I'm going to offer her a marriage in name only."

Grayson's expression turned thunderous. "Still, no."

There was something in Grayson's tone—an unmistakable warning—that put Tristan on edge. "You were willing to let me marry Emma with the same constraints."

"That's because Emma has always been unnaturally shy. Even as a young girl she was awkward and uncomfortable around people. A marriage of convenience would have suited her personality. She would have been happy mothering your daughters and—"

Female laughter rang out from the other side of the room. Emma, the unnaturally shy woman she was, had just linked arms with Maggie and now the two were twirling around the room together. Abigail Black, now Abigail Hewitt, picked up her mandolin and played a jaunty tune to accompany the women's impromptu dance.

"Maybe you don't know either of your sisters as well as you think."

"I know Rachel. I know she won't agree to a marriage of convenience."

Tristan didn't think she would agree to his terms, either. That didn't mean he wasn't going to ask.

No matter her answer, he could guarantee Grayson one thing for certain. "I would never intentionally hurt your sister."

Grayson studied Tristan closely, his eyes boring into him with ruthless regard. At last, he relaxed his stance. "Go ahead and ask Rachel to marry you. *If* she agrees to your terms, then I won't stand in the way. I'll even give you my blessing."

Tristan felt his jaw tighten at the other man's superior tone. "Magnanimous of you."

"What can I say?" Grayson slapped him on the back with unnecessary force. "I'm a generous man at heart."

Chapter Eleven

Rachel needed a break from her well-meaning siblings and their equally considerate spouses. To be fair, she supposed the occasional looks of concern thrown her way were reasonable and not entirely unexpected. She was, after all, the youngest. That often put her on the receiving end of too much worry and excessive amounts of sheltering.

The irony? For the past six years *she'd* taken care of *them*, at least in terms of their physical needs. After their father had grown ill, and Emma had taken over the duty of nursing him, Rachel had cooked and cleaned and generally kept the house running smoothly. She would have to find another way to pull her weight in the family but not today. Not now.

Seizing the moment, she slipped out the back door when her siblings and their spouses were distracted while singing along to a familiar tune Abby strummed on her mandolin.

Tall, craggy mountains rose up on Rachel's right, strong, shadowy faces like sentinels guarding the land. To her left, the sun crept close to the horizon, hovering just above a thin band of puffy white clouds. Brilliant colors filled the sky, a breathtaking mix of golden orange, pink and blue. Rachel breathed in the cool air, realizing this would be the first night in months that she would sleep indoors.

She would miss the freedom of bunking beneath the stars, but couldn't deny she was looking forward to spending the night in a real bed. Still, after five months on the trail, she'd grown to appreciate the ever-changing mood of the evening sky. How the air could be stifling hot one night or surprisingly cold the next.

A stiff breeze suddenly kicked up, whipping her hair around her face. She pulled her shawl tighter around her shoulders and shoved at the tangle of curls.

The sound of familiar footsteps brought a smile to her face. She'd know that purposeful stride anywhere.

"It's a beautiful night," she said without turning around.

Tristan drew alongside her and eyed the horizon. "I don't look at this view often enough," he admitted. "I certainly don't appreciate it the way I should."

"That's perfectly understandable. You're in a hectic season of life."

He rubbed a hand over the stubble on his chin, creating a scratchy sound Rachel found immensely appealing. "I fear my life's about to get even more hectic in the coming days."

Though she already knew the answer, Rachel asked the question, anyway. "More hectic, how?"

"Bertha Quincy will no longer be able to watch the girls for me."

This was the opening Rachel had been waiting for since meeting Tristan's daughters this afternoon. Turning slightly, she considered him from boot to brow. A subtle, nearly invisible smile had crept across his lips, as if he had a secret. Or maybe that was nerves sh\ detected in his expression. Or *maybe* the nerves came om her.

"I have a possible solution to your problem, he said.

"As do I."

Her heart slammed against her ribs. Perhaps they had the same plan. That would certainly make this go easier.

"What...what if..." Her tongue suddenly felt thick and her breathing took on a sporadic cadence. Why couldn't she speak her mind? Where was this awkwardness coming from?

She bought herself a bit of time. "Your daughters are everything you claimed," she said in a rush. "Even more adorable than I expected."

"I'm a very blessed man."

"Oh, you are." And yet she sensed he was not at peace. She sensed his life had been especially difficult since his wife died.

Though Rachel would never dare attempt to replace Siobhan, she wanted to give Tristan some relief from his everyday burdens. He deserved happiness, every drop that came his way. She could help him with his household and care for his daughters, at least temporarily, until he found another, more permanent solution.

"Tristan, I—" she began, while he said, "Rachel, I—"

They broke off at the same time and laughed. The tension between them lifted ever so slightly.

"You first," he offered.

This is it, she told herself. *This is your chance to make your offer.* "I was thinking I could help you with your daughters."

He turned to face her, smiled. "That's what I came to discuss with you."

So, he *had* followed her. She'd suspected as much. But just to be clear...

"You followed me out here to talk about your girls?"

He went very still and studied her face with that intensity she found so disconcerting, as if he were trying to look into the depths of her soul. "In a manner of speaking."

Unsure what he meant, she swallowed. This wasn't supposed to be so hard. Tristan needed her. His girls needed her. What she had to offer made sense for all of them. "So you agree I should take over for Bertha."

"No."

No? She waited for him to expand. When he didn't, she blinked at him in confusion. *That's it*, she thought. *Just...no.* Not a single word of explanation?

She blew out a frustrated puff of air. "You realize I'm offering to take care of your daughters. It's the perfect solution. I adore them. I'm pretty confident they like me."

He was already shaking his head before she finished stating her case.

She frowned at him. "I don't understand your refusal. You need help immediately. I'm available. I can start tomorrow."

"I had a more permanent solution in mind."

Oh. *Oh.* An odd sensation—part hope, part horror—settled over. The feeling grew more intense when she saw the resolve in his eyes. Something was about to change between them.

"Rachel Hewitt." He took her hand in his. "Will you marry me?"

One.

Two.

Three.

Tristan ticked off each passing second silently in his mind. Four. Five. Six. He assumed Rachel's continued silence meant she was seriously considering his marriage proposal. Surely, if she meant to say no she would have done so already.

Could it be this easy? Could they come to terms quickly, without a lot of fuss?

"You..." Her eyelashes fluttered several times. "You truly want to marry me?"

He couldn't tell exactly what he heard in her voice, but at least she wasn't telling him no.

"Yes." He attempted a smile but wasn't sure he pulled it off. "I want you to become my wife."

Eyebrows lifted, she watched him, waiting, as if she expected him to say more.

The muscles in his back tensed at her dry expression. Had he insulted her? He couldn't think how. For a split second, he considered retracting his offer then decided to stand his ground.

"However—" he paused "—before you give me your answer, I should tell you that there are conditions to my proposal."

"Conditions?" She cocked her head at a puzzled angle.

Tristan gritted his teeth. This conversation was not going the way he'd planned, but he'd started it and now he would finish it. "I'm offering you an arrangement that would allow you to care for the children permanently and yet give you more liberty than would be afforded you as a single woman."

"You mean..."

"We will have separate living arrangements in the house." He gave her a moment to process the meaning behind his words.

Apparently, she needed two.

She opened her mouth, closed it and then simply gaped at him for several endless seconds. "Why?"

"Pardon me?"

"*Why* would you want a marriage that wasn't really a marriage at all?"

He blinked at her, then nearly laughed. Of course she would want more information. This was Rachel Hewitt, after all. "I should think it obvious."

Her brow creased in absolute bafflement before her gaze cleared. "It's because you're still in love with your wife."

Tristan didn't know what was worse—her unquestionable conviction she had the situation figured out or the quiet understanding he saw in her eyes.

For a moment, he couldn't seem to formulate a response. Time bent and shifted, drawing him back to Ireland, back to his first marriage proposal. He'd been seven years old, Siobhan nearly the same age. He'd asked her to marry him. She'd said yes. And that had been that. They'd said their vows eleven years later.

He didn't have a single childhood memory without Siobhan in it. He'd never once considered giving his heart to anyone else. The grief he'd experienced after losing her had nearly destroyed him.

He couldn't go through that pain again.

"While I'll admit my wanting a marriage of convenience is partly because of Siobhan, it's perhaps not for the reason you seem to think."

In truth, Siobhan would want him to move on with his life. She would want him to find love again, not only for the girls' sake but for his own. Her last words had been to encourage him to find happiness again someday.

Problem was he didn't deserve to be happy. Siobhan had died because of him. If she hadn't been carrying his child she wouldn't have died. "I'll not subject another woman to the horrors of childbirth," he blurted out.

"Oh, Tristan." Rachel's voice was soft with emotion.

"That's the reason you're offering a marriage in name only? Because you don't want me to die in childbirth?"

"Yes."

"Not all women die in childbirth. Take, for instance, Clara."

He'd said nearly the same words to Grayson this afternoon. Logically, he knew Rachel was right—not all women died giving birth. Nevertheless, he couldn't release his reservations.

He liked Rachel. He liked her a lot. A weary, neglected part of him craved her company, her kindness and her smiles. Especially her smiles. But he couldn't—*wouldn't*—risk her life. That meant he couldn't allow himself to get too close to her, not physically, never that.

"I'm not a man prone to falling in love. I can't give you a real marriage, Rachel. But I can promise I'll provide for you to the best of my ability. I'll keep you safe and do everything in power to make you happy. I won't ever hurt you. We can have a good life together."

He absolutely believed it to be true.

"I'm sorry, Tristan. My answer is no. I want a marriage as God intended."

He heard the slight waver in her voice and the regret. His gut twisted with a corresponding emotion. "I understand."

He wouldn't try to change her mind. He meant what he said. He wanted Rachel to be happy. Part of him wanted her to be happy with him, but that wasn't possible. Not when they wanted two very different things from marriage.

"That's not to say I plan to walk away from you and the girls." She placed a hand on his shoulder. "I can still watch your daughters. At least until you can find a woman who will accept your conditions for marriage."

She sounded sincere and yet also sad. He wanted to

tell her he'd figure out another solution, except he didn't have any other options at his disposal.

"The hours will be long," he warned.

"I'm not afraid of long hours and hard work."

"I'll need you to arrive at sunup and stay past sundown." Was he really considering her offer? Did he have any other choice? "I'll need you to fix all of the girls' meals and I'll pay you a decent wage. It would also be helpful if you—"

She interrupted him with a hand in the air. "Why don't we work out the particulars later? It's been a long day and we could both use some sleep before we get into all that."

He said nothing for a long moment, then found himself nodding in agreement. "You're right. We'll wait until tomorrow for the rest of this discussion."

"I won't let you down, Tristan. I promise I'll take good care of your daughters."

"I trust you, Rachel, completely." He wouldn't have proposed otherwise.

She gave him one of her prettiest smiles, the one that reached into his heart and squeezed. "Then we have a deal."

"So it would seem."

"Shall we shake on it?" She thrust out her hand.

Why not? He closed his hand over hers, palm to palm, and felt an instant jolt in the vicinity of his heart.

He quickly pulled his hand free.

"I say we go back inside and tell the girls. What do you say, Tristan?"

"Lead the way."

Later that night, Rachel was unable to fall asleep. Grayson had given her a room on the second floor. The full moon shone bright through the lone window, a big fat ball of light beckoning her outdoors. She nearly answered the call, despite the chill that now hung in the evening air.

And in her heart.

Tristan had asked her to marry him, but with *conditions*. He wanted a marriage in name only. She wanted so much more.

She thought of Reverend Pettygrove's words at the wedding ceremony this afternoon. *Honor your commitment to one another the way the Lord intended from the beginning...be fruitful and multiply.*

Rachel wanted the kind of marriage the preacher had described. Would she ever find that?

She was still young. There was a lot of time for her to meet a wonderful, caring man and fall in love.

She shut her eyes, tried to picture the man she would one day marry. An image of Tristan flared to life. She'd been sorely tempted to accept his offer. She'd been equally wise to turn him down.

He didn't want her, not really. He wanted a wife in name only. Having just recently come out from beneath Emma's shadow, Rachel would not accept being second-best ever again.

Tossing onto her stomach, she scowled at the floor. Accepting the inevitable sleeplessness, she sat up and lit the lamp on the table next to her bed. She reached for her Bible and opened to the middle of the book. For several minutes, she searched around for something to catch her eye, but came up short.

The Psalms usually calmed her. Not tonight. Tonight, emptiness filled her. A vast loneliness she feared would become a part of her if she didn't take care. She felt as if she were losing her family, though she knew that wasn't precisely true. Still...

She set the Bible back on the table and reached for

the lamp. Her eye caught the other book sitting on the nightstand. She'd nearly forgotten about her mother's journal. Without thinking too hard about what she was doing, she turned to the first page, ran her fingertip over the pretty, looping writing that now defined Sara Hewitt in Rachel's mind.

She picked up reading where she'd left off in Fort Nez Perce, savoring the words slowly, lovingly.

> *Rachel is a good baby. I find such joy in her. She hardly cries and only when she's hungry, which tends to be often. Emma helps bathe her and feed her, treating the baby with the innate caring that seems such a part of her. Grayson, though only nine years old and all boy, is fascinated with her. He's very protective, understandable under the circumstances.*

Rachel stopped reading, her hand hovering over the page. What circumstances did her mother mean?

Shaking her head, she read on.

> *Grayson already takes his role as big brother to the child seriously.*

The child? What an odd reference.

Shrugging, Rachel continued reading the rest of the entry, which was nothing more than a retelling of the day's events. She read two more entries, both full of her mother's love for her and anecdotes of interactions with her siblings.

Feeling less alone and closer to the woman who'd given her birth, Rachel marked her place, then put the journal atop the Bible on her nightstand. She would continue reading tomorrow night, one entry at a time. She wanted to savor every moment of this new connection she felt with her mother.

Rachel thought of the three sweet little girls next door.

She knew she could never replace their mother. It would be wrong of her to try. But she would do everything she could to give them the same tenderness and affection she'd received as a child herself. She would care for Tristan's daughters as if they were her own.

If some of that kindness and tending spilled onto their father, well, that wasn't necessarily a terrible thing. Tristan could use someone on his side, someone to lighten his load, who understood the depths of his grief.

Rachel had a new purpose for the coming days, one she would embrace with joy and happiness for as long as it lasted. All she had to do was guard her heart around Tristan. Easy enough. She would simply think of him as nothing more than a friend. It was a good plan, a wise plan.

What could possibly go wrong?

Chapter Twelve

To Tristan's complete and utter relief, a knock sounded on the front door only moments after the first golden rays of sunlight peeked through the gray dawn. The corners of his lips lifted. Rachel Hewitt was a woman of her word. She'd said she would arrive at sunup, and so she had.

After the first wash of relief passed, he realized he was standing in the middle of his house, frozen, blinking at the shut door. *It won't open itself.* Right. He made quick work of moving across the room when Lily's squeal of delight had him nearly stumbling over his own two feet.

"Miss Rachel is here! Miss Rachel is here!" The child chanted this while bouncing on her toes. "Miss Rachel is here!"

Violet mimicked her older sister, but with one notable exception. Her squeals were garbled by the thumb in her mouth.

They really needed to work on that, Tristan reminded himself, making a mental note to discuss the problem with Rachel.

Daisy danced and skipped around him in small, tight circles, breaking into one of her made-up songs that lacked specific words other than *la-la-la* followed by a *la-la-dee-da-da-da*.

A laugh bubbled in Tristan's chest.

For the span of two full heartbeats, he looked from one beloved daughter to the other.

Another knock came at the door, this one more insistent, followed by a muffled, "Anyone going to let me in? It's cold out here."

Striding around his daughters, Tristan swung open the door and connected gazes with his children's new nanny. The prickle of awareness caught him off guard and he felt his heart catch hard. His reaction made little sense. This was the woman who only last night had turned down his marriage proposal.

She twisted her hands together in front of the waist of her plain pale blue dress, watching him as a rabbit might watch a circling hawk. "H-hello, Tristan."

"Rachel."

When he continued staring at her, one hand on the door, he watched her nervousness vanish as if it had never been there, replaced by a wide, appealing grin. Lightning quick and just as powerful as a punch to his gut.

"Can I come in?"

"Of course." Hurriedly stepping aside, he gestured for her to enter ahead of him.

The girls rushed to greet her. She opened her arms and pulled them close. Childish giggles mingled with her deeper, throatier laugh.

While the four of them got reacquainted, Tristan took his time shutting the door behind him. His chest rose and fell in perfect rhythm with his quickening heartbeat. As impossible as it would seem, Rachel Hewitt had become prettier overnight. Why hadn't he remembered how lovely her hair was, how engaging her smile?

That smile. It had nearly knocked him off his feet just now. He'd actually felt a tangible impact in his gut, the kind that made him think of things he had no right thinking.

He put an immediate halt to his thoughts.

Nothing had changed since last night. Rachel had agreed to help him out on a temporary basis until he could find a woman to marry who would accept his terms. Terms he would not be amending, ever.

Even if he suggested a compromise, it wouldn't be enough. Rachel wanted what amounted to a love match. Tristan had married the love of his life. She'd died because of him.

Blessedly unaware of his troubling thoughts, Rachel released the girls. They flitted and twirled around her, their hands flapping so quickly they reminded Tristan of three little hummingbirds. His head grew dizzy watching them.

"Girls." His voice came out gruffer than he'd intended. He cleared his throat and tried again. "Let's everyone step back and give Miss Rachel room to breathe."

He turned his attention to her.

She favored him with another one of her smiles.

He looked quickly away.

"Miss Rachel." Daisy tugged on her arm. "We've been waiting for you for *hours*."

"Hours and hours and hours," Lily confirmed.

Since when had his daughters become prone to exaggeration? Tristan assumed it must have happened when he was on the wagon train.

"Well, now that I'm here let's have a look at your house." Rachel spun in a slow circle. "Oh…my."

Tristan attempted to view his home from her fresh perspective. He cringed at what he saw—unnatural amounts of clutter, layers of dust on the tabletops, a complete lack of order.

"I'm not much for keeping house," he admitted, but made no further excuses. There were, after all, only so many hours in the day.

"It's perfectly fine, Tristan." Rachel's tone was gentle. "This is why you hired me, to take care of you…I mean, your household."

They exchanged smiles—his tentative, hers full of warmth.

Violet shoved in between them. "I'm glad you're here with us."

Smile firmly in place, Rachel glanced down at the child. "Oh, me, too, Violet. We're going to have lots of fun together."

The girls cheered.

"*After* we finish our chores."

The declaration reminded Tristan of his own work waiting for him across town. "That, I believe, is my cue to depart."

He kissed each of his daughters on the head and told them to. "Mind Miss Rachel today."

A nod in her direction and he set out to meet up with James Stillwell at the jail. They had to come up with a schedule for guarding the stolen money. Once they figured out the various rotations they'd formulate a plan to lure the Tucker brothers out of hiding.

With his head on possible scenarios, Tristan walked the five blocks from his house to the jail. At this early hour there was usually very little activity on the streets. Not today. Because of the significant size of the most recent wagon train, the large influx of emigrants had already changed the face of his town.

The sights and sounds that accompanied Tristan on his

walk to work were similar to what he'd encountered on the trail. He could hear the snap of campfires in the distance, babies crying, hammers striking iron. With winter rapidly approaching, the new arrivals had to erect their shelter quickly. Some would end up with leaky shacks and tents. Others, like the Hewitt clan, would fare much better by sharing homes with family members already settled in the area.

Unfortunately, the wet and cold of the next few months would take its toll. There would be illness and death.

He knew he couldn't save everyone, but he would try. What was the point of becoming sheriff if he didn't attempt to protect and defend the people of his town?

"Tristan." A familiar voice called out from an open doorway. "Got a minute?"

"Not much more than that." He changed direction and strode toward Grayson Hewitt's mercantile.

The moment he entered the store, the pleasant aroma of spices and lavender filled his nose. He was also able to pick out the scent of oats and—his daughters' favorite— licorice.

A quick glance around told him there were no customers milling about. Too early. But there was an astonishing amount of merchandise stacked atop shelves or in neat piles from floor to ceiling. Clearly, Grayson anticipated an increase in business due to the new arrivals from the wagon train. Smart.

"So…" He shot his friend a questioning look. "What can I do for you?"

Grayson leaned against the counter at his back and crossed his arms over his chest. "After significant fishing for information, Rachel admitted that you asked her to marry you and she said no."

Tristan made a sound of annoyance deep in his throat. "Did you call me in here to gloat?"

"Not at all." Grayson surprised him with a sympathetic grimace. "I'm sorry it didn't work out between you and Rachel. The more I thought about you two getting married the more I realized it's not such a terrible idea, after all."

"Yeah, well…" He gave the other man a wry twist of his lips. "I'm growing used to disappointment when it comes to the Hewitt women."

Grayson chuckled softly. "Apparently, I have two very strong willed sisters who seem to know their own minds."

"Apparently, you do."

Impatient to get to the jail, Tristan waited one beat, then two, but Grayson seemed content to continue shaking his head in frustration over his sisters.

Tristan lifted his eyebrows. "Was there anything else you needed from me?"

Something hard came into Grayson's eyes. "Ben told me about the robberies on the trail."

A muscle shifted in Tristan's jaw. He swept his gaze over the interior of the mercantile, seeing the vast quantities of merchandise from a thief's perspective. "You'll want to think about tightening security until we catch the Tucker brothers."

"Already done. Ben and I have agreed that one of us will always be in the store during the day."

"What about at night?" If Grant and Amos attempted a break-in, they would probably do so during the evening hours when there weren't a lot of people around.

"Now that Nathan and Emma are living temporarily in the rooms upstairs, Nathan has agreed to keep an eye on things after we close up for the night."

Tristan pondered this new piece of information. As

a former trapper Nathan Reed had spent years alone in the dangerous wilderness. He'd faced down wild animals, flash floods and many other unthinkable threats. He could handle Grant and Amos Tucker if they showed up unexpectedly.

"Tell me what you know about the Tucker brothers," Grayson requested.

Tristan considered his response. He'd done a lot of thinking about Grant and Amos over the past week since he'd discovered their treachery. He had a good idea who they were—and who they were not.

"They aren't hardened criminals. They're opportunists. They steal what's easy and accessible." He glanced around at all the *easy* and *accessible* items in the store. "That's not to say you should underestimate them. They're unpredictable and that makes them dangerous. Be prepared, Grayson."

Even as he spoke the words, Tristan knew the mercantile wouldn't be their first—or their only—stop. The Tuckers would want to retrieve the money they'd lost, money they believed was rightfully theirs.

"Nathan and Ben had a similar assessment of the two. We'll take the necessary precautions. Hewitts protect their own."

"I'd like to speak with both your brother and brother-in-law, just to make sure we're all in agreement."

"I'm here." Nathan Reed stepped out of a back room. "We can speak now."

From the glint in the other man's eyes it was clear he had very strong opinions about Grant and Amos Tucker. Still, Tristan needed to be absolutely certain the entire Hewitt family understood who—and what—they were up against.

The brothers had collected a sizable quantity of valuable items while on the wagon train. They would not only be destitute now that they'd lost everything, but desperate and dangerous, as well.

Tristan had no doubt they would be looking for ways to reclaim their booty. They would probably attempt to steal from businesses in town, all of which needed to be warned.

He had a long day ahead of him.

"I'm heading over to the jail to discuss the situation with James Stillwell," Tristan said, dividing a look between both men. "I'd like both of you to join us."

A customer entered the store before either man could respond. Grayson hesitated, clearly torn.

"Take care of business," Nathan told him. "I'll go with Tristan and report back what we discussed."

"Good enough."

While Grayson tended to his customer, Nathan followed Tristan outside. They fell into step together, their strides eating up the ground at an identical pace.

Nathan broke the silence first. "I understand you hired Rachel to watch your daughters."

Not liking what he heard in the other man's tone, Tristan fought back a wave of impatience. He had enough to worry about without having to defend his relationship with Rachel. "She's good with the girls and has agreed to help me out with them temporarily. I will pay her fairly for her time."

The explanation was short and truthful but didn't seem to satisfy Nathan's concerns. "Rachel is family now. I won't stand by and watch you hurt her."

Tristan bit back a hiss. He could tell the other man he had no plans to hurt Rachel but realized that wouldn't satisfy him any more than his previous response. Tristan didn't fault Nathan's devotion to his sister-in-law. He actually admired his loyalty. Thus, in the same spirit as before, he kept his response simple and to the point. "Understood."

"Good." Nathan fell silent.

Tristan did, as well, fully aware tension still simmered between them. He knew why and decided to be forthright about the cause. "I never congratulated on your marriage to Emma. I wish you years of happiness together."

Nathan's feet ground to a halt. Eyes narrowed, he studied Tristan with a hard glare. After a moment, his entire bearing relaxed. "I believe you mean that."

"I am sincere."

"Thank you," Nathan said, and actually smiled around the words.

"You're welcome."

They resumed walking. The hostility between them dissipated one step at a time. A block later, they arrived at their destination. Taking the lead, Tristan opened the door to the jailhouse and called out to James Stillwell.

It was time to set a trap for two slippery rats.

Rachel glanced around Tristan's house, feeling a sense of accomplishment now that she'd restored some order to the chaos she'd encountered this morning. The decor was simple, if somewhat austere, and could use a few feminine touches. She'd make curtains first. Maybe hang wallpaper. Add a couple of doilies here and there.

Despite the Spartan conditions, Rachel had spent a delightful morning with Tristan's daughters. She'd taught them basic household chores. Not wanting to overwhelm them, she'd turned each task into a game.

They folded blankets in teams of two, racing to see who could finish first. They sang "Mary Had a Little Lamb" as they swept the dirty floor, timing the strokes to the rhythm of the song. When it was time to dust the furniture, she'd taught them a different tune that Daisy continued singing the rest of the morning.

Brushing her palms together, Rachel decided it was time for a break. "Who's hungry?"

Three hands shot in the air.

Rachel's heart took a direct hit. She'd been right to take this position in Tristan's home. His daughters were so sweet, so obedient.

Smiling, she led them into the kitchen and studied the small area with a sinking heart. Austere was several steps up from this household tragedy. There was a battered table and chairs that had seen better days three decades ago, a tidy row of well-made cabinets and an ugly black stove that spread its squat body in the far right-hand corner of the room.

Bulky, with what looked like rust showing around the seams, it had a sad, neglected look about it, as though the stove had been shoved in the corner with every intention of being forgotten.

It was silly to feel a connection to an inanimate object. And yet, Rachel's heart swelled with sympathy. Ignored. Dismissed. Overlooked. She knew the feeling.

She moved closer and took a lengthier inspection. A dirty pot sat on top of the stove, the contents burned black.

Oh, Tristan.

Head tilted at a curious angle, Daisy came to stand beside Rachel. The child stared at the stove a moment, as if searching for a reason behind Rachel's fascination.

"Who made the oatmeal?" she asked the child.

Daisy gave a woeful sigh. "Da." Lowering her voice to a whisper, she added, "He's not very good at cooking. But Miss Bertha says we mustn't hurt his feelings."

Oh, Tristan.

Rachel's sympathy doubled for the father who'd tried—and regrettably failed—to cook a simple meal for his children. Tristan truly needed her. What woman didn't want to feel needed?

Lifting her chin, Rachel spun to face her young charges. "Who can tell me where the food pantry is located?"

All three pointed to a door on Rachel's right.

Fearing what she would find, Rachel peered inside. A heavy burst of air leaked out of her before she could censure her reaction. She should have known, should have expected there would be little to no food in the house.

Why hadn't she checked the supplies sooner?

"Looks as if we get to make a trip to the mercantile this morning."

Grayson had mentioned last night that he wanted to show her around the new store. Though proud of what he'd accomplished, Rachel had been hesitant to agree to a specific time for a tour. The loss of their family's mercantile business in Philadelphia had been the beginning of their father's demise.

She'd have to set aside her reticence. The children needed to eat and Rachel couldn't provide a meal without actual food in the house. She bundled the girls up and the four of them headed out.

Main Street bustled with an excess of sights and sounds. A horse's whinny mingled with a mother shouting after her laughing children. Two young boys ran past, rolling a large hoop between them, each taking turns with a stick. Rachel remembered playing a similar game in Missouri, sometimes racing against other children.

The girls were a bit too small to play that particular

game, but now Rachel's mind was reeling with other possibilities. Hopscotch, cat's cradle, jump rope.

Breathing in the scent of sawdust, Rachel focused her attention on the town itself. Buildings at various stages of construction lined the street, firmly declaring that the Oregon City was a growing town.

A jaunty voice called out to her. "Good morning, Miss Hewitt."

"Oh, hello." Rachel waved at Reverend Pettygrove as he passed by on the other side of the street.

"That's the man from the church," Lily whispered to Violet. "The one who said all those long words at the wedding."

Rachel was shocked at the surge of emotion that whipped through her. The reminder of yesterday's wedding wasn't supposed to make her feel so...wistful.

"I love weddings," Daisy announced. "They make me smile."

Violet agreed with her sister. "Me, too."

"When Da gets married again," Lily told Rachel, "we get a new mommy, too."

Another bout of wistfulness took hold. If Rachel had agreed to Tristan's marriage proposal, *she'd* be these girls' new mommy. "I'm sure he'll find someone to marry very soon."

She prayed she didn't sound as miserable as she felt. Unfortunately, what she'd told the girls was true. Tristan was a good man, kind and thoughtful, extremely handsome and generous. Any number of women would want to marry him, even with his...conditions.

Thankfully, she had no time to contemplate that depressing thought. They'd arrived at the store. "We're here."

Rachel twisted open the door. The girls rushed inside

ahead of her and ran straight for the counter filled with jars upon jars of colorful candy.

Rachel's heart took a hard tumble and she could no longer deny the truth. She was fast falling in love with Tristan's daughters.

Chapter Thirteen

By the time Tristan left the jailhouse that afternoon, the sun had already slipped below the horizon. The dull light of dusk cast the town in a murky gloom. Usually he enjoyed these final moments of the day, when a soft hush seemed to fall over the land. But now, as the world poised just on the brink of surrendering to night, something felt...off.

Perhaps this lingering sense of unease was due to the conversation he'd had with James Stillwell and Nathan Reed, followed by another one with Ben and Grayson Hewitt. They were all eager to lure Grant and Amos Tucker out of hiding and had designed a concrete plan. Of course, any number of things could go wrong.

Any number of things could go right.

A shadow elongated in front of Tristan, passed over his feet, then melted down a back alleyway. He tracked its path but couldn't seem to locate the original source.

Was he being followed?

He scanned the surrounding area. Finding nothing out of the ordinary, he continued on his way. He was alone on the street. Or was he?

Every third step he stabbed a glance over his shoulder, then to his right, then to his left. As he turned onto the next block, he couldn't shake the notion that he was being watched.

By the Tucker brothers? Possibly. Tristan and the others had already set their plan in motion. They'd each taken turns wandering through town today. In the guise of friendly conversation, they'd let it slip out that the stolen money was locked away in an old beat-up safe at the jailhouse.

As the days wore on, Tristan and Stillwell would make it appear as though they were leaving the money unattended for long periods of time. The idea was to lure Grant and Amos into a false sense of security. What the twins wouldn't know was that someone would always be watching the jailhouse from a spot inside one of the two buildings across the street.

When the Tucker brothers eventually made their move, Tristan and the other men would be ready. He'd already hung wanted posters and had warned the business owners of the ensuing threat. But the twins weren't stupid. Tristan doubted they would come out in the open unless absolutely necessary. He needed to draw them out.

Mind on catching the thieves as quickly as possible, Tristan stepped onto the front stoop of his home. He froze at the sweet sound wafting over him. His children's voices were pitched in song.

For a moment, he couldn't seem to move his feet, couldn't reach out and open the door. Memories of a different time, *a different life*, assaulted him. Music had been a part of Siobhan, as conspicuous as her red hair and blue, blue eyes. She was always humming some tune or another.

Trapped between past and present, Tristan stared straight ahead while the beautiful voices drifted over him. The longer he listened, the more he noticed the childish laughter mingling inside the song.

It was the embodiment of pure joy.

He'd forgotten that sound. For a moment, he closed his eyes and a more recent memory replaced the ones of Siobhan. Abigail Black had shown Rachel how to hold her mandolin and then pluck the strings in such a way as to get the exact note she wanted.

As he stood on the front stoop, listening to the sound of his children singing, Tristan realized Rachel had mastered the instrument.

He opened his eyes and reached for the doorknob. He wanted to enjoy this moment with his children, and with Rachel. Hands slightly shaking, he shoved inside the house and quietly shouldered the door shut behind him.

The music turned sweeter, his daughters' young voices beautifully harmonizing with Rachel's.

Tristan swallowed the lump in his throat.

A portion of a long-forgotten Psalm came to mind— "weeping may endure for a night, but joy cometh in the morning."

Not wanting to interrupt, he refrained from announcing his arrival. Rachel's soft, lyrical direction guided the girls through the song. Tristan remembered her voice being just as pleasant on the trail when she'd sung around the campfire with Abigail and the rest of her family.

Now that he listened more closely to the lyrics, he discovered that his daughters sang a simple nursery rhyme. He mouthed the familiar words along with his daughters. *Baa, baa, black sheep, have you any wool? Yes, sir, yes, sir, three bags full.*

Violet was pretty shaky on the words, but she had the tune conquered. Her voice closely matched the notes from the mandolin. More heartening, it didn't sound as though her thumb was anywhere near her mouth.

The singing stopped, only to be replaced by clapping. "Well done," Rachel praised. "You girls sing beautifully."

The children giggled.

"Will you teach us another one?" Lily asked.

Rachel's response was muffled, but Tristan thought he heard something that sounded like a promise to do so later, after supper.

Heart lighter than it had been in years, Tristan took a tentative step forward, past the small entryway into the larger living area. His gaze landed on his oldest daughter first. She was sitting on the ground, facing Rachel, her eyes full of adoration.

His throat closed and he felt his eyes burn with emotion.

Rachel had her back to him and hadn't noticed his arrival yet. Sitting on the floor with her, flanked on either side, were Lily and Violet.

As if sensing his presence, Rachel looked over her shoulder. Their gazes met and held. Her eyes filled with some unreadable emotion, and then…

She smiled. It was the same smile she'd given him this morning, the one that had nearly flattened him.

"Your da is home," she whispered to the children.

The three immediately leaped to their feet and flocked around him. They spoke on top of one another as they told him about their day, maybe. Their words came at him too fast, garbled, at an octave more suitable for dogs.

Their happiness was infectious.

Caught up in their joy, Tristan fought to catch his breath. He attempted to listen to his daughters chatter and managed to nod at what he thought were appropriate places, but then he looked back up. And straight into Rachel's delighted, albeit watery, eyes.

She was watching him, not the girls.

He lost his breath completely and thought he might suffocate, but finally managed to drag in a hard tug of air. He'd once thought only Siobhan would ever be able to steal his breath.

But now, *now*, Tristan realized Rachel had accomplished the feat, as well. He told himself his reaction was because she'd taken excellent care of his daughters today. There was nothing more appealing than the sight and sound of his children's happiness.

All true. But deep in his heart, he knew his reaction was also due to the woman herself. The sight of her wild, untamed hair escaping from a long, thick braid appealed to him on a purely masculine level.

Her sweet, uninhibited smile was enough to give any man cause for concern, especially a man determined to set limits on any future relationship with a woman.

Yet, as he continued staring into Rachel's pretty brown eyes he felt something new, something life-altering. In that moment, Tristan wasn't grief stricken or overwhelmed or guarded.

He was…happy.

Rachel dragged her gaze away from Tristan's. Heart racing, she set the mandolin on a nearby end table, then untangled herself from her position on the floor. It took her two attempts to gain her feet.

A quick deep breath and she forced herself to look at him again. "Welcome home, Tristan."

He continued watching her. And there she went, getting all caught up in his stare once again.

Daisy tugged on her father's arm. "Da?" She tugged

again with a bit more force. "Why are you staring at Miss Rachel like that?"

Shaking his head, he shoved a hand through his hair, drew in a quick breath, then pulled the little girl into an fierce embrace. "I was thinking about your beautiful singing." He met Rachel's gaze over his daughter's head. "It's been a while since music filled this home."

Rachel heard what he wasn't saying. The music had died with Tristan's wife. She tried not to sigh. She'd taught his daughters several songs this afternoon, without first attempting to discover if he wanted music in his home.

"I'm sorry, Tristan." She twisted her hands together at her waist. "When we stopped by Grayson's house earlier today, and I saw that Abby had left her mandolin there last night, I made a spontaneous decision. I never meant to overstep or—"

"I'm glad you brought the mandolin with you." He lowered a kiss onto Daisy's head. "Will you sing another song for me?"

There was something soft in his manner as he asked the question, but something vulnerable, too. Rachel wanted to go to him, to show him she meant only to lighten his burdens, not take over. She resisted, barely, and only by curling her fingers into loose fists.

Lily tapped her on the arm. "Can we show him 'Little Red Robin'?"

Rachel nodded. She dropped a kiss to the child's head as Tristan had just done with Daisy. "I think that's a wonderful idea."

She organized the girls in a straight row, shoulder to shoulder, oldest to youngest, then pointed Tristan to a chair facing the girls. "Sit there."

"Whatever you say, Miss Rachel."

Realizing she'd used her bossy tone, she gave him an apologetic grimace. "Or…" Her voice caught in her throat. "You can sit wherever you wish."

"Here suits me just fine." His eyes twinkled with amusement as he lowered into the chair she'd indicated.

She felt her own amusement return. On the trail, she'd heard several people refer to this man as stern. How could anyone think that of him? Tristan McCullough was accommodating and easy to be around. He might be tough in his role of sheriff, and protected his town with fierce determination, but he had a keen sense of humor. And dearly loved his children.

He personified the Scripture: "Be wise as serpents and gentle as doves."

And…she'd been staring at him long enough. Putting her back to him, she reminded the girls, "We start on the count of three."

They nodded.

Extending her splayed fingers, she made the shape of a bird by crossing her arms then hooking her thumbs together, palms facing inward, and flaring out her fingers.

The girls copied her movements.

"Ready?" she asked, fluttering their fingers to make them look like wings in motion.

"Ready," they repeated.

"One, two…three."

"'Little Robin Redbreast sat upon a rail,'" the four of them recited. "'Niddle went his head, and waggle went his tail.'"

On the last word they wiggled their fingers.

"Excellent, simply wonderful." Rachel smiled her encouragement. "Let's try it again."

They ran through the verse several more times. Violet

had trouble saying *niddle* but she had no problem shouting out the last four words, *"'waggle went his TAIL'!"*

By the fourth go-round Tristan was singing the song with them, mimicking the hand motions, as well.

Rachel had never seen Tristan look so…relaxed.

The girls lost their rhythm sometime during the seventh go-round. Their words trailed off into fits of giggles.

Laughing with them, Tristan opened his arms from his perch on the chair and the three launched themselves at him.

He caught them tightly to him and hugged them. His expression was fierce with love.

Rachel's heart dipped. *Oh, Tristan*, she thought. During his abrupt marriage proposal he'd told her he wasn't a man prone to falling in love.

Oh, but he was wrong. So very, very wrong. Tristan McCullough had enormous amounts of love inside him, waiting to burst free. And yet, he resisted letting himself love again.

Apparently, the loss of his wife had been so great that he was willing to go through the rest of his life alone, with only his daughters welcome inside his heart.

What a sad way to live.

Rachel's stomach roiled hot with anguish for the man.

Violet scrambled out of his arms ahead of her sisters. "We did chores today."

She announced this with the same level of excitement that she might use to tell him she'd learned a new game.

For the first time since arriving home, Tristan looked around the room. "I…" His eyes widened. "I see that."

"Miss Rachel taught us how to fold blankets," Lily said.

"We also learned how to sweep and dust," Daisy added. "And it was really fun."

"Fun?" He lifted a skeptical eyebrow in Rachel's direction. "You managed to make cleaning house…fun?"

She shrugged. "Chores don't have to be drudgery."

"No, I suppose not." He sniffed the air. "Something smells good."

"We helped with supper, too," Lily announced. "Miss Rachel said we could eat as soon as you got home."

"Then let's eat." He waited for his daughters to step back, then stood.

The five of them paraded into the kitchen. With a finger poised in the air, Tristan counted the plates laid out on the table. "There are only four place settings."

"That's because there are only four of you."

He frowned. "You aren't eating with us?"

She shook her head.

"Please, Rachel." He touched her hand. "I'd like you to eat with the family."

The girls added their vocal support of this idea in the form of pleas or, in Violet's case, little-girl whines.

Still, Rachel hesitated. Tristan had been gone for weeks on the trail. Surely he would want to spend time alone with his daughters. She started to say as much but saw the sincerity in his gaze. "Yes, thank you, I'd like very much to stay and eat with the family."

Turning quickly around, she kept her hands busy setting the food on the table.

Tristan's eyebrows rose. "Where did all this come from? I know for a fact I did not have food in the pantry, certainly not a cured ham, or the makings for—" he grinned in genuine pleasure "—biscuits."

Yet again, Rachel realized she'd made a decision concerning his household without consulting him first. This time, however, she felt no need to apologize for her actions. The man had hired her to take care of his home.

"The girls and I went to the mercantile this afternoon. I stocked your cupboards with the basics. And before you ask, Grayson started an account in your name. He'll let you know how much you owe at the end of the week."

Humor lit in his eyes. "It's a good thing you have connections with the mercantile owner."

"A very good thing."

Supper went without a hitch. By the end of the meal Violet kept rubbing at her eyes with the heels of her palms and yawning loudly.

"I see we have a tuckered-out little girl," Rachel said.

Tristan smiled fondly at the exhausted child and then took in the faces of his other two daughters. "Make that three tuckered out little girls."

"We had a busy day," Rachel said by way of explanation.

"Come on, girls." Tristan pushed away from the table and rose to his feet. "Time for bed."

Not a single argument followed this pronouncement.

Putting Daisy in charge of her sisters, Tristan sent the three of them to change into their nightgowns. Once they were gone, he started to clear the table.

Rachel shook her head at him. "Go take care of your daughters. I'll finish up in here."

Nodding, he left the kitchen without a backward glance.

Alone for the first time all day, Rachel took the opportunity to look out the lone window while she washed the dishes. The sun had set a full hour ago and now the sky had taken on a deep purple tint.

This was her least favorite time of the day, when she felt the loneliest. Even on the trail, when she'd been surrounded by literally hundreds of people, she'd had moments of feeling apart from the others. The sensation had increased when Ben fell in love with Abby, and again when Emma fell in love with Nathan.

A burst of melancholy swept through her. She'd had a wonderful day with the girls, nearly perfect, but she couldn't forget her time here was limited. It wouldn't be long before Tristan found a woman to marry him on his terms. Once that happened, he would no longer need her.

What then?

The sound of laughter cut through her despair. Rachel's mood instantly lifted. It was as if the Lord was reminding her to live in the moment. Seize whatever joy she could. All would turn out as it should.

Smiling, she carried the tub of dirty dishwater outside and dumped the contents into the hard ground. She set the empty tub upside down near the door and returned to the kitchen.

The sound of tiny feet pounding on the wooden floor heralded Daisy's arrival mere seconds before the child appeared in the doorway. She wore a long white nightgown and a big smile. "Da said you should come join us for bedtime stories."

"I'd be delighted." Touched by the invitation, Rachel took the child's hand and escorted her back through the house. Halfway to their destination, she felt a burst of yearning break free, a painful hope that spread all the way to her soul.

If only this family were mine.

Her breath hitched in her throat. *They can be yours,* she reminded herself. *All you have to do is agree to Tristan's conditions for a marriage in name only.*

Sorrow dug a foothold in her heart. Rachel knew herself too well. She'd never be satisfied with such a cold, impersonal arrangement. She wanted more out of marriage than convenience.

She wanted love, family, *forever*.

She guided Daisy the final steps to her room in silence.

Tristan met them on the threshold. His handsome face looked tired beneath the muted light from the wall sconce. Rachel barely resisted the urge to reach up and smooth away the exhaustion she read on his face.

"I was told a bedtime story is the final event for the evening," she said, in what she hoped was a nonchalant tone.

"It is, indeed." He cracked a lopsided smile and reached out to her.

Rachel took his offered hand. It felt incredibly right to have her fingers linked with his.

Under the circumstances, there was only one course of action at her disposal. She pulled her hand free.

Chapter Fourteen

Tristan hadn't realized he'd taken Rachel's hand until she drew away from him. He felt the brush of her fingertips slide lightly across his palm. The subsequent roll in his gut was both unexpected and agonizing. Even more unsettling, additional waves of...*something* stabbed at the back of his throat.

He sucked in a harsh breath.

Rachel's easy smile faded, replaced by an anxious grimace that marred her lovely features ever so slightly. She was clearly distressed. Tristan hated knowing he was the cause of her uneasiness.

Keeping his gaze averted, he moved past her and helped Daisy into bed.

The little girl blinked up at him. "Da, can she live with us forever and ever *and ever*?"

Though the request came seemingly out of nowhere, Tristan didn't need to question his daughter about the meaning behind her words. He knew Daisy wanted Rachel to move in with them. By the sharp gasp coming from behind him, he figured the woman in question knew this, too.

"Oh, Da, please?" Lily sat up in her bed and swept her

gaze between him and Rachel. "Can she come live with us? Please, please, please?"

He swallowed back another burst of that same... *something* in the back of his throat. In a tender gesture, he pulled the covers up to Daisy's chin, then patted Lily on the head.

"Miss Rachel already has a home. She lives next door with her brother and his wife, remember?"

Both children's lower lips jutted out. Violet sucked hard on her thumb.

"It's not the same as her living with us here," Daisy argued.

No, it wasn't.

But Tristan had asked Rachel to marry him and she'd said no. That was the end of it, at least from his perspective. No matter how well she'd handled her first day with the girls, he and Rachel wanted two very different things from marriage.

Unless one of them changed their minds, they would never come to a satisfactory agreement.

He turned his gaze to Rachel, who'd been suspiciously quiet throughout his exchange with his daughters. Her eyes had grown tender, almost wistful. Would she agree to his terms for the sake of the girls?

It would be unfair of him to ask.

Tristan cleared his throat and returned his attention to his daughters, making a point to look at each one in turn.

"Miss Rachel has been in our home for only a day." Choosing his words carefully, he lowered into the chair next to Daisy's bed. "We don't need to..."

"Decide anything just yet," Rachel finished for him, pushing deeper into the room. Holding his gaze, she sat in the chair at the foot of Violet's bed. "For now, how about I tell you another Bible story?"

"Oh, yes, please." Daisy spoke for all three of them.

Rachel looked at Tristan. "Do you have a preference?"

He thought for a moment, remembering the last time she'd asked the same question. "I'd like to hear the rest of the story about Jacob and Rachel."

"I already finished that one, this afternoon at naptime."

Well, that was…disappointing. "What about Daniel in the lion's den?"

"Excellent choice. That's one of my favorites." She punctuated this with a smile.

He couldn't help himself. He smiled back.

She shifted in her chair, stretched out her legs and began the tale. "Daniel was a young man who loved and obeyed the Lord from a very early age. Unfortunately, his homeland was conquered by an enemy king and he was taken into slavery…"

As Rachel explained how even in captivity Daniel remained a man of conviction and valor, Tristan allowed the tension in his shoulders to leak out him, one exhale at a time.

Her soft, lilting voice filled the room, wrapping them all in a safe cocoon of her making.

Peace settled over him like an invisible balm.

He closed his eyes and allowed the story to wash away the concerns of his day. He appreciated the way Rachel told the story with her audience in mind. His own mother used to tell this same story to him when he was a boy. Rachel focused on slightly different details—less lion-teeth-gnashing—but the overall impact was equally exciting.

Tristan opened his eyes and found himself transfixed by the way the flickering lantern cast a golden glow over Rachel's face. No denying, she was an attractive woman. Her features were well-defined and in perfect proportion to one another. Her eyes had an exotic tilt to them that set her apart from the other members of her family.

In truth, she didn't look much like any of her siblings.

As he continued watching her, Tristan wondered why Grayson had intimated that Emma was prettier than Rachel. Emma was certainly more striking upon first glance, but Rachel had a unique, rare beauty that revealed itself over time. To Tristan's way of thinking, that made her far more beautiful.

An unsettling thought occurred to him. If her own brother thought Emma the prettier of the two, had others dismissed Rachel in favor of her sister, also? Something dark tugged at Tristan's heart, a sensation that felt like anger, anger on Rachel's behalf.

He had a sudden urge to slay all her dragons, to make the world a safe place for her.

A soft breeze wove through the cracked window, creating a pleasant feel to what was becoming a tender moment, at least in Tristan's mind. He tried not to read too much into the situation. Rachel was merely telling a Bible story to his daughters with him in the room.

For all intents and purposes, she was merely performing the job he'd hired her to do. Yet he couldn't take his eyes off her.

Perched on the edge of her chair, she leaned forward and lowered her voice to a hushed whisper. "The guards approached the lion's den with Daniel locked in chains. A terrible, frightening roar from the hungry lions filled the air and—"

"How many lions were in there?" Daisy asked, eyes wide.

Taking the interruption in stride, Rachel smiled over at the child. "No one knows for sure, but definitely a lot."

"Do you think there were hundreds of them?" Lily asked.

"I don't know about hundreds." Rachel reached out and patted the child's foot. "But definitely enough to kill Daniel the moment he was thrown in the den."

Lily's eyes widened. "Did he die?"

"You'll have to wait and see." Rachel sat back in her chair and continued the story.

As she wove the rest of the adventurous tale, she glanced over at Tristan and caught him watching her. He didn't attempt to look away. He couldn't.

She kept talking even as her beautiful brown eyes searched his, her gaze full of profound gentleness and something more. Something he'd only ever seen in one other woman's gaze.

He swallowed back a surge of emotion.

Get out, he told himself, *before it's too late.*

Good advice. But he couldn't move, couldn't breathe.

Lips pressed in a grim line, he tore his gaze away from Rachel's and returned his attention to his daughters. All three fought to keep their eyes open. They'd be asleep in a matter of minutes.

When their eyes finally did close and their breathing evened out, Tristan seized the opportunity to make his break.

Unsure if they were completely asleep, he climbed silently to his feet and padded out of the room without making a sound.

Once he was safely in the hallway, he leaned back against the wall and took in several long pulls of air.

There was no other sound in the house but the sweet melody of Rachel's voice. Even in speech, her voice had a musical quality to it. Tristan could listen to her tell stories all evening.

In the span of a single day Rachel had completely taken over his household. She'd won over his daughters, and him. She'd brought music back into all their lives. And hope for better days.

If Rachel had accomplished that much in a single day, what feats would she be able to pull off in a week, a month?

A year?

He wanted to know. He *desperately* wanted to know. Enough to make another offer of marriage? Enough to change the rules between them and agree to a union with Rachel as God intended?

No, Tristan would not ask her again to marry him, primarily because he found her far too attractive to settle for a marriage in name only. He recognized the irony, of course. The very reasons that made him contemplate a real marriage with Rachel were the very same reasons he couldn't marry her.

The soft sound of footsteps threaded through his thoughts. Rachel had joined him in the hallway.

"They're asleep," she whispered. "I continued with the story until I was sure."

He nodded, then directed her to follow him through the house and out onto the front stoop. He pulled the door closed but left a slight crack in case one of his daughters stirred or cried out for him in their sleep.

The moon was full tonight, casting a veil of golden light over the land and a dreamy feel to the moment. "The girls adore you."

Rachel laughed softly. "They're wonderful children, Tristan, and so very lovely."

As are you.

He met her gaze, then instantly regretted it. Several long, dark strands of hair had come loose from her braid and now curled around her face. Even in her disheveled state she was remarkably pretty. A woman shouldn't be this stunning after wrangling three young girls all day.

As though uncomfortable under his stare, she smoothed an unsteady hand over her hair, then tucked a small portion behind her ear. The gesture drew his attention to the flawless skin of her face in the moonlight.

A light breeze swirled around them. When he breathed in her scent, a pleasant blend of lavender and fresh linens, everything in him settled and simply…let…go.

"By all accounts it appears your day with the girls went well."

"Far better than I expected." She blinked very slowly, her brown eyes nearly black under the night sky. "You once told me your daughters were shy and entirely too timid for children their age."

"I remember." At the time, he'd been telling the truth.

"That doesn't describe the little girls I cared for today."

"They like you," he said simply.

"I like them." She braided her fingers together in front of her and smiled fondly at something in the distance, as if caught up in a memory. "The girls and I really had a wonderful day together. Did you know Violet dances as well as she sings? And that Lily is already showing an aptitude for drawing? And that Daisy has a heart for small animals? She rescued a grasshopper from being trampled under one of her sisters' feet."

Tristan hadn't known these things. "Tell me more."

As she launched into the specifics, something powerful passed between them, a moment of complete contentment that went beyond words. He could get used to this, hearing Rachel tell him about her day with the girls. He enjoyed laughing with her over something one of them had said or done.

"It's getting late," he said, cutting her off midsentence. It was either that or pull her into his arms and...

He cut off the rest of the thought. "You should head home, before Grayson comes looking for you."

She blinked at him in puzzlement, then dropped her head and stared down at her hands. "Yes, all right."

He wanted to walk her to her doorstep, but he couldn't leave his daughters alone in the house, even for that short amount of time.

"I'll watch from here until I know you're safe."

She hesitated a moment, seeming to have something more to say, but then nodded. "I'll see you and the girls first thing tomorrow morning."

"We'll be here."

She set out. When she was midway between the houses, Tristan opened his mouth to call her back. He couldn't say why he wanted her to return to his side, only that he didn't want her to leave him just yet.

He shoved aside the selfish wish. She'd had a long day. Best to let her go.

Rachel could feel Tristan's regard on her. She resisted the urge to peek over her shoulder and smile at him. She seemed to smile a lot in his presence. How could she not?

He was handsome and kind, a good man and father who adored his daughters. Was it any wonder Rachel found herself smiling at him? A lot?

Giving in to temptation, after all, she climbed onto her brother's front stoop and glanced over at Tristan.

He was still outside his house, still watching her from the spot where she'd left him. Though his face was cast in shadow she could feel his intensity. She tossed him a wave over her head.

He gave her a short nod, before she disappeared inside

the house. Grayson was waiting for her in the entryway. "You're home late."

She bristled at his impatient tone. Crossing her arms over her waist, she frowned at her ever-vigilant, overprotective big brother. "Not that it's any of your concern, but I stayed to help Tristan put the girls to bed."

His gaze narrowed over her face. "Are you sure that was wise?"

Why wouldn't it be? She felt her frown dig deeper at the odd question. "Tristan hired me to take care of his daughters. Putting them to bed is part of my job."

"Perhaps, but I urge you not to get too attached to the McCullough family."

His words were a harsh reminder that she was only a temporary solution to a permanent problem in Tristan's home.

"I may have turned down Tristan's marriage proposal, but I made a promise to help him out until he finds another woman to marry." She lifted her hands, palms facing forward, to forestall whatever response he thought to give. "I will follow through on my commitment."

Grayson's shoulders visibly tensed. "Now, see, that's the problem. You go at everything too hard, Rachel, and put too much of yourself into every task you undertake."

At his accurate assessment of her, she felt her own shoulders tense. "As Christians we're called to serve."

It was true. She shouldn't sound so defensive.

"Don't get me wrong. I admire your capacity to put others ahead of yourself." He blew out a slow whoosh of air. "However, in this situation, I fear you will put too much of yourself into Tristan's family and wind up getting hurt."

Her brother's worry seemed a bit exaggerated, especially since this was *her* life and *her* choices they were discussing. "You of all people should know Tristan is a good man. I trust him. You should, too."

He blew out another frustrated push of air. "I do trust him, with my life."

"But you don't trust him with mine?"

"It's not your life I'm worried about, it's your heart."

Too late, a voice whispered in her head.

"Stop worrying about me, Grayson." She heard the unsteady cadence of her breathing and forced herself to speak slower. "I know what I'm doing."

"I don't think you do." He touched her arm, the gesture full of brotherly concern. "I was there when Tristan's wife died. I witnessed firsthand what the loss of Siobhan did to him. He hasn't been the same man since."

Oh, Tristan. Heart hurting for him, Rachel felt every part of her fill with sorrow. She had to blink several times to clear away the threat of tears. "He's been grieving, Grayson. It's no different than what you went through in Missouri after Susannah died."

Eyes turning bleak, lips flat, her brother rubbed a hand across the back of his neck. "You deserve the best a man has to offer a woman. I wouldn't object if I thought Tristan could be that man, but he can't, Rachel. He gave everything he had to Siobhan. There isn't enough left for you"

"You were willing to have him marry Emma."

"I admit I was wrong. I see that now. Don't misunderstand me. Tristan is a good man, but I couldn't bear watching him inadvertently hurt you because you have expectations he can't meet."

Though she feared her brother was right, Rachel couldn't help but feel insulted on Tristan's behalf. She'd seen him with his daughters. He had the capacity for great love.

"Grayson, do you love Maggie?"

His eyes immediately softened. "With all that I am."

"Do you love her as much as you loved Susannah?"

His expression changed, turning dark again. Her point had hit home. "Yes, I love Maggie as much as I did Susannah. But Tristan's situation is different."

"How?"

"He has three daughters who resemble their mother. Every time he looks into one of their eyes, he's reminded of the woman he lost."

Rachel had no response, because what her brother said made sense.

Grayson closed his hand over hers and squeezed gently. "Don't put your hope in Tristan. Although I think you'd be good for him, I don't believe he would be good for you."

She nodded. There was no arguing with a truth that had been laid out for her so clearly.

"I'm tired. I want to go to bed now." She pushed past her brother. "I'll see you in the morning."

She heard his frustrated hiss but kept walking toward the stairwell. Rachel needed to spend time with her mother, or rather with her mother's words.

Conquering the steps with a heavy heart, she entered her room, shut the door and then twisted the lock in place.

A chill had crept into her bones that grew colder with each breath she took. She changed her clothes quickly and climbed into bed.

Snuggling under the covers, she picked up her mother's journal and settled in to read.

Chapter Fifteen

With one hand pressed to her heart, the other resting lightly on top of the journal, Rachel experienced a moment of profound uncertainty. Some instinct warned her not to read any more of her mother's private thoughts tonight, that if she continued she would regret it.

She drew in an uneven breath and smoothed her fingertip across the worn page she'd opened to at random. She was so tense that her neck ached. Was the impulse to turn out the lantern and burrow under the covers simply the result of a long day?

Or was it because of her disturbing conversation with Grayson concerning her arrangement with Tristan?

Hot tears pricked in her eyes. She refused to let them form. She'd entered into her agreement with Tristan knowing the rules. She would not regret her decision to watch his daughters until he found a more suitable bride.

Still.

Tonight, alone in her room, Rachel felt discouraged and so very alone. She wanted her mother, with a passion that turned her breath ragged in her lungs.

Without thinking too hard about what she was doing,

she flipped back to one of the earlier entries and settled her focus at the top of the page.

The Lord has finally answered my prayers. He has given me a precious baby girl. Jeremiah and I have decided to name her Rachel.

Rachel smiled. Her mother's love for her leaped off the page. Reassured, she skimmed over the rest of the entry, then read several more. Her mother had taken great pains to keep meticulous records of her daily growth.

Now that Rachel has finally accepted my milk, her color is better. The sickly gray pallor is all but gone. Her cheeks are beginning to fill out, as are her spindly little arms and legs. She must survive. She must. I don't know what I will do if she dies. She quite literally saved my life.
It is my turn to save hers.

Rachel paused in her reading. She hadn't known she'd been perilously close to death. Was that the reason behind Grayson's overprotective behavior toward her?

She caught her bottom lip between her teeth and read on.

Today was my first attempt to leave the house with Rachel. I should have stayed home. Just one block into my stroll and I ran into that dreadful Kathryn Marlow from the Ladies Church League. That woman wields far too much power in our section of Philadelphia. Most believe her to be a godly woman. I have always had my doubts.

Rachel frowned. What had this Kathryn Marlow done to her mother? One easy way to find out.

She continued reading.

> *She was so condescending to me about my pre-cious baby girl. How dare she call Rachel a charity case, and then diminish my love for her by insinu-ating I only took her in out of Christian duty. I'm grateful the baby is too young to understand the meaning behind that horrid woman's words. Chris-tian duty, indeed. Kathryn Marlow has no under-standing of the concept.*

Swallowing back the bile rising in her throat, Rachel looked down at her hands. They were shaking. And her fingers were cold, as cold as the dread collecting in her heart.

She knew this feeling, had experienced it two other times before. Once, right after her father had taken ill, and again when Grayson's wife had fallen deathly still in the midst of birthing their son.

Rachel looked down at her mother's journal, to the spot where she'd left off reading. She couldn't seem to take a decent pull of air. Her breath iced in her lungs. For a dangerous moment, she had an urge to toss the book into the fire crackling in the hearth across the room. Did it really matter what her mother had written about her nineteen years ago?

Somehow, she knew that it did.

Her mind became so clear it hurt to think. She forced her gaze back onto the open journal, backed up a bit and continued reading once again.

> *My Christian duty, indeed. Kathryn Marlow has no understanding of the concept. Rachel is a mem-*

ber of our family. Despite how she came into our home, she is a Hewitt.

Rachel's heart hammered against her ribs. She pressed on, hardening her focus onto the page.

I asked Jeremiah about the day he found Rachel in the alley behind the mercantile. He assured me he'd searched for her kin and gone through all the proper channels to make her a part of our family. Rachel is not a charity case.
She is my daughter.

Rachel's vision blurred. She wanted to cry, to beg God to take away the pain clutching in her throat. Her head grew thick, her thoughts muddled.

She flipped to the next page, and then the next. She kept turning pages without actually seeing the words. But then, something caught her eye. A word. One word. *Missouri.*

Her heartbeat slowed. Now there was only a dull drumming at the base of her skull. She skimmed the rest of the entry.

I've convinced Jeremiah we must leave Phila-delphia. Rachel must never know she isn't a real Hewitt. We will head for Missouri, where no one knows the truth about her. Our secret will be safe.

Rachel choked back a sob. Beneath her ice-cold skin, she burned.

Because of her, her family had left Philadelphia. No, not her family. The Hewitts. Rachel wasn't one of them. She'd never been one of them.

No, Lord. Please, it can't be.

She sank her face into her hands and hid within her palms. Her breathing came too fast, in hard snatches that burned in her lungs. Her father—or rather, Jeremiah Hewitt—had found her in the back alley behind his mercantile.

Rachel wasn't a Hewitt. Not…a…Hewitt.

She dropped her hands to the bed and pounded at the mattress with clenched fists. Her real parents had tossed her away like a piece of garbage. Unwanted. Unloved. Unworthy.

A charity case.

She cried out in agony before she could slap her hand over her mouth.

How could her family have lied to her all these years? No, she reminded herself, not her family. The Hewitts. The people who'd taken her into their home because her own parents hadn't wanted her.

She'd always felt different, a little set apart from her siblings. Now she knew why. She wasn't one of them. She was a…a…charity case.

She choked back another sob. When the next one threatened, she let it come unhindered. Her misery sounded in every ragged breath she took, in every tear that fell from her eyes.

What was so wrong with her that her own mother and father hadn't wanted her? What deep-seated flaw flowed in her blood?

She glanced down at the journal still in her lap. With a furious swipe of her hand, she tossed it to the floor. A wail of fury gurgled in her throat. She choked it down with a hard swallow. Her effort was only partially successful. The sound that came out of her was that of a wounded animal.

Shame tasted bitter on her tongue. Blood pounded in her ears. Unwanted. Unloved. Unworthy.

"Rachel." An insistent knocking entered her consciousness. "Rachel, let me in."

Scrambling from beneath the covers, she rushed to the door and checked to make sure the lock was in place. "Go away, Grayson."

"Open up." He knocked again and again and again, the sound growing louder with each strike of fist to wood. "I heard you cry out. What's wrong? Are you hurt?"

With great deliberation, she wiped all inflection from her tone. "I'm not hurt."

Not physically, at any rate.

The doorknob rattled. "Let me in or I'll get the key and let myself in."

"No." She looked frantically around. "I...I stubbed my toe on the trunk beside my bed. That's what made me cry out."

"Perhaps you broke it. Open the door so I can check the injury."

No. She couldn't face Grayson right now. She couldn't look into his false blue eyes and pretend she didn't know the truth. All these years, she'd thought she was a Hewitt. She'd thought her cooking skills had come from her mother. A lie. Her whole life had been a lie.

The door shook on its hinges.

Grayson wasn't going away. Why wasn't he going away?

The answer came from some of the first words she'd read in her mother's journal. *Grayson has taken a special liking to the baby. He's become very protective of her.*

And yet he'd lied to her every day of her life.

"Rachel, this is your last chance. Open the door or I get the key."

She heard the determination that sat upon his words.

Swiping at her eyes, she unlocked the door and stepped back, chin lifted at a determined angle. Grayson would answer for his betrayal.

When the door swung open, she lost her nerve and turned her back on the man who'd pretended to be her brother. The thought was enough to keep her eyes dry and her voice hard.

"As you can see—" she gave a little hop from one to the other "—my foot doesn't hurt anymore."

Now she was the one telling lies. No better than them. She felt dead inside.

"Rachel, I didn't mean to upset you earlier." Grayson spoke with such tenderness, such caring, she thought she might scream. Or weep.

Or demand answers.

Now was not the time. She needed to pull her thoughts together before she confronted him.

"When we spoke about you and Tristan earlier," he continued, "I was only looking out for your best interest."

Her best interest? The gall.

Furious at his interference, now more than ever, she spun around to face Grayson Hewitt directly.

At the sight of his brow wrinkled with concern for her, a portion of her anger vanished.

"Rachel, all I was trying to say is that you deserve to be loved by the man you marry."

Did she?

If her own mother and father hadn't loved her, had thought her worthy of abandonment, how could she expect anyone else to—

Rebellion surged at the direction of her thoughts.

She was a child of God. *For you created my inmost being; you knit me together in my mother's womb.*

"I deserve to be loved," she whispered.

"Yes, you do." The tenderness was still in Grayson's voice. He reached up and touched her wet cheek. "Please don't cry."

She firmed her chin. "I stubbed my toe. It hurt."

"Let me have a look at it."

"No, it's fine." She wrapped her foot behind her calf.

She would not feel guilty for telling a falsehood to this man. But, of course, she felt nothing but guilt. There were so many things she wanted to say to Grayson and the other Hewitt siblings. But she didn't know where to begin. Didn't know *how* to begin. "I'm tired, Grayson."

So very tired.

He pulled her into his arms, always the big brother, even to a little sister who wasn't a true member of his family.

A charity case.

Her heart felt as if it was tearing apart in her chest.

With slow, purposeful movements, she slipped out of his arms. "I'm going to be fine. There's no cause to worry about me."

"I'll always worry about you, Rachel." He kissed the top of her head. "You're one of my two favorite sisters."

She felt the tears coming again. From somewhere deep within herself, she managed to step back and drum up a smile. "We'll talk tomorrow. Good night, Grayson."

"Good night, Rachel." He gave her a head another kiss. "Now get in the bed," he ordered with mock severity. "Tomorrow is a new day full of endless possibilities awaiting you."

A new day? Endless possibilities? She'd never felt more hopeless in her life, or more betrayed. All she had left was her dignity.

Chin high, eyes unblinking, she waited until Grayson shut the door behind him before rushing to her bed. Face buried in her pillow, she burst into tears.

* * *

As days turned into weeks, life fell into a pleasant routine for Tristan and his daughters. Rachel arrived every morning just after sunup. She took excellent care of the girls during the day, then made her way back to her brother's house in the evening.

Other than catching the Tucker brothers, Tristan had very little to worry about in his life. Save for one, nagging problem he couldn't figure out how to solve. Rachel was sad. It was the only word he could think to define the change that had come over her since that first day in his home.

To be fair, the transformation wasn't immediately discernible and only showed at times when Rachel didn't think anyone was watching her. Because Tristan watched her frequently, he caught the melancholy that hummed beneath her carefree smiles.

She did not let her guard slip often.

With his daughters she was the same sweet, guileless woman he'd gotten to know on the wagon train. In fact, when she was around the girls, Rachel seemed happy.

Mostly.

But Tristan couldn't shake the notion that something terrible had happened to her, something she kept buried deep inside. He wanted to ease her suffering.

As he did every day at this early hour, he opened the door to Rachel's light knock. But instead of moving aside and letting her into the house, he joined her on the front stoop.

In the early dawn light the skin beneath her eyes was bruised with fatigue. She'd had another sleepless night.

He wanted to make her pain go away. He couldn't do that until he knew the source. He took a subtle approach. "Good morning, Rachel."

The smile she gave him didn't quite meet her eyes. "Good morning, Tristan."

She attempted to push past him.

He pulled the door almost closed, leaving it slightly ajar. "Before we go inside, I want to speak with you."

Casting her focus to a spot just above his right shoulder, she fidgeted from one foot to the other. "Is there a problem?"

"You tell me." He placed his hand beneath her chin and gently guided her face around to his. "What's happened to make you so sad?"

Before she lowered her eyelashes he caught the vast range of emotions moving across her face. "I'm not sad."

The way her voice hitched told its own story.

"Who's hurt you, Rachel? Give me a name, and I'll toss him in jail for a night or two, however long it takes for him to see the error of his ways."

He was only half kidding.

She finally cracked a real smile. "Oh, Tristan, that's about the sweetest offer anyone has ever made me."

He took her hand and pulled her close, close enough to feel her slight trembling. And the sadness she claimed didn't exist. "Tell me how to make your pain go away."

"It's...complicated."

Just as he opened his mouth to mine for more information, a thud came from inside the house, followed by a muffled *uh-oh*.

Looking more than a little relieved by the interruption, Rachel threw her shoulders back. "I better check on the girls."

This time when she tried to push past him, Tristan let her. He wasn't through with their conversation, but now wasn't the time. He'd catch her again tonight, after the girls were tucked in bed.

By the time he entered the house, everything appeared to be in order. Rachel held Violet in her arms and was whispering something in the child's ear. The little girl erupted into giggles. Lily and Daisy were already laughing.

He smiled at the picture the four made. After nearly two weeks, he was no longer amazed at the changes in his daughters. He was merely grateful. Rachel's presence in his home was a blessing he'd not seen coming.

He didn't want to lose her. He couldn't imagine anyone else laughing with his daughters or telling them bedtime stories or teaching them nursery rhymes.

Perhaps he could convince her to marry him, after all. He couldn't love her, not the way she wanted or deserved, but he already cared about her more than he'd thought possible. Tristan had seen marriages built on less, and…

He was being completely selfish, putting his own needs ahead of hers. He cleared his throat and four pairs of eyes swung in his direction.

"I have to get to the jail." He reached out to Rachel. "Walk me to the door."

"Of course." She set Violet on the ground and placed her hand in his.

Her fingers were ice-cold.

He led her back outside before letting go of her hand. "I'll be at the jail all day if you need me for anything, anything at all."

She nodded.

In a fit of spontaneity, he wrapped her in his arms and pressed a light kiss atop her head. Before she could protest the move, he released her.

"We'll finish our conversation later tonight."

Eyes wide, she stared up at him for three long seconds. "There's no reason. I'm all right, Tristan. Truly, I—"

He pressed a brief kiss to her lips, cutting off whatever argument she'd been about to voice.

Frozen in shock, she gaped at him.

"Tonight," he said, his tone brooking no argument.

Jamming his hat on his head, he left her staring after him. Ten minutes later, he pushed into the jailhouse. And stopped cold. Grayson Hewitt was in an animated conversation with James Stillwell.

"Grayson, something I can do for you?"

Lips compressed in a flat line, the man in question stepped away from the insurance agent. "We had a break-in at the mercantile sometime before dawn."

Tristan's blood ran cold. "Anybody hurt?"

Grayson shook his head. "The thieves were in and out before Nathan made it downstairs."

"What did they take?"

"Mostly food, a few blankets, a lantern, several tools." Eyes hard, Grayson rattled off the list of items, then paused. "And an entire jar of lemon drops."

"Had to be the Tucker brothers," Stillwell said, shaking his head in disgust.

"That would be my guess," Tristan agreed. Grant's sweet tooth had been legendary on the trail. "How'd they get in the store?"

If possible, Grayson's eyes hardened even more. "Threw a brick through the glass."

Of course they did. Finesse had never been the brothers' favorite mode of operation. "Let's go have a look."

"Follow me." Grayson led the way out of the building.

Stillwell's voice stopped Tristan at the door. "I'll stay behind and guard the safe. Something tells me our boys are about to make their move any day now."

"I'll be back shortly. When I return, we'll discuss how best to lure Grant and Amos out of hiding." He met Stillwell's gaze. "It's time to end this."

Chapter Sixteen

Rachel pressed a finger to her temple and wished the pounding behind her eyes would subside. Now that it was just her and the girls in the house, she attempted to let down her guard and simply relax.

But no matter how many deep breaths she took, the brittle feeling in her bones wouldn't go away. She'd been holding in her sorrow for nearly two weeks, pretending all was well, acting as though her heart wasn't shattered. She didn't know how much longer she could keep up the charade.

Tapping into the remaining scraps of her composure, she lowered to a chair and watched the girls play jacks on the floor at her feet. She felt immediately less restless for the span of three whole seconds. Then a suffocating pressure squeezed in her lungs and breathing became difficult once again.

She shut her eyes and prayed for the Lord to take away the heaviness that had settled in her heart. No relief came down from above. It was as if the Heavenly Father had abandoned her as surely as her own parents had nineteen years ago.

Everything she'd ever known about herself and her

family was a lie. She needed answers, deserved them. But each time she attempted to broach the subject with Grayson, her words came out a little too loud, a little too panicked, and she would rush away before she even began.

All her life, she'd been taught that family turned to each other in times of trouble. That was the Hewitt way. How was Rachel supposed to turn to a family that wasn't really hers?

Tears welled in her eyes. She knew she couldn't go on like this. Tristan had seen through her pretense this morning. It was only a matter of time before the others did, too.

Would they react with the same tenderness and concern that Tristan had shown her? He'd been unbearably kind. And then, *then*, he'd kissed her. It hadn't been much more than a brief press of his lips to hers. She sensed he'd only done it to keep her from arguing with him. But… he'd…*kissed* her.

She didn't know quite what to make of his behavior.

"Miss Rachel?" Violet climbed onto her lap and leaned her head against her shoulder. "I'm bored."

The grown-up word made Rachel smile even as she rested her chin on top of the child's head. Of course she was bored. At two years of age, Violet didn't have the skill—or the inclination—to play jacks.

Perhaps it was time for some fresh air. A change of scenery would also do Rachel good. She set Violet on the floor. "All right, girls. Let's put on our coats."

Daisy paused in the middle of tossing the ball in the air. "Where are we going?"

Rachel smiled down at the child, seeing a lot of herself in the inquisitive eyes staring up at her. At Daisy's age, Rachel had also asked unceasing questions.

Her brothers and sister had indulged her curious nature with unending patience. Had it been out of obligation? Had their parents insisted they treat Rachel with kindness because she'd been abandoned?

Hating the doubt that pulled at her, Rachel curled her fingers into fists. Would all her childhood memories be forever tainted now that she'd stumbled upon the truth? Would she always question if her siblings truly loved her, or merely pitied her?

Confront them.

The thought came at her in a whisper. She shoved it aside and focused on the little girl waiting for an answer from her.

"We're going visiting," she said.

With confusion knit across her brow, Daisy set the ball on the floor amongst the scattered jacks. "What's visiting?"

"It's when we drop in on friends to say hello."

"Oh." Her expression still looked puzzled.

"We aren't going far," Rachel added. "Just next door to see Mrs. Quincy's sister, Clara, and her new baby."

The pronouncement had the intended effect. All three girls hurriedly put on their coats. After adding hats, gloves and scarves, Rachel steered the three of them out the front door.

A cold wind swept off the mountains, carrying the scent of snow in its wake. The sky had turned a dingy gray, but at least the misty chill in the air was refreshing, sweeping away some of the heaviness in Rachel's mind.

When they arrived at the Quincy home, she rapped lightly on the door, then told the jabbering girls to speak softly.

"Why?" Violet asked in a voice loud enough to be heard two blocks over.

"Shh." Rachel pressed a finger to her lips. "We don't want to disturb the baby if she's sleeping."

The door swung open.

Bertha Quincy stood on the threshold, her mouth spread into a wide grin. "Well, look who it is, three of my favorite little girls and their pretty nanny."

"We've come to see the new baby," Daisy announced, taking a step forward.

Rachel placed a hand on the child's shoulder to keep her from taking another. "As long as we aren't disturbing you. If this is a bad time, we can stop by later."

"Nonsense, you're here now." Bertha opened the door wider. "Please, come in."

The girls scurried into the house. Rachel followed at a more sedate pace.

"Rachel, I thought I recognized your voice." Clara beamed at her from a seated position on an overstuffed, comfortable-looking couch. "And look, it's the McCullough children. Come closer, girls, and meet my daughter, Emma Leigh."

Rachel blinked. "You named your baby after...after Emma?"

"I did." Glowing from the inside out, Clara smiled down at the bundle in her arms. "Emma was the first person to befriend me on the trail. She kept me going when I thought I couldn't bear another moment. It only seemed right to name my child after her."

There was unmistakable gratitude in Clara's voice. Rachel couldn't imagine what the journey had been like for the other woman. Alone and grieving her husband, she must have been incredibly frightened.

"I think Emma Leigh is a fine name." Rachel took a look at the baby with light brown hair and sweet, round features. "She's beautiful."

Daisy marched up to Clara, set her hands on her hips

and peered at the baby with obvious intent in her eyes. "Can I hold her?"

"Only if you sit here beside me." Clara patted an empty spot on the couch.

Daisy quickly crawled into place. After showing her how to support the infant's head, Clara placed the baby in the little girl's arms.

Once their sister was settled, Violet and Lily moved in for a better look.

"She's so tiny," Violet whispered.

"You were smaller." Looking much older than her six years of age, Daisy touched the baby's face very gently with her fingertip. "Da used to let me hold you like this."

Rachel went very still. If Daisy remembered holding Violet as an infant, did she also remember her mother's death?

Daisy opened her mouth as if to continue, but a noisy burp came from the baby and whatever she'd been about to say turned into a giggle.

Laughing with her, Lily reached out and touched the very edge of the baby's blanket. "She looks like a doll."

"She's a really good baby," Clara said with no small amount of pride.

"Does she cry a lot?" Daisy wrinkled her nose. "Violet used to cry a lot."

"She does, sometimes," Clara confirmed. "But only when she's hungry or has a soiled diaper."

Now Lily's nose wrinkled.

Violet popped her thumb in her mouth and sucked hard.

Happy to entertain her captive audience, Clara proceeded to tell the girls when the baby ate, when she slept and what she did in between. Love sounded in every word she spoke.

Bertha drew closer to Rachel. "She's a wonderful mother."

Rachel smiled. "It's nice to see her so happy." She lowered her voice. "The journey was very hard on her."

"From what I understand, your sister was a godsend."

"Emma rarely left her side." Now Rachel understood why.

Disguised as a man, Clara must have endured some harrowing moments. Even without the threat of someone seeing past her disguise, carrying the baby in her belly across treacherous terrain and through difficult weather couldn't have been easy. Men were not supposed to ride in the wagons as women and children could on occasion.

"Praise the Lord she made the trip relatively un-scathed," Rachel said, watching Clara reach inside the blanket to show off the baby's fingers and toes.

Longing rippled down her spine.

I want one, Rachel thought. *I want a baby of my own. I want to hold a child who shares my blood.*

"Not to diminish your sister's kindness on the trail," Bertha said, "but carrying Adam's child kept my sister from completely giving up after his death. That baby saved Clara's life."

Rachel's throat seized on a gasp. Sara Hewitt had written nearly the same words in her journal. She'd claimed Rachel had saved her life, too. Momentarily overwhelmed, she lowered her head to hide a fresh bout of tears. Anger at her real parents, thankfulness for the Hewitt family—both emotions took up residence in her heart. She didn't know which was more unsettling.

The sound of Clara taking the baby back from Daisy had her looking up again. At some point while she'd been staring at the ground, Violet and Lily had climbed onto the couch and now snuggled in around mother and child. Three fascinated gazes were riveted on the infant.

Was that how Rachel's siblings had looked at her when she'd first arrived in their home? With wonder and awe in their eyes?

Why, then, had they deceived her? What good had come from telling her lies?

The truth shall set you free.

Rachel didn't feel free. She felt…betrayed. Even if her family had wanted to protect her from public ridicule and the stigma of being adopted, they could have told *her* the truth.

She'd had enough of doubts and indecision. She would confront Grayson tonight. Until then, she would focus on three little girls she loved as if they were her own. Something new and humbling slipped just of out of reach in her mind.

Violet hopped off the couch and hurried over to Rachel. Before she knew what the child was about, she flung her arms around Rachel's waist and held on tight.

Eyes burning, throat going scratchy, Rachel hugged the little girl fiercely to her. Love filled her to near bursting. She opened her mouth to ask what had inspired this sudden display of affection but couldn't seem to find her voice.

Out of the corner of her eye, she caught Clara hiding a yawn behind her hand. That was their cue to leave.

"Time to say goodbye, girls."

"Already?"

"I'm afraid so." Rachel carefully peeled Violet's arms from around her waist. "The baby needs her rest."

The children reluctantly said their farewells and, heads hung low, feet dragging, they followed Rachel outside.

Halfway between the two houses, Lily tapped her on

the arm. "Can we have a new baby come live with us, too?"

The question brought an image immediately to Rachel's mind. She was holding her own child, a baby girl who had her dark hair and eyes the same intense green as Tristan's.

"Can we, Miss Rachel?" Violet bounced up and down on her toes. "Can we have a new baby in our home?"

If it were up to me...

"It's not that simple." She brushed the backs of her fingers across Lily's forehead, touched Violet lightly on the head. "Your father needs to find you a mother first. Then, *maybe*, in time, there will be a new baby after that."

But probably not. Tristan had made it clear there would be no more children in his home. And that, Rachel realized, was the very issue standing between them. She wanted a real marriage. She also wanted children, a whole houseful of them.

Tristan had already decided to stop at three.

"Can *you* be our mommy?" Violet asked with a slight catch in her voice. "Then we can have a new baby right away."

A spurt of longing clutched in Rachel's heart. *If it were up to me...*

"Even if your father and I were married, making babies is complicated. It's not as if we can order one from the catalogue at the mercantile."

As soon as the words left her mouth an idea struck her. Rachel may not be able to give the girls a new baby, but she could give them a new baby doll.

"Who's up for a short walk?"

Tristan strode through town, checking all the possible hiding places Grant and Amos might be holed up in, but the rats had gone underground since breaking into the mercantile.

He paused midstep, thinking he heard the sound of his daughters laughing in the distance, but that couldn't be right. He was probably hearing things, a clear indication of how much he'd missed the girls when he'd been on the trail.

Never again would he leave his children for an extended period of time. They'd weathered his absence well enough, but he'd missed them with a burning ache that had reached deep into his soul. If he was going to find his daughters a mother, he must accomplish the task closer to home.

The laughter rang out again, louder, closer. And very real. He hastened toward the sound, rounded the next corner and spied his family just as they disappeared into the mercantile on the other side of the street.

Curiosity had him increasing his pace. Why were his girls heading into the mercantile in the middle of the afternoon? It wasn't until he was halfway across the street that it occurred to him that the term—*his girls*—included Rachel.

His feet ground to a halt and a sense of inevitability rolled over him. *She's not for you*, he reminded himself. *You can't give her what she needs.*

Shoulders taut, mouth set at a determined angle, he entered the mercantile. Grayson had already boarded up the broken window, Tristan noted with approval.

He looked around, not sure where Rachel and the girls had gone. Then he heard his daughters' laughter again, coming from deep within the store. A few steps later he spotted his family standing at a counter near the backdoor.

The girls were appropriately dressed for the cold weather.

Equally bundled up, Rachel hovered closely behind them. Emma Hewitt, or rather Emma Reed, stood on the other side of the counter.

While Emma conversed with his daughters, Rachel took a step back. And another. And then one more. Tristan could practically feel the tension rolling off her in waves.

He was reminded of their conversation earlier that morning, of the sadness he'd seen in Rachel's eyes, and the sorrow that now seemed a part of her. Wanting to comfort her, he reached out a hand, silently willing her to look in his direction.

The move caught her attention. Expression softening, she headed toward him, leaving his daughters in Emma's capable care.

Stopping a few feet in front of him, Rachel gave him a shaky smile, one that seemed to require a heroic effort on her part.

Something profound moved and shifted inside him, pulling him toward her, not just physically but also emotionally. He wanted to take her in his arms and chase away the hurt that wavered beneath her smile.

"I wasn't expecting you on this side of town today." He somehow managed to speak around the lump in his throat. "Are we out of something at the house?"

As soon as the question left his mouth, he realized that he'd said *we*. As if they were a family of five, him, Rachel and the girls.

He took a large step back, distancing himself from the connection he felt with a woman who could never be his.

Rachel didn't seem to notice his discomfort. "Not to worry, we have plenty of food in the cupboards."

We. She'd used the term in the same manner as he, the word slipping out of her just as naturally. Tristan couldn't help but smile even as he sensed how foolish he must look, perhaps even besotted.

Maybe he *was* besotted.

He was definitely staring.

But, then, so was she.

Neither of them seemed to be able to break free of the tender moment that held them captive.

Tristan let out a strained breath. It wasn't an altogether awful feeling, this closeness he felt toward Rachel.

With great effort, he swung his attention to the back of the store. All three of his children were studying the shelves of toys behind Emma.

They were huddled close together, hands joined, heads bent at identical angles. They seemed to be trying to make up their minds about something. Emma continued engaging them in conversation, but it was mostly one-sided on her end.

At last, Daisy released her sisters' hands and pointed to the highest shelf behind Emma. "I want that one."

"A lovely choice." Emma retrieved a doll with dark hair nearly the same color as Rachel's.

Lily took her turn next. She pointed to a similar-looking doll with the same color hair, but her toy wore a green dress with white lace. When Lily cradled the doll in her arms, understanding finally dawned.

Rachel was giving his daughters each a doll. The cost was an issue, but worth the expense given the children's reaction.

Why hadn't he thought to do that himself? Because he was a man and men didn't think to give their daughters dolls. It was yet another stark reminder he needed to find the girls a mother.

His chin jerked very faintly, then he took off toward

them. Rachel followed along beside him. The girls hadn't noticed either of them yet.

After handing Lily and Daisy their choices, Emma waited for Violet to make hers. The child pointed to a doll with a cloud of silvery-blond hair wearing a light blue dress.

"She's very pretty." Emma took the doll off the shelf. "One of my personal favorites."

The child's eyes widened, but she didn't make a move to accept the doll right away. She merely skimmed a fingertip along the doll's sleeve.

Watching his daughters, Tristan was transported back in time. His pulse roared in his ears. His throat worked, but no sound came out. A memory of each of them as infants flashed in his mind. They'd been incredibly tiny, fragile and precious to him at first sight. He'd held them in much the same way Daisy and Lily held their dolls.

He swallowed.

"Is this the one you want?" Emma asked Violet.

Violet shook her head. "I want one that looks like Miss Rachel."

The request yanked Tristan back to the present and a gruff sound erupted in his throat. Violet peeked over her shoulder, caught sight of him and squealed in delight. "Da!"

His other daughters looked at him but then turned their attention back to their dolls without a single word of greeting.

Before he could absorb the impact of their obvious dismissal, Violet skipped over to him. "Miss Rachel is letting us get a dolly of our very own."

Rachel sighed. "I overstepped again, didn't I? But I want you to know this is my treat."

"That's a kind gesture. Every little girl needs her *very*

own dolly." He gave her a smile of appreciation. "I should have thought of it myself."

Something came and went in her eyes. "That's why you hired me, to think of these sorts of things."

There was a lesson here, one he wasn't ready to learn. "Thank you, Rachel."

"You're welcome, Tristan."

He reached out to her, not sure why, but Violet wedged herself between them and he dropped his hand.

"I wanted a real baby, but Miss Rachel said you have to find us a mommy first."

"Miss Rachel is right," he said in a raspy voice. For the first time since deciding to marry again, he feared the task of finding a wife was bigger than he could handle on his own.

He'd always thought himself capable of making anything happen as long as he put his mind to the task. He'd never relied completely on faith. Waiting for the Lord to answer his prayers had never appealed to Tristan.

"You know, Da." Violet studied him closely, then turned to look at Rachel with equal force. "If Miss Rachel was our mommy, then you and she could—"

"Here you go, Violet," Emma interrupted the child. "A doll with dark hair and brown eyes just like your nanny."

Thankful for the interruption, Tristan reached out to take the doll himself then passed it on to his daughter.

"I love her." Violet hugged the toy tightly in her arms. "I love her. I love her. I love her."

Such simple pleasure, such pure joy, he thought. A lesson he *was* willing to learn today. Smiling, he glanced in Rachel's direction, but movement out on the street caught his attention. Snow had begun falling since he'd arrived. Big, fat, fluffy flakes floated in the air. "Weather's turned."

Rachel glanced over her shoulder. "Oh, my. We better get going."

In her usual efficient manner, she gathered up the girls, then turned her pretty smile on him. "Will you be home for supper tonight?"

"Nothing could keep me away."

Chapter Seventeen

Nothing could keep me away. Except something *had* kept Tristan away. Rachel told herself not to fret. He was a competent lawman and could take care of himself.

Still, she worried.

The sun had set hours ago. Sticking to their daily routine, she'd already put the girls to bed, which left her alone with her anxious thoughts.

Pressing her lips tightly together, she moved to the window in the kitchen and searched for Tristan's tall, dark form. She couldn't see much past the white swirls of sleet and ice whipping around in the wind.

The snow had been falling sporadically on and off since early afternoon, turning the already gloomy night a cheerless void of gray upon black and—

A movement caught her attention.

Leaning forward, Rachel pressed her nose to the glass and squinted into the murky, austere night. A moving shadow elongated, shifted over the ground, then formed into the shape of a man.

Tristan.

He was home at last.

Relief nearly flattened her. Shocked by the intensity

of her reaction she suppressed a heavy sigh and stepped away from the window.

As was his habit, Tristan entered the house through the back door. Rachel could hear him kicking off the snow from his boots in the tiny mudroom off the kitchen.

She met him in the doorway with a smile and a full plate of food. The appreciative light in his eyes reminded her of their time together on the banks of the Columbia River, when she'd sat with him beside the crackling fire while he ate.

It seemed an eternity since they'd shared those brief interludes under the stars. She longed for those moments when it was just the two of them discussing his daughters, his town and what she could expect from life in Oregon City.

Nothing had turned out the way she'd hoped or planned.

"You didn't have to save me a plate of food," he said in the same tone and pitch he'd used on the trail.

Did he remember their time together?

From his fond expression, she thought he might.

Aware of the same, warm pull she felt every time he was near, she allowed a portion of her guard to drop.

"You work hard, Tristan. Someone needs to make sure you're well fed."

The smile he gave her transformed his face and she realized that he, too, had let down a portion of his guard. "If it gets me more of your buttermilk biscuits, I'm all for putting in a long, hard day at the jail."

Her heart lurched at the hint of Ireland wrapped around the words. She recalled feeling the same thrill the first time she'd heard him speak.

"I enjoy cooking for you, Tristan." She paused, then added, "And for the girls."

As they'd done in the mercantile earlier this afternoon,

they stared at each other longer than necessary. Rachel tried to keep her face calm as she struggled with the sad truth. *He can never be mine.*

At least not in the way she wanted him to be hers.

"The girls are already in bed. So…I guess…I'll see you in the morning."

She started for the mudroom, where she'd left her coat, but Tristan reached out and stopped her with a touch to her arm. "Sit with me while I eat. You can tell me about the rest of your day and I'll tell you about mine."

"I'd like that." She hesitated, but only for a second. Moments later, she was pouring them each a cup of coffee and taking a seat across the table across from him.

He chomped a bite of biscuit and sighed in pure masculine pleasure. "Good."

She adopted a tone of mocked outrage. "Not great?"

"Excellent, actually," he amended with an amused grin. "Best biscuit I've consumed since…last night."

She laughed. "I should say so."

Catching her light mood, his mouth curved with a slow, easy grin. Rachel was thankful to be sitting down. Had she been standing, no doubt her knees would have collapsed beneath her.

"Anything special happen after you left the mercantile?" She was quite proud her tone didn't give away the worry she'd felt for him since sunset.

He eyed her a moment before responding, then lifted a shoulder. "A few unexpected issues came up."

That was certainly vague. "I…see."

"Do you?"

"No." She gave a strained laugh. "But it seemed the right thing to say."

His lips twitched.

Silence fell over them. While he ate the rest of his

meal, Rachel shifted in her chair and watched the snow fall against the window. The flakes were coming at a much slower rate than earlier in the day. "Looks like the storm is letting up."

"About time."

Not sure what she heard in his voice, Rachel turned back to face him. Something had altered in Tristan's overall bearing. It wasn't anything she could pinpoint, precisely, a slight strain in the angle of his shoulders, a small muscle twitch in his jaw.

She couldn't think what had brought on this change. The evening had started out easy and comfortable. They weren't strangers anymore. In many ways, this man knew her better than most. He'd even kissed her lightly on the lips this morning.

Oh. *Oh, no!*

Did Tristan regret kissing her?

She twisted her hands together in lap. She'd become quite the sighing sort since their first meeting. Her mind raced back to that day. She'd been so naive back then, so trusting and determined to protect her sister from making a mistake.

Much had changed in recent weeks. Did she regret standing up for Emma? For interfering in Ben's relationship with Abby? Her behavior had been out of love for her family, a family that wasn't even hers.

Tristan set his fork down. "Rachel, won't you tell me what's bothering you?"

She cleared her expression. "I was about to ask you the same question."

They shared a smile and suddenly everything felt... better.

A quiver went through her as his fingers closed momentarily over hers. His brief hold was gentle and, in that instant, she knew she could tell Tristan what she'd discovered about her past without him passing judgment.

She wanted to unburden her heart. But her lungs felt too tight, constricting with such force she had to fight for each breath. When she finally opened her mouth to begin, Tristan was already speaking.

She'd missed the opening portion of what he said but caught up quickly.

"...and with the change in weather, I fear the Tucker brothers will make their move sooner rather than later." He held her gaze. "I was late coming home because James Stillwell and I were finalizing our plan to trap them."

Of all the things that could have put that quiet gravity in his voice, Rachel would not have expected Grant and Amos Tucker to be the cause. "You really think they'll come to Oregon City?"

"I believe they're already here." He shoved his empty plate aside and leaned his forearms on the table. "They have to be behind the series of break-ins in town. The two today had the same entry and exit scenarios."

She thought a moment, her mind reviewing what she knew about the Tucker twins. "You mean a place with easy access that allows for quick grabs and even quicker exits."

"Exactly." He shook his head in obvious distaste. "Grant and Amos aren't ones for creativity, but they're still dangerous. I'm telling you this so you'll be aware of the potential threat to your safety and that of the girls. No more impromptu trips to the mercantile."

She answered without hesitation. "Of course not— the children's safety is far too important." She let her mind settle over the reality that the Tuckers were not only thieves but also dangerous. "It's amazing how they managed to fool everyone for so long. Looking back, their laziness and unscrupulous tendencies were always there, hidden beneath the charming manners."

"They've shown themselves to be tricky and cunning. In my mind, that makes them the worst kind of degenerates."

She didn't disagree.

They contemplated each other for a long, wordless moment, enough for Rachel to catch the shadows in Tristan's eyes and the signs of weariness on his face. She also saw anger in him, an emotion she shared.

"I want Grant and Amos out of my town." His voice turned stony, a little ruthless even. "I won't rest easy until they're in custody."

Neither would she.

She reached for his empty plate. He stopped her with a shake of his head. "I'll take care of that later."

"But it's my duty to—"

"Not tonight." He rose from the table, a sweet, almost shy smile lifting at the corners of his mouth. "I have a gift for you."

Surprise had her leaning back in her chair and staring up at him in silent wonder. "You brought me a gift?"

"I'll be right back."

She watched him disappear into the mudroom. He was such an appealing man: tall, sinewy muscled, with broad shoulders and lean hips. Rachel doubted she would ever grow tired of looking at him.

When he returned to the kitchen, one hand behind his back, green eyes glittering in his tanned, handsome face, she had to swallow several times to hold back a surge of emotion.

"For you." In an unusually awkward movement, he thrust a paper bag at her.

Her heartbeat tripped over itself.

"Oh, Tristan." Her hand flew to her mouth. He'd brought her licorice, an entire bagful, with at least twenty individual strings tucked inside. "How did you know that's my favorite candy?"

"Grayson told me." His expression softened. "Your brother said he used to sneak you pieces when your father and mother weren't looking."

The backs of her eyes stung. She had to pull in several gulps of air to keep the tears from falling. "Grayson remembered doing that for me?"

"He did, quite fondly."

Clutching the bag close to her heart, Rachel couldn't stop a few tears from sliding free. She swiped at her cheek, to no avail. More fell. And then several more after those.

Tristan angled his head, his gaze full of masculine puzzlement. "Are those happy or sad tears?"

"I don't know. Both, I suppose." Tears continued spilling down her cheeks, coming faster than she could swipe at them. She gave up trying. "I'm happy. *And* I'm sad."

"Will you tell me why?"

"I want to." She lowered her head, surprised at the urge to share her secret pain with this man. "I *need* to tell someone what I discovered."

"Then let it be me."

He drew her into the living room, directing her to sit on the sofa. With a gentle tug, he took the bag of licorice from her. She'd all but strangled the candy in her merciless grip.

Settling on the sofa beside her, Tristan took both her hands. "Tell me what's happened to put that sad look in your eyes."

She lowered her head. "I don't know where to start."

"The beginning is always a good place."

Yes. But where was the beginning? Was it with Sara Hewitt's stillborn babies? Or when Jeremiah Hewitt found Rachel behind his mercantile?

She discarded both options and opened with the most relevant piece of information. "I recently found out I'm not a Hewitt."

He blinked at her for several long beats. "I'm not sure I understand. What do you mean you're not a Hewitt?"

Rachel struggled for control, but a burst of shame had her drawing her hands free of Tristan's and curling them into fists.

"Jeremiah Hewitt found me in the alley behind his mercantile." She drew in a shaky breath. "I was but an infant."

"Are you certain of this?" He sounded as shocked as he looked. Of course he was shocked. How could a good man like Tristan understand the ugliness in some people's hearts?

"My mother, I mean…Sarah Hewitt, wrote about me in her journal. She chronicled every detail of the night the Hewitts took me into their home." Her eyes filled with another onslaught of tears. This time Rachel choked them back with sheer force of will. "My real mother and father thought so little of me, they wanted rid of me so badly, that they dumped me in an alleyway."

A hum of raw pain sounded deep in his throat as Tristan's eyes filled with sorrow and what looked like unshed tears. He reached out again and closed his hand over hers a second time.

His concern for her was evident in his tender grip.

"Say something," she whispered.

"Praise God that Jeremiah Hewitt found you and took you home with him."

Rachel processed his words. For the first time since

reading her mother's journal, she understood the blessing in Jeremiah Hewitt's act of kindness toward her. Things could have ended very differently had he not brought her into his home and raised her as one of his own children.

She attempted to smile but only managed to lift one side of her mouth. "What I can't seem to reconcile in my mind is why my real parents abandoned me in that alley." She worried over the rage that churned in her heart, feared it could stay with her for years, perhaps forever. "Why did my own mother and father leave me out there, knowing I could die?"

The reality of what Rachel had endured as a baby broke Tristan's heart. His throat burned with sorrow for that small, abandoned child. Muttering under his breath, he pushed to his feet and then pulled Rachel up with him.

Hands resting lightly on her shoulders, he only had one thought in mind. Make her pain go away. "There aren't words for what your parents did to you."

She lowered her chin, offering her bent head to him.

The dejection in her stance sent a ripple of fury along the base of his skull. He'd like nothing more than to have *a word* with the people who'd left her to die alone in a back alley.

Something about her story didn't sit well with him. It had to do with the way she'd found out this information, by reading her mother's journal rather than hearing it from her siblings. There had to have been a reason they'd kept silent so long.

"Have you spoken about this with Grayson?"

"Every time I try I can't seem to find the words." Head still lowered, her pale fingers fluttered in a helpless gesture beside her skirt. "He's known the truth since I arrived in the Hewitt home yet hasn't said a word. How do I confront him? What do I say that won't come out sounding bitter?"

Tristan didn't know. He couldn't understand why Grayson had kept the truth from her even after she became an adult. One thing, Tristan did know. "He loves you, Rachel, as do Ben and Emma."

"Not enough to tell me the truth about my childhood. They call me sister, yet they lie to me on a daily basis." She lifted her head and the pain he saw in her eyes cut him to the core. "I'm clearly not one of them, I'm—

"You're a Hewitt, Rachel—maybe not by blood," he added when she tried to interrupt, "but a Hewitt all the same."

"No." The cold restraint in her voice was gut-wrenching. "I keep asking myself, if I'm not a Hewitt, then who am I?"

"You're a beautiful child of God." He pulled her a step closer to him, compelling her to look back into his eyes. "You're a woman who has brought music and laughter back into my home."

"People in Philadelphia called me a charity case."

"I don't believe that and neither should you. You're a bold, courageous woman who lives every moment to the fullest and is teaching my daughters to do the same."

Though she struggled to moderate her breathing, a soft light came into her eyes at the mention of the girls. "I didn't do much more than pull out what was already there. Your daughters are easy to care for, Tristan, even easier to love."

A crack opened in his heart.

"The transformation in them has been remarkable, all because of you. Rachel, hear me when I say this." He pulled her closer still, wrapped his arms around her and pressed his forehead against hers. "They aren't the only ones in this family you've inspired to change."

She trembled. "No?"

"You've inspired me to embrace life once again. Because of you, because of knowing you, I want to do more than survive from one day to the next."

"Oh, Tristan."

He lifted his head to look her directly in the eyes. "You are a blessing straight from God."

She gave him a watery smile that broke through his well-laid defenses. The crack in his heart opened wider. Before he could think too hard about what he was doing, he pressed his lips to hers.

She stiffened for less than a second. Then, as if allowing herself this one moment of abandon, she relaxed into him.

He tightened his hold as the kiss rocked through him, landing straight in the middle of his heart. Everything in him softened, let go, and he knew he would never be the same. He also knew he needed to release her. Now. He savored the feel of her in his arms for three more seconds.

When he finally pulled back, he was vastly surprised at the effort it took to force his arms to drop down to his sides.

At least Rachel's eyes were now round with surprise and wonder instead of sorrow. That counted for something, made it easier to accept that what had begun as a need to offer her comfort had turned into something much more complicated.

He'd taken advantage of her vulnerability. What kind of man did that make him? "Rachel, I'm sorry, I—"

"No, Tristan, please don't say you're sorry." She briefly pressed her fingertips to his mouth. "I can't bear knowing you regret kissing me."

"I'm not sorry I kissed you. I'm sorry I took advantage of the situation. You were feeling vulnerable and I—"

"Offered me comfort," she finished for him. "Let's not make more out of this than what it was, just one friend demonstrating to another that he cared."

The kiss had been more than that, much more. They'd made a connection that went beyond comfort and friendship, beyond rules and restrictions. But this wasn't the time to discuss it. Not with her feeling lost and vulnerable and him feeling…incredibly…renewed.

"I'll walk you to the door."

She nodded.

In the mudroom, he helped her into her coat. With slow, careful movements, he turned her around to face him. Gaze locked with hers, he pressed a chaste kiss to her forehead, then another to her temple and one more to her lips.

She gave him a shaky smile in return.

A silent message passed between them, a quiet understanding that went beyond words.

Perhaps it was time to move on from his grief, for his daughters' sake *and* for his. Perhaps it was time to say goodbye to Siobhan, to quit holding on to her and the past they'd shared. Perhaps it was time to step embrace the future.

With Rachel by his side?

He wasn't sure. *Set it aside*, he told himself. *Deal with this later*.

In the meantime, Tristan would do what he could to help Rachel, but the work would be on her. In the same way, the work of letting go of Siobhan fell on him.

Reaching behind Rachel, he twisted open the door. A blast of frigid air swirled over them. Smiling into her pretty eyes, he lifted the collar of her coat and sent her on her way.

He watched her hurry across the small strip of land between his house and her brother's.

"Rachel," he called out over the wind. "Hold up a moment."

She paused, looked at him over her shoulder.

"I'll be right back." He hustled into the house, retrieved the bag of licorice and then trotted over to where she waited.

Her gaze widened as he handed over the candy.

He took her face in his hands and smiled tenderly down at her. "Thank you for sharing the secret of your past with me." He wiped a tear off her cheek with the pad of his thumb. "You can trust me to keep the information to myself."

"I know."

It took every ounce of willpower not to kiss her again.

He lowered his hands and let her go. He watched her until she entered Grayson's house and shut the door behind her.

Another minute passed and, still, Tristan remained rooted to the spot, one part of him desperately clinging to the past, the other ready to step into the future.

He predicted a long, sleepless night.

Chapter Eighteen

Early the next morning, Rachel stood by the window in her bedroom and stared out at the cold, gray dawn. She'd wept through the night—endless, endless night—and now, empty of tears, her eyes felt dry and gritty.

She wasn't supposed to be sad this morning. She was supposed to be filled with happiness. Tristan hadn't turned away from her after finding out the secret behind her adoption. In fact, he'd kissed her. They'd had *a moment*. Of course, as she pressed her fingertips to her mouth and attempted to savor the memory of his lips meeting hers, reality set in. Tristan hadn't really meant to kiss her. He'd only been trying to comfort her. Kindness, maybe even pity, had driven his actions.

After all, her own parents hadn't wanted her. They'd actually left her to die. If they'd cared even a little, they would have brought her to a church or a foundling home or any number of other places where she'd have been safe.

She continued staring out the window. The first rays of sunlight split through the dawn. Spun gold over muted lilac. The start of another day.

Not just any day, the Sabbath.

Rachel couldn't imagine attending church today, worshipping the Lord and pretending all was well. She couldn't *lie* like that. Not to her siblings. Not to herself. And certainly not to God.

She swiveled away from the window and caught a glimpse of her mother's journal on the nightstand beside her bed. She glared at what had once been her most treasured possession. Now it was the source of her misery.

A portion of an oft-recited prayer flashed in her mind. "Forgive us our trespasses, as we forgive those who trespass against us."

Guilt came fast and hard. The Lord called her to forgiveness. How was she supposed to forgive the people who left her to die? She buried her face behind her palms. She couldn't attend church with this rage in her heart.

Pretending illness was not an option. She would not stack her own lies atop all the others. Perhaps she could find somewhere else to go. But where?

Think, Rachel, think. An idea struck. A rather brilliant idea, actually.

Just as she reached for the door handle, a firm knock came from the other side. Grayson.

You can't avoid him forever.

No, she couldn't. The time for running was over.

She set her chin at a determined angle, pulled in a deep breath and opened the door.

Grayson stood in the hallway, a wide smile on his face. "Excellent. You're ready for church. We'll be leaving shortly, once Maggie finishes dressing."

Rachel remained perfectly still, stunned by a need to slam the door in his face. *No, no more avoiding the difficult conversation.*

She opened her mouth but closed it when she realized Grayson's smile seemed especially happy.

"You're certainly cheerful this morning."

Her voice sounded too sharp, too fragile, but he didn't seem to notice.

As his expression filled with unmistakable pleasure, he leaned a shoulder against the doorjamb. "God has blessed me more than I can fathom, and definitely more than I deserve. I'm going to be a father."

For a moment, Rachel simply stared at her brother. At the announcement, she felt strangely unmoored, disoriented, as if unsure how to react to the news.

Happy, she should be happy for her brother and his wife.

"Maggie is with child?"

Emotion chased across his face and she wondered what he was feeling. Love, certainly, but she also saw fear in his eyes, just behind the joy.

"We think she's about three months along. So far, all is well." A portion of the excitement left his eyes. "I keep telling myself that Maggie is healthy and strong. I trust the Lord will keep her safe."

The shadows in his eyes, shadows he could no longer disguise, reminded Rachel how Susannah had died. In childbirth.

Her own concerns faded, seeming almost petty in the light of what Grayson had suffered. She rushed forward and wrapped her arms around the man she'd always thought of as her brother, a man who'd shown her all manner of kindnesses.

"Oh, Grayson, of course God will keep Maggie safe." *Lord, Lord, let it be so.* "This is wonderful news. I'm so pleased for you both."

She clung to him a bit longer, setting aside her anger. Grayson deserved this second chance at happiness.

Stepping out of her brother's embrace, Rachel's gaze alighted on the bag of licorice Tristan had given her last night. He'd known what she liked because Grayson had told him.

"You'll make a great father," she whispered, tears slipping along her lashes.

"Ah, Rachel, my sweet little sister, I hate to see you looking so sad."

Solid, steady Grayson, always the protective big brother, always putting her needs ahead of his. She felt another, uglier stab of guilt. "I'm happy for you and Maggie. Truly. I am."

She heard the strain in her voice, the shrill note to her words. Apparently, so did her brother.

"Is it Tristan?" Grayson set his hands on her shoulders and searched her expression. "Has he done something to hurt you? Because if he has, I'll—"

"Tristan has been nothing but wonderful to me." Her cheeks heated as the memory of his kiss sparked to life. She wanted him to kiss her again. Not out of sympathy, or kindness, but because he really, truly wanted to kiss her.

Oh, my.

She lowered her gaze to hide her inappropriate thoughts.

"Rachel, I can't help you if you won't tell me what's wrong."

"I'm…tired, that's all. I didn't sleep well last night."

"Won't you at least tell me why?"

The genuine concern in his question was her undoing. Her control slipped and the tears began to flow again. How she missed the brother she'd always counted on, the one who'd sneaked her pieces of licorice as a child.

Unable to stop herself, she leaped back into his arms and tried not to sob into his shirt.

He patted her head as he had when she was a child. "Rachel, something's happened to you recently, that much

I know. If it's not Tristan, then it must be something to do with our family."

She stepped out of his arms and drew her bottom lip between her teeth. Why couldn't he be her *real* brother?

Why couldn't she unread what she'd read in Sara Hewitt's journal?

Grayson continued staring at her. "Help me understand why you're determined to avoid the family, me especially."

Before she could censure the move, her gaze shot to the bed, to the loathsome book that had shattered everything she'd ever known about herself.

Following the direction of her gaze, he made a sound of alarm deep in his throat. "Is that our mother's journal?"

She nodded.

After a long hesitation, he released a sharp, shallow breath. "How much have you read?"

"Enough." Eyes burning with a fresh onslaught of tears, she choked them back, then lifted her chin at a proud angle. "I know I'm not a Hewitt."

"You weren't supposed to find out." Eyes dark and turbulent, he swiped the back of his hand across his mouth. "Not this way, not ever."

His candid response only managed to fuel her anger. Bitterness rose up in her throat. "Why, Grayson? Why did you let me believe that I was a part of this family, when I'm not?"

"You are a part of this family. You're a Hewitt, in every way that counts." Arms wide, he approached her, presumably to hug away her concerns.

She stepped back so that his hands met nothing but empty air. "You should have told me."

"Why tell you? It never mattered to us how you came into our family. You're our sister, that's the truth of it."

No peace surfaced with his announcement, no sense of triumph. Just bone-deep sorrow, and loneliness such as she'd never known before. "How could it not matter that our fa—that *your* father found me behind his mercantile?"

Lips pressed into a grim line, Grayson paced through the room, paused, then came back to stand beside her. "You make it sound so cold, when your arrival in that back alley was a blessing straight from God."

She frowned. "How could my abandonment be a blessing?"

"After our mother lost her third baby she became inconsolable. She was no longer the mother I'd always known. She was dying, little by little, day by day, from the inside out."

Rachel picked up the journal, ran her hand over the binding. She knew Grayson spoke the truth. Sara Hewitt's despair practically jumped off the pages of her first entries.

"Your arrival changed everything. You made her happy and when she became your mother, she became our mother again."

Rachel continued staring at the journal in her hands.

"Rachel." Grayson touched her arm with a tentative brush of his fingertips. "You saved our mother's life. You were the answer to our prayers."

She recalled her mother's final words to her every night at bedtime. *Rachel, my beautiful, precious daughter. You're my very own, special gift from God.*

Stomach quivering, she finally lifted her head and met Grayson's gaze. "Do you know who my real parents are?"

"No." She saw nothing but truth in his eyes. "I only

know what Pa told us the night he showed up with you in his arms. He said he found you nestled in a pile of blankets in a snowdrift behind the mercantile."

A snowdrift? Sara Hewitt hadn't included that piece of information in her journal. Rachel had been left out in the cold. She'd been left to die…in…the…snow. But she'd been rescued by a wonderful, loving family that considered her their own.

"Grayson? Rachel?" Maggie called out from down the hall. "It's time to go. Church starts in twenty minutes."

"I'm not going." Rachel's fingers clutched at the journal.

Grayson nodded. "I understand." There was a slight pause, then he added, "Will you be all right on your own?"

No. Yes. Eventually. Maybe. "I'll be fine."

He dragged her into his arms and pressed a kiss to the top of her head. "I love you, peanut, always have, always will."

She said nothing, not when he stepped back and looked into her eyes. Not when he turned to go. Not when he shut the door behind him with a soft click.

Alone at last, she fell back on her bed and wept. Unlike the tears she'd shed last night, these carried a trace of healing.

A vicious wind thrashed off the mountains in bone-chilling blasts. Tristan hunched his shoulders against the driving cold and hurried his daughters along toward the small wooden church up ahead.

A sharp gust kicked up, whipping Tristan's coat tightly around him. On mornings such as these, when the temperature dropped by the hour and the wind blew in cold and furious off the water, he was reminded that living in Oregon City came with a cost.

Tristan didn't regret moving his family here. The weather could be just as unpleasant on the Irish coast. Besides, Siobhan's death could have just as easily occurred in Ireland. Though he would still carry his share of the blame.

An image of Rachel came to mind.

His thoughts turned to last night, to the moment he'd taken her into his arms. He shouldn't have kissed her. He was opening her up to heartache, making silent promises he couldn't keep.

Still.

Their kiss had been coming on for days, maybe even weeks. Rachel had brought warmth back into his life, into his heart. She'd slipped past his guard and was systematically transforming every part of him. He felt like a new man, as if he were waking from a long, deep sleep.

"Can we sit with Miss Rachel?" Daisy asked over the howling wind, her new doll held securely in her arms.

"If she's willing to join us in the back pew, then yes. Of course." He'd welcome her company, as he did more and more each day.

Narrowing his gaze over the milling crowd, he searched for her pretty dark head. He didn't see her anywhere. He maneuvered his daughters around a pile of slushy mud and ushered them inside the church. Warm air immediately enveloped them while the wind continued battering angry fists against the exterior of the building.

He steered his daughters toward the back pew. The girls caught sight of Bertha Quincy and her sister, Clara. Squealing something about *playing with the baby again*, Violet hurried over to the women. His other two daughters followed closely behind their little sister. All three showed off their new dolls.

Tristan looked around for Rachel but saw no sign of

her inside the church. He did, however, see the rest of her family up near the front.

"Where's your baby?" he heard Lily ask Clara.

"We left her at home with Rachel," Clara said. "It was very thoughtful of her to offer to watch Emma Leigh this morning. I haven't been out of the house since her birth."

So, Rachel had chosen to skip church. Tristan wasn't completely surprised. But he knew from personal experience that distancing herself from the world wouldn't make her pain go away. He suddenly wanted to see her, *needed* to see her, to ensure with his own eyes that she was all right.

He pulled Bertha aside and asked her if she would watch his daughters during the service. "I need to speak with Rachel about an issue concerning their care," he explained.

"I'd consider it a treat." Bertha smiled over at the girls. "I've missed the girls terribly these past few weeks."

"Thank you."

He hastened out of the church and then tightened his coat at the collar as the frigid air frosted his breath. The streets were relatively deserted. The only sound came from the muted squeak of a wagon wheel in the distance.

He looked to the sky, took a moment to watch the clouds collide into one another. Jamming his hat on his head, he set out.

Grayson's voice stopped him at the bottom of the church steps. "Where you going, Tristan?"

"To speak with your sister," he said, turning back around. "I'm worried about her."

Their gazes clashed and a brief, tumultuous silence followed.

"I'm worried about her, too," Grayson admitted at last. There was evidence of guilt in the man's dark expression. Tristan figured he knew why. Rachel had confronted him last night or possibly early this morning.

"You must know that keeping secrets, no matter how well intentioned, is never a good idea," he said. "Someone always ends up hurt when the truth comes out."

Sighing heavily, Grayson rubbed the back of his neck with a frustrated swipe. "How much did she tell you?"

"All of it." Tristan's breath turned hot in his lungs. Righteous anger moved through him, anger on Rachel's behalf. "She's devastated, Grayson."

"I know. We withheld the truth from her because we never wanted her to think she wasn't one of us. She *is* one of us."

Grayson's explanation made sense on a certain level, but the man was ignoring an important piece of the puzzle. "Nevertheless," Tristan said. "She's feeling betrayed and abandoned right now. It's as if her parents left her in that alley only yesterday."

And Tristan needed to get to her. He needed to make sure she knew she wasn't alone. That someone cared. That *he* cared. "I have to go."

Grayson lowered his brows. "I don't think that's a good idea."

"She shouldn't be alone right now."

"And you think you're the one to help her through this?"

"I don't know. I guess I'll find out soon enough."

Without explaining himself further, he left Grayson staring after him. Walking with purpose, Tristan made his way across town in record time.

Rachel opened the door almost immediately after his knock.

"Did you forget something—" She broke off. "Tristan, I wasn't expecting you."

"And yet, you're just the person I came to see."

She cautiously stepped back to let him into the house.

"How are you doing?" he asked as he moved beyond the entryway and deeper into the main living space.

"I'm fine." Her tone said otherwise.

Stepping around the bassinet where Clara's baby slept, he saw the strain in Rachel's eyes, the exhaustion etched around her mouth. "You had a bad night."

She nodded.

"Because of our kiss?"

"No." A small smile played at the corners of her lips. "The kiss was—" her cheeks turned a pretty shade of pink "—quite lovely."

"I thought so, too."

Her smile spread to her eyes, until sorrow chased the hint of joy away.

"Oh, Tristan." She worried her hands together as if she didn't know what to do with them. "I can't seem to come to terms with what my parents did. How could they just leave me in a…back alley? And never, ever come back?"

Her pain was palpable. "I don't know."

Absently, he shoved at his hair. He hated not being able to erase her hurt. At least he could listen, for as long as she wanted to talk. Perhaps a sympathetic ear was all she needed from him.

He prayed it was enough. It had to be enough. Because deep down in his gut he knew he would never rest easy as long as Rachel was unhappy.

Chapter Nineteen

Rachel wasn't sure what she saw in Tristan's eyes. His silence seemed to suggest he was prepared to listen closely, as if what she had to say was important. Had she become more to him than his friend's little sister, more than his daughter's temporary nanny?

Afraid to hope for such a thing, Rachel broke eye contact. Why did her shoulders feel so tight?

She knew, of course. Tristan was standing too close. She could smell the scent of crisp, fresh air on him and something indefinably male that reminded her she was a woman.

Oh, my.

Taking several steps back, she randomly plucked at the fringe of a blanket. She'd lost her ability to think in full sentences now that she was aware of Tristan's…nearness.

She decided to wait him out, let him do the talking.

But when he simply watched her from his side of the room, she couldn't stand the silence any longer. "Was there a specific reason you sought me out this morning?"

She shook her head. She hadn't meant to sound so defensive.

Intent, he moved a step closer. And there went her train of thought again.

"I know why you didn't come to church this morning. I even understand your reasoning. However…" He hesitated, as if contemplating how best to continue.

"However…" she prompted.

His face suddenly softened, and he looked at her with such tenderness she thought she might weep. He *did* care about her. He really, truly cared.

"However," he repeated, his tone now as gentle as his face, "you can't avoid your siblings forever. Distancing yourself from them won't get you the answers you're seeking."

He was right, of course. She lowered her head. "I know."

"The longer you wait to talk with them, the harder it will be to have the conversation."

She knew that, too.

"I will speak to them. Soon. I promise." She raised her chin and squared her shoulders. "I just need a bit more time to gather my thoughts and figure out how to begin—"

She broke off when she heard the baby moving around in her bassinet. A whimper soon followed. Rachel reached for the infant and cuddled her close.

The impromptu act had a calming effect on them both.

Tristan smiled down at the baby, rubbed a finger across the tiny cheek, then looked once again into Rachel's eyes. "Don't wait too long to speak with your family. It'll only get harder with each day that passes."

Wise advice, especially now that Grayson knew she'd discovered the secret of her birth. He would tell Ben and Emma as soon as he found a chance. Maintaining her distance at this point would only make her seem small and petty.

Well, she was feeling small and petty.

"Rachel."

She shivered at the way her name sounded wrapped inside Tristan's Irish brogue. "Yes?"

He took the baby from her and placed the infant back in her bassinet. He rocked the tiny cradle until Emma Leigh fell asleep once again. Then, with slow movements, carefully gentle, he pulled Rachel into his arms.

Wanting his warmth, reveling in his closeness, she settled in his embrace and pressed her cheek against his solid chest.

"It still hurts," she whispered. "So very much."

"I imagine it does." His hold tightened around her ever so slightly. "Every choice your siblings made, every lie they told and every truth they withheld, was done out of love. They were acting out of a need to protect you."

He seemed so confident and, oh, how Rachel yearned to accept his words as truth. She desperately wanted to believe that her family had deceived her for all the right reasons.

She didn't know if she could.

"How can I be certain they acted for my protection and not theirs? What if they didn't tell me because they didn't want to have to deal with my reaction?" The moment she posed the question, she heard the flaws. Her siblings didn't indulge in selfish acts. It went against everything their parents had taught them.

Tristan released his hold and moved back several steps. She didn't like the distance between them but didn't feel comfortable saying so.

"Rachel, I speak from experience when I say I understand the need to protect a loved one from an unpleasant discovery." He approached her again and took her hands.

His manner was casual, but his eyes were grave. "You know how I lost Siobhan."

Pain clutched at Rachel's heart, pain for all this man had endured. "I do."

His grip loosened, then his hands fell away.

"Siobhan passed only moments after giving birth to Violet. She smiled at the infant, then at me, and then she was gone." His voice was carefully modulated, as if he was retelling someone else's tragedy rather than his own. "I will never, under any circumstances, tell Violet how her mother died."

Rachel's mouth trembled and she sobbed, just once. For the terrible loss Tristan had suffered, for the little girl he loved so completely despite the way she'd come into the world.

"I'm sorry, Tristan." The words felt so inadequate. "I know what I'm going through pales to what you've endured."

"I'm not telling you this to earn your sympathy." His frustration showed in the way his jaw tensed. "I've never actually put any of this into words. But it's important to me that you understand why I plan to withhold the truth from my own child."

Rachel understood completely. "You want to protect her."

"I don't want her to think, even for a moment, that she was the cause of her mother's death."

How could Rachel fault him for that? The tragic loss of his wife had brought the glorious blessing of his youngest daughter. But if Violet discovered the truth, it would change how she saw herself. The sweet, impish light that personified the happy child would be dulled. She might even begin to question why she'd been spared over her mother.

"Siobhan's death is my burden to carry, not Violet's."

Aware her heartbeat had quickened, Rachel touched his sleeve, then slid her hand down his arm until her palm met his. "Thank you, Tristan. Thank you for explaining this to me from such a personal place."

She was humbled that he'd told her why he planned to keep the circumstances of his wife's death a secret from his daughter. What a giving man. He'd shared a very private decision because he wanted Rachel to understand why her own family had deceived her.

In that moment, she fell a little in love with him.

Tristan placed their clasped hands atop his heart. He held on for several beats before letting her go. "Forgive your siblings, Rachel. They acted out of love."

"I see the situation more clearly now. I—"

The creak of the front door moving on its hinges cut off the rest of her words. A blink later, in walked Clara. Tristan's daughters crossed the threshold next, followed by Bertha Quincy and her husband, Algernon.

Clara went straight for the bassinet, picked up her baby and placed a kiss on the downy-soft cheek. "Were you a good girl while I was gone?"

Rachel smiled. "The very best."

Tristan's daughters crowded around Clara, cradling their dolls in an identical manner as the new mother held her baby. The scene touched her—undeniable evidence they would be sweet, caring big sisters to a newborn babe.

Brows lowered over his eyes, Tristan watched his daughters mimic Clara. His gaze started out thoughtful then turned shattered. Several hard, fast blinks and his expression closed completely, as if a shutter had fallen over his eyes.

Siobhan's death is my burden to carry...

Rachel bit her lip. If only Tristan could learn to forgive himself. Bertha came up to stand beside her. "Your brother has invited us to eat Sunday dinner at his house." She leaned over to peer at Tristan. "The invitation includes you, Sheriff, and your daughters."

Rachel couldn't be more pleased by this turn of events. Although she needed to speak with her siblings, her emotions were still in tatters. She welcomed this opportunity to prepare for the difficult conversation ahead.

"Did Grayson mention a time he wanted us over there?" she asked.

"Right away, but Algernon and I will be several minutes behind the rest of you." Bertha smiled at her husband, who was already moving through the room. "He refills the lanterns with oil every Sunday while I wind the clocks. It's our weekly tradition."

How…utterly…sweet. The two working together to accomplish simple household chores. Rachel wanted tradition and teamwork. And she wanted them with Tristan.

"I'll stay behind with you," Clara said, patting her baby's bottom. "I want to change this little girl's diaper before we walk over."

Rachel, Tristan and his daughters made the short hike to Grayson's house five minutes later. As they drew closer, laughter spilled out into the cool afternoon air. Rachel recognized the individual voices, so familiar, so dear to her. She heard the unmistakable sound of happiness in the laughter, heard the unconditional love in the muted tones.

Her heart filled to overflowing and she lost her footing.

Tristan helped her find her balance with a hand on her arm. Before he let her go, he dipped his head close to hers. "You aren't alone. I'm right here with you."

Everything in her calmed.

No, she wasn't alone. She'd never been alone, not really.

She might not be a Hewitt by blood, but she'd been raised as one of them. The only person who considered her an outsider was Rachel herself.

Chin lifted, she pushed into her brother's house.

Warmth and noise and the smells of home wafted over Rachel, calming her, giving her the courage to continue into the main living area where her family had gathered.

She halted at the edge of the room as the girls rushed in, announcing their arrival with high-pitched cheerful voices.

Daisy immediately engaged Emma and Abby in conversation. One of her small hands waved in the air as she spoke while the other clutched her baby doll. Lily and Violet showed off their dolls to Abby's father and Nathan. Both men appeared sufficiently impressed.

On the other side of the room, heads bent close together, Grayson and Ben were in a deep discussion. Rachel had seen them strike that same pose more times than she could count.

How had she allowed herself to believe she didn't belong with those she loved? Her place was here, with this family.

Her family.

The nameless, faceless people who'd left her in a back alley to die were nothing to her. Jeremiah and Sara Hewitt were her parents. Grayson, Ben and Emma were her siblings, as surely as if she shared their blood.

Head down, Rachel voiced a silent prayer straight from the heart. *Forgive me, Lord. Forgive me for missing the blessings You've bestowed on me, blessings that began the moment Jeremiah Hewitt rescued me from certain death.*

Determined to set aside her anger and feelings of betrayal, Rachel stepped fully into the room. "I'm home."

* * *

The next morning, Tristan silently observed Rachel move about his kitchen with practiced ease. He enjoyed watching her. She had an inherent grace that he'd noticed from the very beginning of their acquaintance.

She was her usual efficient self as she cleaned the breakfast dishes with confident strokes of the scrub brush. But today Tristan noted a sense of peace in her manner that hadn't been there yesterday.

He didn't have to guess what had brought on this change. "You spoke with your siblings."

The smile she shot over her shoulder was so full of joy he felt the impact of it in his heart.

"I spoke with them last night," she said. "Grayson had already informed Ben and Emma what I'd discovered in our mother's journal. We didn't have to rehash the particulars. Healing came surprisingly quick."

Tristan had countless questions he wanted to ask her. He voiced none of them. The individual words Rachel and her siblings said to one another were between the four of them. What mattered was they'd come to reconciliation. "I'm happy for you, Rachel."

Abandoning the pot she'd been scrubbing, she wiped her hands on a dry rag and turned to face him fully. "I want to thank you. You helped me put the situation in perspective and see their motives had been driven by love. If I'd been in their place I probably would have acted in the same manner."

A brave speech, but he knew how much she'd suffered these past few weeks. "I'm sorry you had to find out about your past the way you did."

She sighed. "Me, too. But it's over and done with now. I choose forgiveness. From this point forward, I'm looking ahead to the future and forgetting what came before."

Another brave speech, Tristan thought, praying she was successful. *He* certainly hadn't been able to forget the past. Everything he did, every choice he made, was shaped by what had come before.

"Or at least," Rachel amended, as if sensing the direction of his thoughts, "I plan to let go of my bitterness. I can't change what happened to me, but I don't have to let it define me, either."

Tristan's past defined him. His marriage to Siobhan, how she died and the motherless daughters she'd left behind influenced every portion of his life. He didn't know any other way to live.

"I have to get over to the jail," he said, his voice as tight as the knotted muscles in his back.

Rachel followed him to the door in silence.

He paused to kiss each of his daughters on the head, then turned to Rachel. "I'll be home at the usual time."

"We'll be here waiting." She gathered the girls around her and smiled.

"I'm counting on that." More than he cared to admit.

He left the house without another word. When he arrived at the jail, James Stillwell stood out front, looking anxious.

Tristan broke into a trot. "What's happened?"

"Another break-in, this one especially distasteful, even for the Tucker brothers." Stillwell ground out the words. "The church offering from yesterday's service has gone missing."

Tristan's gut roiled. "Grant and Amos stole money from the church? Have they no sense of honor?"

"Apparently not." Disgust hiked Stillwell's chin up a notch. "Reverend Mosby came by this morning, deeply concerned that he'd been careless. He'd locked up the money in the small safe in his office. The safe has disappeared. With the money inside."

Tristan shook his head. "The preacher couldn't have known they'd steal the entire safe."

"I told him exactly that." Stillwell went on to give the rest of the particulars, then finished with, "The reverend asked to see you as soon as possible."

"I'll head over there now."

Along the way, Tristan stopped in at several businesses to warn them that the Tucker brothers were still in town. He stopped in at the mercantile last.

"Grant and Amos stole the church offering," he said without preamble.

Grayson's face hardened. "I'll let Ben and Nathan know to be on the lookout."

"Good enough." Tristan headed for the door.

"Before you go, I want to thank you."

Tristan lifted a shoulder. "No need. I'm alerting all the businesses in town."

"I meant, I want to thank you for encouraging Rachel to come to Ben, Emma and me with her questions."

Tristan frowned. "She told you that I—"

"Your name never came up in the conversation." Grayson stuck his hands in his pockets and rocked back on his heels. "I just figured you were the one who influenced her to come to us. Am I wrong?"

Uncomfortable with the way his friend studied his face, Tristan shrugged again. "She'd have gotten there on her own, eventually."

"Maybe. Maybe not. The point is that she came to us because of your encouragement. So, again, thank you."

"You're welcome." A beat passed. "We through here?"

Amusement filled Grayson's gaze. "Guess we are."

At the door, Tristan had to stop and shift several steps back so a young woman could enter.

She looked familiar, though he couldn't quite place her face. She must have been on the wagon train. Her brown hair and brown eyes were nearly the same color as Rachel's, but she wasn't nearly as pretty as Rachel. There was certainly no mischievous spark in the woman's eyes.

Her smile brightened as she drew closer to him, turning her ordinary face less…well, ordinary. *Still not as pretty as Rachel*, he thought.

"Good morning, Sheriff."

He tipped his hat. "Ma'am."

An awkward silence fell between them. Tristan couldn't retrieve her name from his memory. He finally came up with a single, salient point. She'd been one of several unattached young women on the wagon train. She'd hired herself out to the—he thought a moment—Beecher family. With five young children, they'd needed the extra pair of hands.

The young woman's name was…it was…

Tristan truly couldn't remember.

Thankfully, Grayson stepped into the conversational void. "Can I help you, Miss…?"

"O'Brian." Looking somewhat reluctant, she moved her focus away from Tristan. "My name is Lucy O'Brian. I arrived on the wagon train last month."

When Grayson politely asked her about her journey and she answered in great detail, Tristan made his break. Nodding a silent farewell to them both, he exited the mercantile. But not before he heard Miss O'Brian say, "I was wondering, Mr. Hewitt, if you knew of anyone looking for a cook or a nanny or—"

Tristan shut the door on the rest of her words.

So, Miss O'Brian was in need of work. He doubted

she would remain unemployed for long. She was young, healthy and unattached, with considerable experience caring for young children. If Tristan had met her a month ago, he might have considered her a potential candidate for his bride.

It wouldn't have worked out.

Lucy O'Brian had a very large, extremely glaring flaw. She wasn't Rachel.

Chapter Twenty

Later that night, Rachel braided Violet's hair with surprisingly unsteady fingers. She wasn't accustomed to Tristan watching her so intently. He'd observed her in a similar fashion this morning.

As he had then, he seemed distracted...by her.

It wasn't that he was ignoring his daughters, precisely. It was that he kept glancing over at Rachel. Often. Nearly every other second. She knew this because she couldn't stop looking at him. She tried to tell herself it was because he'd arrived home late this evening and she'd missed him at supper.

There was an easy way to stop all the staring. Rachel simply had to discontinue looking at Tristan.

With that in mind, she focused her full attention on the thick, glossy red hair between her fingers. She made one final back and forth twist then secured Violet's braid with a ribbon. "All done."

The little girl swung around and grinned up at her.

Smiling in return, Rachel reached around Violet and lowered the covers so the child could crawl underneath.

Out of the corner of her eye, Rachel noted that Tristan helped Daisy into her bed with the same careful attention she herself gave Violet. He repeated the process with Lily. Once all three girls were snug in their beds, he turned back to look at Rachel.

She looked at him. And…

Here we go again. They were back to staring at one another.

With the quirk of a single eyebrow, she shot him a silent question.

He didn't respond to her unspoken query, but neither did he look away. He simply continued watching her, as if he were seeing her for the first time.

Or perhaps Rachel was reading things that weren't there. Perhaps the strange mood in the room was merely a by-product of the low lighting cast by the wall sconces. Shadows played on surfaces throughout the room, dancing across tabletops and dressers. Was it any wonder she attached a mysterious quality to Tristan's silence?

She let out a long breath and settled atop the chair at the foot of Violet's bed. "Who wants to tell your da what we did today while he was at work?"

"Me!" Lily immediately launched into a detailed account of their day. She spoke so quickly Rachel wondered if Tristan caught any of what the child said. Rachel barely understood the little girl's exchange and she'd been involved with each activity.

Finally, Lily came to the end of her report. "…and then you came home and, and—" she paused to catch her breath "—we ate supper and, and now it's time for bedtime stories."

Tristan's mouth twitched. "Sounds like you had an active day."

"Oh, we did." Lily gave him a fast head bob. "It was great fun."

"No doubt."

"We made muffin bread." Daisy smiled smugly at her sister in that superior yet loving manner only the oldest in the family could pull off without offense. "Lily forgot to tell you that part."

"I'm not sure I've ever heard of muffin bread." Tristan angled his head toward Rachel.

She smiled.

The girls giggled. Rachel explained, "Muffin bread is what Violet calls pumpkin bread, and now it's what we all call it."

"Because it's funnier to say," the three girls said in unison.

"McCullough Muffin Bread is the bestest of the bestest," Lily declared.

"Is it, now?" Tristan relaxed a little, even chuckled a bit. "Well, since you've officially attached the family name to this wondrous confection, I believe, as head of the family, it's imperative I sample a piece. For quality purposes, of course."

Rachel thought her heart might explode with affection for this family. Oh, how she loved them, with her entire being. Each and every one of them was special to her. Violet with her sweet, trusting nature. Lily with her adventurous spirit. Daisy with her bold, protective tendencies.

And then there was Tristan.

He was so many things. Handsome and steadfast. Kindhearted and compassionate. A loving father determined to find his daughters a mother. The heartbroken widower who carried the burden of his wife's death so deep within his soul that he refused to put another woman through the risk of childbirth.

Rachel's heart pounded so hard in her chest she thought it might leave an imprint on her ribs. She felt scared. She felt jubilant. These young girls were the daughters of her heart, as surely as she was the daughter of Sara Hewitt's heart. Tristan was the only man she wanted in her life.

It was time to accept her feelings for him, at last.

She loved him. She *loved* Tristan.

The truth settled over her like a wet wool blanket. Scratchy and uncomfortable.

It was an impossible situation, because she knew he had feelings for her. She knew! She also knew he would never allow himself to fall in love with her, not fully, not completely.

Was half his heart better than none at all? Was she willing to settle for something short of a great love to gain a family of her own?

Daisy's voice jerked her attention back to the moment. "Whose turn is it to tell us a story?"

"Mine," Rachel said automatically.

"After you say prayers," Tristan interjected.

All three girls interlocked their fingers beneath their chins and closed their eyes.

As the youngest, Violet lifted up her prayers first. "Thank You, God, for the moon and the stars and snow. I like playing in the snow with Miss Rachel. I also like that she braids my hair and teaches me how to sing songs. Oh, and thank You for muffin bread. It's my favorite."

Hearing Tristan's soft chuckle, Rachel connected her gaze with his. They shared a smile over the children's heads. In that moment, a sense of peace settled over her. Loving him would always be the best part of her world, even if he never loved her back.

Lily took her turn next. "Dear God, please keep Miss Clara's baby safe and, if it's okay with You, could You make sure Miss Bertha's baby is a boy? She told me she wants a boy and, well, that would be nice if You could do that for her."

Tristan lifted an eyebrow. Rachel merely shrugged. This was the first time she'd heard that Bertha wanted a boy.

"My turn," Daisy said, cracking open one eye, then shutting it just as quickly when her father caught her peeking. "God, will You make sure my daddy finds a wife real soon? I really want a new mommy."

Mouth tight, Tristan shut his eyes a moment, released a slow breath and opened them again.

"And, God," Daisy continued. "When You see my real mommy up there in heaven, please tell her not to worry about me and my sisters. We have Miss Rachel now and she's taking real good care of us. Amen."

The other two girls echoed their older sister.

Rachel swallowed back the lump in her throat. Before she knew what the child was about, Violet had crawled out of bed and into her lap. "I love you, Miss Rachel."

"Oh, Violet." She hugged the little girl tightly to her. "I love you, too."

She lifted her head and met Daisy's gaze. "I love you, Daisy." She focused on Lily. "And you, Lily."

"What about Da," Violet asked. "Do you love Da?"

Her answer came in a whisper. "Yes, Violet, I love your da." She forced herself to meet his gaze. "I love him very much."

Once Rachel began the evening's story, Tristan made his way to the door. He could feel her eyes tracking his progress, but he didn't glance in her direction. He knew better. If he looked into her eyes, her beautiful, life-affirming, amazing eyes, he wouldn't be able to walk away from her. Not now, maybe not ever.

His gut warned him to get out of the room as fast as he could. He needed to create distance between him and Rachel before he revealed the contents of his heart to her.

That would be a mistake. No matter what he told her, no matter how he really felt about her, he couldn't risk being with her.

Defeat settled on his shoulders as he slipped into the hallway. He was going to break Rachel's heart. That had never been his plan. He hadn't set out to hurt her.

The realization that she loved his daughters brought him great joy. The realization that she loved him, as well, also brought him great joy. A large part of him wanted to tell her that, yes, he loved her, too.

Only he couldn't.

In his mind, love and a real marriage would be the equivalent of issuing her a death sentence. Logically, he knew he hadn't actually killed Siobhan, but something in him warned that if he led with his heart he would destroy Rachel.

Rachel. Longing washed over him. He wanted to ask her to marry him again. He wanted to raise his daughters with her by his side. He just plain wanted her in his life.

Was there a way?

He leaned his head back against the wall and closed his eyes. The situation was too big for Tristan to handle on his own. He thought about praying to the Lord for guidance.

The moment he lifted up the request, an image of Rachel flashed in his mind. It was as if the Lord was reminding him of the blessing she'd become in his life. Hope blended with fear. Neither sensation was very comfortable.

As much as he liked her, maybe even loved her, he had to let her go. She deserved a man who could give her the life and family she wanted, without restrictions, without reservations.

Problem was, he knew she wouldn't leave the girls. She was too loyal, too much a woman of her word. The only way he could ask her to leave his home was to find someone else to watch his daughters in her stead.

He remembered his chance encounter in the mercantile earlier today. Lucy O'Brian was looking for a position.

Had the Lord answered his prayer already? Or was Tristan grasping for a quick, easy solution to a complicated problem?

Too many questions, not enough answers.

"Tristan?"

He opened his eyes but didn't lower his gaze. He didn't trust himself to look at Rachel. "Are the girls asleep?"

"Yes." The sound of crushed dreams was in her voice. He'd done that to her.

He'd done it to them both.

"I better get home," she said to a spot near his feet.

"I'll walk you out." He headed down the hallway.

Her soft footsteps sweeping over the wooden floor told him she trailed in his wake. They entered the mudroom minutes later, a painful silence weighing heavy between them. They'd become strangers again. He wanted to reach out, pull her to him and tell her what was in his heart.

For her sake, he must remain strong.

Still not looking at her, he retrieved her coat from its hook and held it open.

She let out a fast exhale and then stuffed her hands through the armholes. "I'm sorry I made you uncomfortable in there." Her breath turned quick and shallow. "That wasn't my intention."

He could tell her she hadn't been the reason he'd left

the room, but that would be a lie. She'd had enough lies told to her in her life. He wouldn't add another.

"This isn't working," he blurted out, which was all too true. "I have to let you go."

"What?" Her eyes flew to his face. "You're…you're letting me go?"

"You're very good with the girls, exceptional even, but—"

"It's because I said I love you."

"No." But, of course, it was. "I need to find the girls a mother. As long as you're here I can't do that."

"Why not?"

Because no other woman could ever measure up to you, was what he should have said. What he actually said was, "The girls like you too much, Rachel. As long as you're watching them they won't be open to any other woman taking over the household."

He wanted to tell her that he was doing this for her own good. He hadn't been able to protect Siobhan and he couldn't protect her. Rachel deserved the very best in life. He needed to let her go so she could fall in love with another man.

The thought made his jaw clench and his gut ache.

"I understand, Tristan." She drew in a shuddering breath. "I'll continue watching the girls until you find my replacement."

Choking on a gasp, she spun around and ran toward her brother's house.

Only when she disappeared out of sight did Tristan respond. "My dear sweet, beautiful Rachel, no one will ever replace you."

Chapter Twenty-One

Ever since Rachel was a young girl, no matter how bad things seemed when she went to bed, they always looked better in the morning. Of course, that was before she'd fallen in love with a man who couldn't or, rather, *wouldn't* allow himself to return her feelings.

Stomach churning, head pounding, she climbed onto Tristan's front stoop, lifted her hand to knock, then dropped it again. Indecision left her torn between running back to her brother's house and honoring her commitment to three little girls who desperately needed her.

Blinking back tears, she let out an unsteady breath very slowly, very carefully. She only had herself to blame for her current misery. Tristan had made his position clear from the very beginning of their acquaintance. Rachel simply hadn't expected him to let her go so soon. Actually, she hadn't expected him to let her go at all.

But he had.

Now she had to gather the courage to face him this morning. How was she supposed to pretend nothing had changed between them, when she knew—*she knew!*—he was already on the hunt for another woman to take her place in his home, in his life?

Tristan McCullough was one very stubborn, closed-minded, hardheaded, stubborn, stubborn, *stubborn* man. And she loved him desperately.

Rachel caught her bottom lip between her teeth. No more stalling. This time, when she lifted her hand she connected her clenched fist with a hard, determined knock.

Daisy immediately opened the door. "You're finally here!"

Rachel laughed despite herself. Such uninhibited happiness, she thought, glad to bask in the child's joy momentarily. A portion of the pain was still with her, would always be with her, but the sick churning in her stomach eased under Daisy's broad smile.

The sound of Tristan's purposeful footsteps announced his entrance into the room. "Good morning, Rachel."

She would not cry.

"Good morning, Tristan." The cool, carefree pitch of her tone surprised her. She hadn't realized she could pretend nonchalance quite so effectively.

A beat passed. And then another. Tristan cleared his throat. "I won't be staying for breakfast. I'm needed at the jail early this morning."

Of course he was. Jaw firm, heart pumping hard, Rachel forced herself to hold his stare. She loved Tristan, but now, instead of joy, the emotion brought her grief.

She would not cry. "Will you be home for supper?"

"Probably not."

She lowered her gaze. "I understand."

He moved smoothly toward her. He stood so close she could feel his warmth, smell his crisp, male scent. "I'm sorry, Rachel."

She said nothing, knowing no response was expected.

A light touch to her arm came and went so quickly

she thought she might have imagined it. "I'll see you this evening."

She would not cry. She would not cry. *She would not cry.* "I'll save you a plate."

"I'd like that." He drew in a sharp inhale. "Goodbye, Rachel."

The finality in his voice had her looking up again. She confronted an unreadable expression, the most hurtful punishment he could have bestowed on her.

"Goodbye, Tristan." Her hands felt like ice as she shut the door behind him with a determined click.

One moment at a time, she told herself. All she had to do was get through one moment at a time.

As if moving through a dream, she made breakfast for the girls, cleaned the dishes while they ate, then directed her young charges back into the main living area. She needed something to do with her hands. "Now that you have baby dolls I think it's time we made more clothes for them."

Her pronouncement was met with their typical enthusiasm. The girls watched with avid attention while she threaded a needle. Although Rachel would do most of the work today, they would still learn the process of putting together a dress. When they were older she would let them do more than watch.

Except…

Rachel wouldn't be here when they were older. Another woman would be in their home. Would she teach them how to sew?

Rachel shouldn't ask herself such questions, not if she wanted to keep from crying.

Footsteps sounded on the front stoop. Her entire body went warm, then ice-cold. Had Tristan returned?

No. He almost always entered the house through the mudroom.

"We have a visitor," she said, a mere second before the expected knock came.

She opened the door to the familiar form of her sister. Rachel blinked in confusion. "Emma? Was I expecting you this morning?"

"No. I took a chance. Is this a bad time?"

"Not at all. Come in." Rachel opened the door wider. "Girls, look who's come to see us."

Tristan's daughters welcomed Emma with bright smiles and a million questions. She did her best to keep up, but it was clear their fast chatter overwhelmed her.

Not for the first time, Rachel marveled at her sister's beauty. She wore a pretty pink dress with white trim that fit tightly at her waist and accentuated her blue-blue eyes. She'd pinned her hair atop her head, but several strands tumbled about her face in soft, casual curls.

When Daisy asked about her husband, Emma blushed prettily, and her lovely eyes turned dreamy. "He's quite wonderful. I left him at the mercantile stocking shelves."

The questions continued several more minutes until the girls' curiosity finally waned.

Once they turned their attention to an impromptu tea party at Rachel's suggestion, Emma pulled her to a spot out of earshot but still close enough to keep an eye on the girls.

"You've been on my mind ever since you read our mother's journal. I'm worried about you."

Rachel sighed. "There's really no need. I'm perfectly well."

Physically, this was true. Emotionally, not even a little.

"How are you *really* doing?" The skepticism in her sis-

ter's eyes was impossible to miss. "Now that you know...
the truth?"

Rachel started to tell her sister she was fine, that she
held no animosity toward her siblings. But then, as if to
mock her resolve to let go of the past, the pain, the bitterness, the sense of betrayal came back to her in a flash.
The emotions were as real and devastating as when she'd
first read the truth in her mother's journal.

She swallowed several times until the pain lessened
enough to speak.

"I'm better than I was," she admitted in a stilted voice.
"I'm sure it'll get easier with time."

Could she say the same about her heartache over
Tristan?

"Mama loved you, Rachel. Never doubt that."

Emma had said something similar back at Fort Nez
Perce.

In that moment, Rachel missed Sara Hewitt with a
keen awareness that threatened to steal the remaining
scraps of her composure. She wished her mother were
with her now.

"You look sad." Emma moved a step closer, brushed
her hand down Rachel's arm. "I hate that we caused you
pain. I'm so sorry."

"I understand why you kept the truth from me, truly,
I do."

"I'm still sorry." Emma angled her head. "And you're
still upset."

"I miss Mama."

"Me, too. Yet, I can't help thinking there's something
else bothering you, something you're not telling me."

Rachel desperately wanted to unburden herself. Her
first instinct was to go to the one person she trusted most.

Since that person was the cause of her current sorrow, she wasn't sure where to turn.

If not Tristan, why not Emma? They'd always been close.

"It's…Tristan. He's…" She looked over at the girls playing with their dolls. As if sensing her eyes on them, Daisy raised her head.

Rachel shook her head. "Never mind."

Emma waited until the girls were occupied with their game once again, then leaned a shade closer. "You've fallen in love with him."

Throat tight, Rachel nodded.

"Why, that's wonderful. I'm pleased for you both. He's a good man and you—" she faltered "—aren't happy about this."

Rachel dropped her voice to a low whisper. "He wants a marriage in name only."

Eyes wide, Emma stared at her a full three seconds. "Oh, well…that…makes no sense. I've seen the way he watches you. It's the same way Ben looks at Abby and Nathan looks at me. He's smitten, Rachel."

Perhaps he was, but not enough to take a chance on her. On them.

Choosing her words carefully, keeping her voice barely above a whisper, she explained Tristan's wife's passing during childbirth. "So you see. It's hopeless."

"Nothing's ever hopeless." Emma dragged Rachel into a much-needed sisterly hug. "All things are possible with God."

"I wish it was that simple."

"It can be." Emma released her. "You just need a little faith, and a lot of patience. He'll eventually realize you two are meant to be together."

Rachel desperately wanted to believe that everything

would work out between her and Tristan. Did she have that much faith?

Was a tiny bit enough?

She and Emma talked a little while longer before Emma said she had to return to the mercantile.

When Rachel escorted her sister to the door, Emma pulled her into another fierce hug.

"Don't give up on Tristan," she whispered. "He's going to come around, I just know it."

"Perhaps." Rachel shut the door behind her sister with a soft click. She felt another sickening churn in her stomach.

Under the circumstances, she did the only thing she could think to do. She prayed.

Across town, Tristan had a hard time concentrating on his work. His mind was full of Rachel and what might have been had he met her at another time, in another life. She was a beautiful, giving, compassionate woman.

He couldn't let her go.

He loved her too much to keep her. He…loved her?

Yes, he did. He loved Rachel. The realization came at him like a sledgehammer to the heart.

Siobhan had been the only woman he ever thought he could, or would, love. She'd been a part of him since childhood, his first love and, for most of his life, his only love. There would always be a place for her in his heart.

But Rachel was the woman he loved now. He wanted to spend the rest of his life with her. He wanted to raise his daughters with her by his side, as his wife and helpmate.

He *loved* her.

It was as simple as that.

For two years, he'd shied away from feeling strong

emotions other than when it came to his daughters. With her inherent kindness and bold personality, Rachel had broken through his defenses. What had started as a crack in his heart was now a gaping hole that only she could fill.

Not only did he want to marry Rachel, he wanted a real marriage with her. But…

If he got her with child, and she didn't live through the birth, then…

His throat seized up with fear, nearly choking the breath out of him. He closed his eyes and railed against God for putting Rachel in his life at all. Tristan and his daughters had gotten along just fine without her.

Of course, he knew that wasn't true. She was the best thing that could have happened to him and the girls.

Why, God? Why did I have to fall in love with Rachel?

As he continued to share his honest feelings with the Lord, voicing his anger, his fears, something remarkable happened. A sense of peace filled him.

Could he let go of his need to control the future? Could he surrender his will to God's and then live out every day with a hope he'd lost long ago?

The outer door swung open and James Stillwell entered the jailhouse. "Grant and Amos were seen coming out of the Winstons' barn this morning."

Tristan leaned forward in his chair. "They take anything valuable?"

"Don't know yet. They may have just been hiding out in the hayloft. I'll know more after I speak with Carl Winston."

Tristan shoved away from his desk and rose to his feet. "This makes four sightings of the Tucker brothers in three days."

"Our boys are getting careless."

"They're getting desperate." Never a good sign.

Tristan glanced toward the backroom where they'd locked up the stolen money. "They'll make their move soon."

Perhaps even today.

Stillwell gave him a flat stare. "It's time to set the trap."

"Yeah, it's time."

After running through the plan, Stillwell left for the Winston homestead. Tristan exited the building a few minutes later and turned in the opposite direction.

He took a roundabout route through town and returned to the jailhouse from a different direction, concealing his movements inside shadows and alleyways.

Behind the building, pressed flush against the wall, he checked his surroundings one last time. He arced a wide glance to his left, another to his right and then one more to his left. Confident no one took note of his presence, he climbed through the window.

He landed deftly on his feet. Alert for anything out of the ordinary, he moved deeper into the room and studied the cheap metal contraption that held nearly fifteen thousand dollars of stolen money.

The safe itself was of inferior quality, certainly nothing compared to the original Thayer & Edwards. And that was the point. If the Tucker brothers had the confidence and skill to break into one of the finest safes in the world, they wouldn't hesitate to breach this one.

The lure was too strong, the promise of reward too large.

Thinking of rewards, Tristan's mind immediately went to Rachel and the blessing she'd become in his life. He needed to tell her how he felt. He needed to trust that the Lord would protect her. They would face the future together, navigate their fears as a couple—

Tristan froze. Narrowed his eyes. Opened his ears. There was no sound, but he felt a shift in the air, the feel of another presence. Someone had entered the jailhouse.

The steps belonged to a man used to sneaking around in the shadows. Tristan concentrated on the slow, slightly off balance cadence. Step, shuffle, pause. Step, shuffle, pause.

One man, not two.

Frustration tightened his chest.

The footsteps slowed. Then stopped altogether. A fat shadow fell across the floor. Tristan moved away from the safe, closer to the door. He shifted his stance, ready to pounce.

A low, masculine clearing of a throat sounded from the interior of the other room. "Anybody here?"

Recognizing Amos Tucker's voice, Tristan held his position, waited for the other man to draw closer.

Another step, shuffle, pause.

Tristan peered around the doorjamb. Amos was just around the corner, hobbling closer. Closer.

Tristan melted into the shadows, balanced on the balls of his feet. Just a few more steps and Tristan could grab Amos.

Another step and…

Amos appeared in the doorway. He didn't notice Tristan. Instead, his beady eyes went straight for the safe.

Tristan held steady.

Releasing a low whistle, Amos entered the room and made his way to the unattended safe. "Well, look at you. Sitting there all by your lonesome."

Tristan slid in behind Amos and placed the business end of his revolver against the man's temple. "Amos Tucker, you're under arrest."

Amos went very still. His only movement was the unsteady rise and fall of his chest. "You can't arrest me," he snarled. "I ain't done nothing wrong. I just came by for a friendly chat about the weather."

"Turn around. Nice and slow."

Amos's shoulders bunched a half second before he pivoted on his heel and made a break for the door.

With his free hand, Tristan yanked him back around and threw him to the ground.

The lanky man went down hard. A boot heel planted firmly in the center of his back kept the sputtering, cursing thief on the ground.

For a split second Tristan stared at Amos sprawled out beneath his foot, astonished at how easy it had been to subdue the thief who had eluded capture for months. He checked the room again, listened for any other sound besides Amos's complaining. Nothing out of the ordinary.

Amos was alone.

Wild-eyed and heaving, Amos dragged in a big gulp of air. "I can't breathe. I can't breathe, I tell ya. I'm hurt."

Lips pressed in a hard line, Tristan holstered his gun, and then wrestled Amos to his feet. A few pushes, several pulls, one hard shove, and then the rangy, dumb man stood inside a jail cell.

Tristan slammed the door shut.

Amos wheeled around, banged two angry fists on the bars. "Let me out."

"Settle down, Amos. Have yourself a look around. Get comfortable. That jail cell is your new home for the foreseeable future."

Amos howled in fury. "You think you're so superior, don't you, Sheriff?"

"I'm not the one locked behind a wall of iron bars."

This earned him another long string of muttered oaths.

Tristan waited for him to wind down. "Where's your brother? Where's Grant?"

A mean, sinister look filled the other man's eyes. "You won't look so smug when I tell you." He laughed at his own joke. "Grant is at your house, taking care of your woman and your three little brats."

Tristan's heart stalled in his chest. *No.*

"Don't worry." Amos gripped the bars and literally rattled his own cage. "My brother ain't gonna hurt your family, long as I show up with the money by noon."

A suffocating pressure squeezed in Tristan's throat, moved down into his chest. He refused to give this man the satisfaction of reacting outwardly. Inside, he burned with rage. With every breath the sensation grew worse. Fear, pain, fear, pain, they became one.

"And if you don't show up with the money?" he asked, keeping his voice cool and even. "What then?"

Amos's lips peeled back to reveal a row of tobacco-stained, crooked teeth. "They're dead."

No.

Grinning now, Amos pressed his face between the bars. The move distorted his features. "Time's running out, Sheriff. You better hand over the money so I can go save your family."

"I've got a better idea." Tristan strode to the front door and jerked it open. "You stay here. *I'll* save my family."

He stepped outside and took off at a dead run.

Chapter Twenty-Two

From her place at the kitchen table, Rachel thought she heard the front door open and close.

Emma must have left something behind or perhaps wanted to share another piece of advice concerning Tristan. Hoping it was the latter, Rachel rose from the table and told the girls to finish their food.

"I'll be right back," she added over her shoulder.

Barely acknowledging her, they happily continued their semi-heated discussion over whether pink was a prettier color than purple. Daisy was the lone holdout, arguing with her sisters that everyone knew purple was the best. They wholeheartedly disagreed.

Rachel carefully picked her way to the center of the kitchen and stopped, not sure why she hesitated. Something told her to move slowly, to take her time, to listen for anything out of the ordinary. "Emma?"

No response.

She raised her voice slightly higher. "Emma, is that you? Did you forget something?"

Still no response.

Rachel's skin iced over. Whoever had entered the house, it wasn't Emma. She would have responded by now. Besides, Rachel remembered locking the door after her sister left.

Heart racing, she motioned for the girls to quiet down.

Three pairs of round, slightly frightened eyes stared back at her, but each child did as she commanded.

She called out, "Tristan?"

Silence.

A nauseating suspicion trembled in her stomach.

Stay here, she mouthed to the girls.

They nodded.

Mouth dry, Rachel advanced to the edge of the kitchen, into the living room. And froze. It took her precious seconds to process the identity of the man glaring back at her.

Grant Tucker.

He looked shaggier than she remembered, more desperate. For a dangerous moment, Rachel's thoughts tangled over one another, pinpointing to one awful, terrifying realization. There wasn't enough distance between him and the children she loved.

"Well, well, well, if it isn't Rachel Hewitt." He grinned at her with a half-crazed look in his eyes. "Fancy finding you playing house with the sheriff."

Her breath hitched in her lungs. "What are you doing here, Grant?"

"Why, Miss Hewitt. I'm paying you a visit."

Fear hit her like a fast, hard punch to the throat. Tristan's girls—*her girls*—were mere feet away from a very dangerous, desperate-looking criminal.

She swallowed hard.

Snickering, Grant moved another step in her direction. Sending up a silent prayer to God, Rachel held her ground.

Grant continued toward her.

She shifted her stance slightly to the right. The new position placed her body directly between him and the girls. "Don't come any closer," she warned.

He kept advancing, one slimy step at a time, until Rachel was forced to back up or have him run straight into her. She thought she might gag from the foul odor coming off his clothes.

Looming over her, he reached up and swiped the back of his hand across her cheek.

She jerked back.

His eyes hardened. "Where did you stash the sheriff's brats?"

She ignored the question.

"What do you want?" She suspected, of course, but Grant Tucker wasn't getting a step closer to her girls. Not without going through her. "The money isn't here."

"Amos has that covered." His gaze filled with frosty disdain. "But first, I have to set things right."

Keep him talking. It's your best defense. "How do you plan to do that?"

"I'm gonna hit the sheriff where it'll hurt most."

No. *No.* Grant planned to harm Tristan's daughters.

"You're mad." She spit out the words.

He reached for her again.

She slapped his hand away. "Don't touch me."

"I'll touch you whenever I please." Breathing hard, expression murderous, he closed his fingers around her throat. "Wonder what the good sheriff will do when he comes home to find you and his brats dead?"

Her stomach pitched.

Lord, help me protect the girls.

She would do anything, sacrifice everything, to keep them safe. No price was too high to pay to protect the children she considered her own.

Grant's grip tightened around her throat. "Where'd you hide the brats?"

Terror gave her courage. She slammed her knee into his groin.

Howling a stream of obscenities, Grant doubled over in pain.

The moment his hand fell away from her throat, Rachel slipped past him and ran into the kitchen. She skidded to a stop in renewed horror. The table was empty. Where were Tristan's daughters? She looked frantically around the room.

Had Amos come through the back door and taken them?

Her skin went hot, and her lungs grew so tight she couldn't pull in a single gasp of air. Out of the corner of her eye, she caught a slight movement. The girls were huddled together in the mudroom.

She started for them. Grant caught her braid and yanked her back toward him.

She cried out.

The girls' mouths gaped open. Tears welled in their eyes.

"Run," she shouted at them.

"You leave this house," Grant warned, "and I hurt her."

To emphasize his point, he twisted her hair around his fist and jerked her back against him.

Pain exploded behind her eyes. Better prepared this time, she swallowed the scream rising in her throat.

"Run," she managed to ground out.

The girls scooted back a step. And another.

"Run," Rachel yelled again.

"Don't take another step," Grant ordered.

They stood frozen in wide-eyed terror and swung their

gazes between Grant and Rachel. Dragging her with him, he reached out and caught Violet's sleeve.

The child screamed.

Rage shot through her. Vision tinged red, Rachel kicked Amos's shin, elbowed him in the stomach, then kicked out again.

His grip loosened—just enough—and, with one more blow to his gut, she wrenched free.

A weapon. She needed a weapon.

Her gaze landed on the iron skillet she'd used to make johnnycakes. Giving herself no time to think, she scrambled to the counter, grabbed the handle and raised the skillet in the air.

Focused on getting a firm grip on Violet, Amos didn't see Rachel coming. She knocked him out with one swipe.

He hit the ground with a loud thud.

"Is he dead?" Lily asked in a whisper.

Rachel noted the rise and fall of his chest. "No."

Keeping her gaze firmly planted on the unconscious man, she nudged him with the toe of her shoe. He didn't budge. "You made a big mistake, Grant Tucker, coming here and threatening my family."

Tristan ran flat out through town, unmindful of his footing, aware that James Stillwell fell into step beside him. The other man had been heading to the jail when Tristan sprinted out of the building.

One look at his face and the insurance agent joined him without question.

Now Stillwell spoke over the sound of their pounding feet. "The Tucker brothers made their move?"

Tristan gave one firm nod.

They rounded the first corner. As they continued, he

explained what happened in the jailhouse. He finished with, "Amos is in a cell."

Stillwell clenched his jaw. "What about the money?"

"Untouched."

Tristan turned onto the next street without breaking stride. Stillwell easily kept up the fast pace.

"Grant's planning to hurt my family."

"We won't let that happen."

Rounding the final block, Tristan slowed, then stopped altogether. He couldn't afford Grant catching sight of him.

"You take up position near the front door," Tristan ordered. "I'll enter through the back."

He prayed he wasn't too late, that Grant hadn't harmed his daughters or Rachel. The four of them were the heart of him, his entire world.

Lord, guide my hands and keep me focused on protecting them, however necessary.

Taking in a fast pull of air, Tristan unlocked the back door and soundlessly slipped inside the mudroom. Flattened against the wall, he mentally calculated how many steps to the kitchen and how many more to the main living area.

Over the roar of his rushing pulse, he listened for voices.

What he heard nearly buckled his knees. A loud thud. And then...

A feral female growl was followed by a fierce declaration. "You made a big mistake, Grant Tucker, coming here and threatening my family."

Rachel's voice was so angry and so lethal that a portion of Tristan's fear quieted. While another escalated. Taunting a dangerous man like Grant Tucker was not a good idea.

Tristan vaulted into the kitchen.

He stopped dead in his tracks, dumbfounded and speechless.

Grant Tucker lay spread-eagled on the ground, no longer a threat. Rachel stood over him, glaring hard. "Attempt to get up, move a single muscle, and I'll knock you over the head again."

Grant remained immobile.

Dropping the skillet to the ground, Rachel gathered up Tristan's daughters into a protective hug. They buried their little faces into her dress. As she soothed them with soft words, she looked larger than life, confident and composed. Tristan had never loved her more than he did in that moment.

His daughters were safe because Rachel had saved them. Awed by her courage, Tristan drew in a sharp breath.

The sound caught Rachel's attention. Her eyes round and watchful, she stared back at him, as if she didn't quite believe he was there.

A thousand silent messages passed between them. He stood perfectly still, staring at the woman he loved, accepting that he wanted her in his life, always.

He said her name on a wordless whisper. He wasn't even sure she heard him. But she wiped her cheeks, sniffled once and then gave him a smile that reached all the way inside his chest and grabbed his heart.

Shaking out of his inertness, he moved quickly. Putting first things first, he went and checked the prisoner. Grant was, indeed, unconscious. He had a sizable lump growing on his head, and his breathing was shallow, his pulse slow but steady.

"Your da's home," Rachel whispered to the girls.

Lily looked up first and squealed out his name. "Da! Da! Miss Rachel saved us from a really, really bad man."

"It was scary. He grabbed Miss Rachel by the hair," Daisy said. "And then he came for Violet."

Frowning, she pulled her little sister close.

In two long strides Tristan reached the center of the kitchen and drew all four of his girls into his arms.

The front door banged open.

Stillwell rushed into the kitchen. The insurance agent took one look at the scene and went immediately to work. He leaned over and slapped Grant in the face.

Grant moaned.

"On your feet," Stillwell ordered.

Only half aware Stillwell was tugging the slumped body to a standing position, Tristan continued holding his loved ones. Rachel clutched at him nearly as hard as his daughters. He wasn't sure how long they stayed in that position, holding tightly to one another. But when Tristan looked up, Stillwell had Grant on his feet, his hands tied behind his back.

The insurance agent caught Tristan's eye. "I'll take the prisoner back to the jailhouse."

Tristan stepped forward, with the idea of accompanying them, but Stillwell held up a hand to stop him. "Your family needs you right now."

Yes, they did. And he needed them. "I'll meet you at the jail later."

"Take all the time you want."

Once the other man was gone, Tristan took Rachel's hands and stared into her eyes. "You're remarkable, Rachel Hewitt, the most courageous woman I know."

Her lips twisted at a wry angle. "It wasn't courage that drove me. It was fury."

Such modesty.

His hand slightly shaking, he tucked a loose strand of hair behind her ear. "I love you."

She swallowed several times. Her throat continued working, but nothing came out beyond a small gasp of surprise.

"I love you, Rachel Hewitt," he repeated for both her and their very attentive audience of three.

"You...you really love me?"

He wiped a stray tear off her cheek. His sweet, stubborn, irreplaceable Rachel, why had he resisted loving her for so long? "I really do."

She inhaled a shaky breath.

The girls crowded around her. Daisy tugged on her sleeve. "I love you, too, Miss Rachel."

"Me, too," Violet and Lily said in unison.

The exuberant declarations got her sobbing—big, gasping, choking gulps of air. She gathered the girls into her arms.

Tristan smiled at the picture they made. He hadn't sought love. He certainly hadn't sought it with Rachel. She was the complete opposite of what he'd once believed his girls needed.

How wrong he'd been. Rachel was everything they needed, everything *he* needed.

"I love you, Rachel Hewitt."

Her lips started to tremble.

"Will you marry me?"

The girls cheered and jumped around them both, adding their very vocal opinions on the matter. "Say yes. Say yes."

Four against one, not exactly fair odds, but Tristan wasn't in the mood to play fair. He was in the mood to win Rachel's kind, tender heart for the rest of his life.

Half laughing through her tears, half crying, Rachel

shook her head. "Oh, Tristan, you know I want a real marriage, while you want—"

"A real marriage, too."

She took a gulping, shuddering breath.

He closed his hand over hers and placed it against his heart. "I never expected to fall in love twice in my lifetime. But I did, Rachel. I fell in love with you. It's just as deep and real as the first time, different, but equally powerful."

"Oh, Tristan, I love you, too. So very much, but—" she lowered her head "—I want a...large family."

"I want that, as well," he said. "I want more children."

The girls cheered again. "Does that mean we can have a new baby soon?" Daisy asked.

Tristan chuckled. "It means I'm willing to consider it."

More cheers.

Deciding the rest of this conversation was for Rachel's ears only, he ushered his daughters out of the room. "Go find your baby dolls and practice being good big sisters while I talk to Miss Rachel in private."

They didn't exactly rush out of the room, but they didn't argue with him, either.

Alone at last, he caught Rachel's face between his palms and kissed her again. "I want to marry you and be a real husband to you, in every sense of the word, the way the Lord intended."

Tempered hope filled her gaze. "You said you didn't want to risk putting another woman through childbirth."

Ah, Rachel, his sweet, bold, outspoken Rachel. Of course she would expect a thorough explanation.

She *deserved* a thorough explanation.

"The thought of putting you at risk still terrifies me. But, as we discovered today, danger comes in many forms."

Her gaze sobered. "When Grant showed up, all I could

think was that I had to protect my girls. And then I worried that Amos was out there somewhere, maybe even attempting to hurt you. I've never been angrier in my life."

"Remind me never to cross you." He kissed her nose. "I took care of Amos. He's locked up in a jail cell as we speak. No need to worry about him hurting me or anyone else."

She released a sigh of relief. "So it's over."

"No, it's only just beginning."

She smiled.

He took her hand again. "I'm sorry I held back from loving you. I let myself get weighed down by memories. Instead of using my past to guide me into the future I allowed it to keep me rooted in fear."

"You lost someone very precious to you." It was her turn to cup his face between her palms. "I don't want to take Siobhan's place in your heart. I know there's room in there for both of us."

Even in that, Rachel proved herself a very wise woman.

"I have no idea what the future has in store for us," he said. "Good or bad, I want to face it with you by my side. I trust God will walk with us every hour of every day."

"I love you, Tristan McCullough."

"Does that mean you'll marry me?"

"Ask me again."

Chuckling at her bossy tone, he lowered to one knee. "Rachel Hewitt, my love, my heart, will you marry me?"

"Yes. Oh, yes, I will." She pulled him to his feet and slipped her arms around his neck. "Now kiss me, Sheriff McCullough."

He couldn't think of anything he wanted more, so he simply did as she requested. He kissed her.

Epilogue

On a cold mid-November morning, with less than five minutes before the ceremony was scheduled to begin, wedding guests continued spilling into the church. Their shoes and coats were dusted with new snow.

A burst of cold air swept into the gathering area where she waited to make her entrance. Clara Pressman hurried into the church with her sister and brother-in-law one step behind.

The two women broke away from Bertha's husband and approached Rachel.

"Oh, my dear, dear girl, you make a lovely bride." Bertha took Rachel's hands and opened them wide, evidently so she could inspect her dress. "Pale blue is definitely your color."

"Thank you, Bertha." Rachel smiled, then turned and greeted the other woman beaming at her. "Hello, Clara."

Clara hugged her. "Congratulations, Rachel, I pray you have a long, happy life with Sheriff McCullough."

"Thank you." Rachel knew how hard it was for the young widow to attend her wedding so soon after her husband's death. "I'm very happy you came today."

"I wouldn't have missed it."

Rachel gave Clara one more squeeze, then stepped back. "Where's your sweet baby?"

"Lucy O'Brian is watching her for me this morning."

Of course. The pretty young emigrant was still looking for a permanent position. Rachel started to say more, but Grayson stepped into view and touched her arm. "It's time."

Oh. Oh, my. Her heart lifted and sighed. Happiness filled her to near bursting.

Clara and Bertha joined the rest of the stragglers hurrying to find seats. By some tacit agreement, the only people left in the tiny gathering area were Rachel and her three siblings.

The Hewitts had known their share of tragedies. They'd lost their wealth, their parents, as well as Grayson's wife and his unborn son. But they'd always had each other and Rachel was one of them. She'd always been one of them.

Had it only been a year since Grayson's letter arrived, encouraging them to come out west? Ben, Emma and Rachel had stuck together. Their dedication to family and faith in God had seen them through every trial along the way, making every triumph that much sweeter.

Ben had married the only woman he'd ever loved. Emma had married the only man for her. Grayson would soon be a father and now…

Rachel was getting her very own new beginning, as well.

Ben was the first to reach for her and pull her into his arms. "I'm proud to call you sister. Be happy, Rachel."

"Oh, Ben, I am happy, so happy."

She had only a moment to cling to him before Emma scooted in between them and took her turn.

"Tristan is a good man and your perfect match," she

said through a sheen of tears. "I'm thrilled you two found one another."

Choked up, Rachel managed a short nod. "Thank you, Emma."

Both still smiling, Ben and Emma each gave Rachel one last kiss on her cheek. Shoulder to shoulder, they headed down the aisle to claim their seats in the front pew with their respective spouses.

Grayson gave her a brotherly kiss on the forehead. "Tristan cherishes you, as only a man deeply in love could. I don't think I would have let you marry him if I believed otherwise."

She quirked an eyebrow. *"Let me?"*

He threw his hands in the air. "Perhaps I should re-phrase that."

"Perhaps you should."

Chuckling, he cleared his throat. "Tristan adores you, Rachel. I predict a very happy life together."

"Why, thank you, Grayson, that's so kind of you to say."

They both laughed.

Impatient now, she linked her arm through her brother's and the two of them took their positions at the back of the church.

Up front, Tristan stood tall and looked as handsome as any groom Rachel had ever seen. Her stomach fluttered with emotion. He would soon be hers, all hers.

Blinking back tears of joy, she noted how Tristan had arranged his daughters beside him, oldest to youngest. All four waited for Rachel to make the short trek to them.

Grayson squeezed her arm. "Ready?"

"Ready." She looked to the ceiling, offered up a prayer of thanksgiving and then allowed her brother to guide her down the aisle.

As she made her way toward Tristan, his gaze never left hers. He seemed to be calling her to him, urging her to fill the empty space beside him, not only during the ceremony but for the rest of their lives.

Rachel was up for the challenge.

The next few minutes went quickly. Grayson gave her away. Tristan took her hand and lowered his lips to her ear. "I love you, Rachel, with all that I am. I will never let you go."

And the ceremony began.

After they said their traditional vows, Rachel lifted her hand to stop the preacher from declaring them husband and wife. "I have one more promise to make."

She lowered to her knees and gathered Tristan's daughters into her arms. "Daisy, Lily and Violet, you have become the daughters of my heart. I promise to love you always, and care for you as my very own for the rest of my life. You are my very own precious gifts from God."

With her thumb nowhere near her mouth, having conquered the problem weeks ago, Violet asked, "Are you our new mommy yet?"

Tristan laughed at the question, as did the rest of the congregation.

"She's *almost* your mommy," he said as he bent over to look his daughter in the eye. "We have to finish the ceremony first."

He took Rachel's hand and helped her stand. At last, the preacher pronounced them husband and wife, then added, "You may kiss the bride."

"Gladly."

Tristan's first kiss as her husband was full of silent promises that Rachel knew he had every intention of fulfilling.

Heart overflowing with love for him, she turned toward the back of the church and, after a quick swipe at her eyes, took Daisy's hand. She reached out and took Lily's hand next. Tristan picked up Violet and the five of them navigated the journey down the aisle.

In the gathering space they were quickly surrounded by family and friends. The girls glowed under all the attention.

Rachel would miss them in the next few days while they were at Grayson's house. But she had to admit she was looking forward to spending time alone with her husband.

Anticipation filled her at the thought.

Nearly thirty minutes passed before the crowd eventually thinned out.

Tristan drew Rachel into his arms. He opened his mouth to say something but was interrupted by James Stillwell.

"Sheriff. Mrs. McCullough." He nodded to Rachel. "I congratulate you on your marriage. I wish you a long, healthy, happy life together."

"What a lovely thing to say." Rachel smiled at the insurance agent who'd joined the wagon train to catch a pair of thieves and had now become a part of their community. "Thank you, Mr. Stillwell, for your kind words."

"You're most welcome." He turned his attention to Tristan. "I've organized transportation back to Missouri for myself and the Tucker brothers. I don't have their trial date set yet, but I'll get word to you when they're officially brought to justice."

Tristan nodded. "When do you leave?"

"As soon as the weather lets up."

"Let me know if there's anything else I can do." Tristan reached out and shook the other man's hand. "If you ever find yourself in need of a job, I could use a deputy."

"I just might take you up on that offer, once the trial is over. In the meantime, this is for you and your wife." He dug into his jacket and pulled out a small brown paper package.

Neither Rachel nor Tristan reached for it. "We requested no wedding gifts."

"It's not a gift. It's a reward for helping me catch the Tucker brothers. I couldn't have done it without either of you."

Rachel shared a look with Tristan. For a moment, they simply stared into each other's eyes, silently communicating their thoughts. Together, they said, "We don't want a reward."

"Nevertheless, someone should take the money."

Rachel swung her gaze to her daughters. They were speaking energetically with Emma and Abby. Maggie stood close by, Grayson's arm around her waist. Ben and Nathan soon joined their wives. All four of them laughed over something one of the girls said.

Gratitude filled Rachel's heart. She had innumerable blessings, more than her share. It didn't seem right to take the reward money.

Tristan must have gone through a similar thought process because he placed his hands on Rachel's shoulders and turned her to face him. "We could donate the money to the church. With Oregon City growing faster than any of us expected, we'll need a bigger building soon."

"I like that idea."

"Then it's settled." Tristan turned to the other man. "Give the money to Reverend Mosby."

"Good enough."

Rachel waited until Mr. Stillwell went in search of

the preacher before she cupped her husband's cheek and smiled into his moss-green eyes. "You're a good man, Sheriff McCullough."

"We have an exciting future ahead of us, Mrs. Mc-Cullough." He kissed her on the lips. "Whether we have five days together, or fifty years, I look forward to every moment I get to spend with you by my side."

Still smiling, she wrapped her arms around his waist. "I say we get started on our life together right now."

"We are of one mind."

Hand in hand, they said their farewells as quickly as possible without issuing too much offense.

They hurried home to embrace their first day together as husband and wife. As Tristan scooped her into his arms and carried her inside their house, Rachel realized she'd found where she belonged. She would always be a Hewitt, but now she was also a McCullough.

The Lord had blessed her with two families instead of one. And that, she decided, was the best gift of all.

* * * * *

Dear Reader,

Thank you for choosing to join me on the final leg of the Oregon Trail with the incomparable Hewitt family. I hope you enjoyed Rachel's journey across the rugged frontier. There were several bumps along the way, but she weathered them rather well, don't you agree? I loved being able to give her a family of her own, with an honorable man who loves her with all his heart and three adorable children in desperate need of a *new mommy.*

This is my third venture into writing a book in a publisher-generated continuity miniseries. It was an honor and a privilege to work with two authors I greatly admire. I found both Linda Ford and Lacy Williams extremely generous with their time and input, a must in these types of projects.

This book was especially fun for me to write because I had the chance to research a time period and setting I haven't explored previously.

I always love hearing from readers. Please feel free to contact me at my website www.reneeryan.com. You can also find me on Facebook and Twitter, @ReneeRyanBooks.

Wishing you a life full of faith, hope and love. Happy Reading!

Renee

COMING NEXT MONTH FROM
Love Inspired® Historical

Available July 7, 2015

THE MARRIAGE AGREEMENT
Charity House
by Renee Ryan

Fanny Mitchell has cared for her boss, hotelier Jonathon Hawkins, since they met. When they're caught in an innocent kiss, Jonathon proposes marriage to save her reputation. Can Fanny turn their engagement of convenience into one of love?

COWGIRL FOR KEEPS
Four Stones Ranch
by Louise M. Gouge

The last thing Rosamond Northam wants to do when she returns to her hometown is help a stuffy aristocrat build a hotel. But her father insists she work with Garrick Wakefield, and now it's a clash between Englishman and cowgirl.

THE LAWMAN'S REDEMPTION
by Danica Favorite

Wrongly accused former deputy Will Lawson is determined to clear his name. His search leads to lovely Mary Stone, who seems to know more about the bandit who framed Will than she lets on...

CAPTIVE ON THE HIGH SEAS
by Christina Rich

When ship captain Nicolaus sees a beautiful woman in a dire situation, he offers to rescue her from slavery. As their friendship grows at sea, Nicolaus wants to offer her freedom—and his heart.

LOOK FOR THESE AND OTHER LOVE INSPIRED BOOKS WHEREVER BOOKS ARE SOLD, INCLUDING MOST BOOKSTORES, SUPERMARKETS, DISCOUNT STORES AND DRUGSTORES.

LIHCNM0615

REQUEST YOUR FREE BOOKS!

2 FREE INSPIRATIONAL NOVELS
PLUS 2 FREE MYSTERY GIFTS

Love Inspired HISTORICAL

YES! Please send me 2 FREE Love Inspired® Historical novels and my 2 FREE mystery gifts (gifts are worth about $10). After receiving them, if I don't wish to receive any more books, I can return the shipping statement marked "cancel." If I don't cancel, I will receive 4 brand-new novels every month and be billed just $4.99 per book in the U.S. or $5.49 per book in Canada. That's a saving of at least 17% off the cover price. It's quite a bargain! Shipping and handling is just 50¢ per book in the U.S. and 75¢ per book in Canada.* I understand that accepting the 2 free books and gifts places me under no obligation to buy anything. I can always return a shipment and cancel at any time. Even if I never buy another book, the two free books and gifts are mine to keep forever.

102/302 IDN GH6Z

Name	(PLEASE PRINT)	
Address		Apt. #
City	State/Prov.	Zip/Postal Code

Signature (if under 18, a parent or guardian must sign)

Mail to the **Reader Service:**
IN U.S.A.: P.O. Box 1867, Buffalo, NY 14240-1867
IN CANADA: P.O. Box 609, Fort Erie, Ontario L2A 5X3

Want to try two free books from another series?
Call 1-800-873-8635 or visit www.ReaderService.com.

* Terms and prices subject to change without notice. Prices do not include applicable taxes. Sales tax applicable in N.Y. Canadian residents will be charged applicable taxes. Offer not valid in Quebec. This offer is limited to one order per household. Not valid for current subscribers to Love Inspired Historical books. All orders subject to credit approval. Credit or debit balances in a customer's account(s) may be offset by any other outstanding balance owed by or to the customer. Please allow 4 to 6 weeks for delivery. Offer available while quantities last.

Your Privacy—The Reader Service is committed to protecting your privacy. Our Privacy Policy is available online at www.ReaderService.com or upon request from the Reader Service.

We make a portion of our mailing list available to reputable third parties that offer products we believe may interest you. If you prefer that we not exchange your name with third parties, or if you wish to clarify or modify your communication preferences, please visit us at www.ReaderService.com/consumerchoice or write to us at Reader Service Preference Service, P.O. Box 9062, Buffalo, NY 14240-9062. Include your complete name and address.

LIH15

Jonathon's eyes roamed Fanny's face, then her gown.
Appreciation filled his gaze. "You're wearing my favorite
color."

"I…know. I chose this dress specifically with you in
mind."

Too late, she realized how her admission sounded, as
if her sole purpose was to please him. She had not meant
to reveal so much of herself.

He took a step forward. "I'm flattered."

He took another step.

Fanny held steady, unmoving, anxious to see just how
close he would come to her.

He stopped his approach. For the span of three heartbeats they stared into each other's eyes.

She sighed.

"Relax, Fanny. You've checked and rechecked every
item on your lists at least three times, probably more. Go
and spend a moment with your—"

"How do you know I checked and rechecked my lists
that often?"

"Because—" his expression softened "—I know you."

There was a look of such tenderness about him that

for a moment, a mere heartbeat, she ached for what they might have accomplished together, were they two different people. What they could have been to one another if past circumstances weren't entered into the equation.

"We're ready for tonight's ball, Fanny. *You're* ready."

She drew in a slow, slightly uneven breath. "I suppose you're right."

He took one more step. He stood so close now she could smell his scent, a pleasant mix of bergamot, masculine spice and…him.

Something unspoken hovered in the air between them, communicated in a language she should know, but couldn't quite comprehend.

"Go. Spend a few moments with your mother and father before the guests begin to arrive. I'll come get you, once I've changed my clothes."

"I'd like that." She'd very much enjoy the chance to show him off to her parents.

He leaned in closer. But then the sound of determined footsteps in the hallway caught their attention.

"That will be Mrs. Singletary," she said with a rush of air. The widow's purposeful gait was easy enough to decipher.

"No doubt you are correct." Jonathon's gaze locked on her, and that was *not* business in his eyes.

Something far more personal stared back at her. She had but one thought in response.

Oh, my.

Don't miss
THE MARRIAGE AGREEMENT by Renee Ryan,
available July 2015 wherever
Love Inspired® books and ebooks are sold.

Samuel waited impatiently for his brother to adjust the pillows behind him. With his eyes covered by thick dressings, Samuel had to depend on his hearing to tell him what was going on around him. Maybe forever.

If he didn't regain his sight, his days as a master carver were over. He wouldn't be of any use in the fields. He wouldn't be much use to anyone.

"There. How's that?"

Samuel leaned back. It wasn't any better, but he didn't say that. It wasn't Luke's fault that he was still in pain and that his eyes felt like they were filled with dry sand. After six days, Samuel was sick and tired of being in bed, and no amount of pillow fluffing would change that, but he didn't feel like stumbling around in front of people looking hideous, either. Only his mouth had been left free of bandages.

"Is there anything else I can do for you? Do you want me to fluff the pillows under your hands?" Luke asked.

Before Samuel could answer, Luke pulled the support from beneath his right hand. Intense pain shot from Samuel's fingertips to his elbow.

"I'm so sorry. Did that hurt?"

Samuel panted and willed the agony to subside. "I don't need anything else."

"Are you sure?" Luke asked.

"I'm sure," Samuel snapped. He just wanted to be left alone. He wanted to see. He wanted to be whole. He wanted the pain to stop.

He caught the sound of hoofbeats outside his open bedroom.

"*Mamm* is back." The relief in Luke's voice was almost comical, except Samuel was far from laughing. He heard his brother's footsteps retreat across the room.

An itch formed in the middle of Samuel's back. With both hands swaddled in thick bandages, he couldn't reach to scratch it. "Luke, wait."

His brother's footsteps were already fading as he raced downstairs. Samuel tried to ignore the pricking sensation, but it only grew worse. "Luke! *Mamm!* Can someone come here?"

It seemed like an eternity, but he finally heard his mother's voice. "I'm here, Samuel, and I've brought someone to see you."

He groaned as he heard the stairs creak. The last thing he wanted was company. "I'm not up to having visitors."

"Then it's a pity I've come all this way." The woman's voice was low, musical and faintly amused. He had no idea who she was.

Don't miss
AN AMISH HARVEST by Patricia Davids,
available July 2015 wherever
Love Inspired® books and ebooks are sold.